www.slough.gov.uk
Slough
Borough Council

SPECIAL MESSAGE TO READERS

THE ULVERSCROFT FOUNDATION
(registered UK charity number 264873)
was established in 1972 to provide funds for research, diagnosis and treatment of eye diseases. Examples of major projects funded by the Ulverscroft Foundation are:-

- The Children's Eye Unit at Moorfields Eye Hospital, London
- The Ulverscroft Children's Eye Unit at Great Ormond Street Hospital for Sick Children
- Funding research into eye diseases and treatment at the Department of Ophthalmology, University of Leicester
- The Ulverscroft Vision Research Group, Institute of Child Health
- Twin operating theatres at the Western Ophthalmic Hospital, London
- The Chair of Ophthalmology at the Royal Australian College of Ophthalmologists

You can help further the work of the Foundation by making a donation or leaving a legacy. Every contribution is gratefully received. If you would like to help support the Foundation or require further information, please contact:

THE COBBLER'S WIFE

Seren James yearns for a child of her own. Married to a man who has little care for her, she longs for something to fill the emptiness within — and fears that she is almost out of time. When Seren meets a woman who says she can help, she thinks her dreams have come true. But the locals suspect Anwen of witchcraft, and any association with her may taint Seren too. And as Seren finds herself growing closer to Elwyn Evans, the local minister, who has made no secret of his attraction to her, she must ask herself what it will take to find happiness — and whether she is willing to pay the price . . .

LYNETTE REES

THE COBBLER'S WIFE

Complete and Unabridged

MAGNA
Leicester

First published in Great Britain in 2019 by
Quercus Editions Ltd
London

First Ulverscroft Edition
published 2020
by arrangement with
Quercus Editions Ltd
An Hachette UK Company
London

This book is a work of fiction. Names, characters, businesses, organizations, places and events are either the product of the author's imagination or used fictitiously. Any resemblance to actual persons, living or dead, events or locales is entirely coincidental.

A catalogue record for this book is available from the British Library.

ISBN 978–0–7505–4827–4

Published by
Ulverscroft Limited
Anstey, Leicestershire

Set by Words & Graphics Ltd.
Anstey, Leicestershire
Printed and bound in Great Britain by
TJ Books Limited., Padstow, Cornwall

This book is printed on acid-free paper

In memory of the men and young boys, who died or were injured, in both explosions at the Gethin Coal Pit at Abercanaid, Merthyr Tydfil, in 1862 and 1865, respectively.

1

Abercanaid, Merthyr Tydfil, 1866

Hollow laughter filled the air behind her as Seren James stood watch on her doorstep waiting for the arrival of her mam and sister, Gwendolyn. Where were they? She was relieved they were late because she wanted *him* gone before they got here. He was already fifteen minutes behind time this morning opening the little cobbler shop he owned just down the road.

'Come here, woman!' he growled from behind her and her gut clenched with fear.

'What is it you want, Morgan?' she asked, trying to keep her voice level, then she turned to see he was closer than she'd imagined. Stepping back through the door, she brought her gaze to meet with his.

'I'll tell you what I want, shall I?' he bellowed, his eyes so enlarged it seemed they might pop out of his skull at any moment. 'I want a son, something you can't give me, you bloody barren bitch!'

She took a step back. There was no use arguing with him when he was in this sort of mood, experience told her that. The alcoholic fumes flowing to meet her caused her to gag.

Oh, dear Lord, no, he wasn't going to try to take her now, was he? Not like this? Her mam and Gwendolyn could turn up at any moment.

She watched in horror as he slipped his leather belt from his trousers, holding it like a whip in his hand. 'What's it to be then, buckle end again?' he shouted. 'Get up them stairs now, or I'll beat you into a pulp!'

She bit her lip, her eyes filling with tears, as she walked backwards to the front door which was slightly ajar. Hearing a voice, he suddenly stopped in his tracks as the belt slid from his hand to the linoleum floor. His eyes narrowed to slits as she breathed a sigh of relief.

It was Iorwen Gruffudd's voice she heard outside, the local minister. 'Mrs James, are you in?' he shouted through the half-open door, his elderly voice cracking with age.

Hitching a breath, Seren pulled the door open a fraction. A moment or two later and she would have been dragged up those stairs, kicking, screaming and beaten like last time, thrashed within an inch of her life and taken forcefully without an iota of love or compassion, just to serve her husband's lustful urges.

'Y . . . yes, Mr Gruffudd!' she shouted back, staring at her husband all the while. He wouldn't dare shout or curse in front of the minister. To all intents and purposes, he was an upstanding member of the community. People in the village thought he was a respectable, hard-working man, they didn't see this side of him like she was forced to.

'Get rid of him, sharpish!' he hissed.

She nodded, though she had no intention of doing so.

Seren drew the door wide open and smiled.

'Mr Gruffudd, please come into the kitchen and I'll make us a nice cup of tea,' she said, relieved that the elderly man had arrived at exactly the right moment to save her skin.

The minister nodded and, removing his hat, followed her into the sparse scullery as Morgan James hovered near the doorway.

'Please sit down, Mr Gruffudd,' Seren said in as bright a tone as she could muster. The old man smiled as he drew out a wooden chair from the table and sat, placing his hat in front of him. Trembling, she filled the kettle with water and placed it on the hob to boil.

Morgan glared at her and she could tell by the expression on his leather-skinned, lined face that he was thinking, 'Why have you asked him to sit down and have a cup of tea, woman? Get rid of him!'

She was just about to say something when the minister, raising his brows, asked, 'Not in work today then, Morgan?'

Morgan narrowed his eyes until they were almost slits, then as if by magic, his face changed. His eyes widened and a big smile appeared on his face. 'Oh aye, I'm off now at any moment. It's Seren's fault that I am late, she didn't wake me in time this morning. A man needs a good wife to get him going in the morning!'

My fault indeed! You drunken pig! If you hadn't stayed out half the night and needed to be put to bed in your alcoholic stupor, you'd have got up this morning on time . . . She gritted her teeth.

The minister rubbed his rheumy eyes and smiled. 'Then don't let me keep you, I'm only here to discuss chapel business with your wife.'

Morgan nodded. He was walking towards her now: what did he want? Her heart thudded a beat so hard, she feared it might burst out of her chest, though she knew he'd never lay a finger on her in front of the minister.

Stooping, he pecked her cheek, taking her somewhat aback as she sensed the contempt he had for her beneath it all. His whole demeanour told her so: the beady-eyed stare, the tone of his voice, the hidden barbs beneath his words, everything. Yet, the minister wouldn't have picked up on any of it as he didn't know him like she did and was slightly hard of hearing anyway.

Still, she was relieved to see her husband lift his metal snap tin that contained a hunk of bread and butter and a lump of cheese for his dinner at the shop. It was always the same, he worked hard all day then went home via the pub. Sometimes she wouldn't see him for hours on end, and it was during those torturous times that she became worried what mood he'd return home in. Sometimes he was frisky, demanding sex from her on the spot and she'd grimace and bear it, other times it involved violence or sometimes both, but the best times were when he got himself so blind drunk he could barely stand, and she'd help him up the stairs to bed, draping his arm around her neck and shoulder as she hefted his heavy weight, step upon laborious step up those bloody stairs. Afterwards, her back would be in half and she'd massage her sore neck, breathless from the exertion, but at least when he was asleep she was safe. Then she knew he was incapable of harming her, or anyone else for that matter. Many a time she'd thought, if she just released his arm, he'd fall down the stone steps and either injure or kill himself and she could blame it on the booze. She'd been sorely tempted to let go on many an occasion, or even to give him a quick push down the stairs, but something inside her stopped her in time.

'Goodbye, Mr Gruffudd!' Morgan said chirpily, and he left, closing the front door behind him.

Seren heaved a sigh of relief and steadied herself by holding on to the counter. She poured them both cups of strong tea with plenty of sugar for her frazzled nerves — today they were jangling.

'W . . . what chapel business did you want to see me about, Mr Gruffudd?' she asked, as she took a seat at the pine table opposite the minister. She was curious to find out. The minister called around the street occasionally to see various parishioners at their homes, but when he called on Seren it was usually because he wanted a favour of some sort. No doubt he realised she was reliable.

Mr Gruffudd cleared his throat before taking a sip of tea from his china cup and setting it back down on its saucer. 'It's like this, you see, Mrs James . . . ' He paused for a moment as if wondering what to say to her. 'Next month I'm retiring . . . '

'Oh?' Why hadn't anyone warned her of this?

She looked at the man and could see the apprehension in his grey eyes.

He doesn't want to go?

He let out a ragged breath. 'I know it's a surprise, I didn't realise myself until I saw Doctor Owen last week. He's advised me to do so. My old ticker isn't what it used to be and he's suggested I retire and take things easy from now on, though you'll still see me from time to time. Anyhow, a new minister called Elwyn Evans, from Pontypridd, will be taking over. He's a good man, young and unmarried so far. And anyway, I was hoping that you and some of the other ladies from the village might make him feel at home here. You know the kind of thing: invite him to your homes for supper, offer to help him at The Manse.' He raised an enquiring eyebrow 'He'll have a housekeeper, but I'd like him to settle into the community.'

Seren found herself nodding in agreement, though she knew the last thing that Morgan would want was a new minister around for supper sitting at his table! And of course, even if invited, there was always the chance Morgan would make a fool of them both in front of the man if he'd been drinking. She supposed, though, she could invite him on a lunchtime instead, maybe for a bowl of cawl, and on the odd occasion offer to help at The Manse when Morgan was in work.

'That's settled then . . . ' Mr Gruffudd said with a hearty grin. 'Now tell me . . . how are things with you, Mrs James?'

* * *

'What's that bastard been doing to you again?' Gwen examined her sister's arm and saw a few dark bruises at the wrist.

'It's nothing, honestly . . . ' She didn't want to worry anyone.

'Mind your language, girl!' Their mother looked at Gwen and then turned to Seren and said, 'I've made my thoughts clear on this and you know there's always room for you back at the family home with us, but I fear for you if you stay with Morgan, Seren.' She shook her head.

'He'll kill you one day, he will!' Gwen raised a fist. 'What I wouldn't like to do to that man. Oh, he fooled us all, he did, before you wed, with his good looks and his fancy patter. We were all taken in and you especially, Seren. The rest of us don't have to live with the blighter!'

Seren couldn't argue, she could only agree, for Morgan James had been one of the best-looking lads in the village of Abercanaid in Merthyr Tydfil. With his dark mop of hair and chocolate-brown eyes, he had brooding good looks and was well built, too, seeming such a catch with his little shop and his cobbling skills. A match made in heaven, she'd thought. He was someone she'd watched from afar over the years as he was a few years older, reminding her of Heathcliff to her Cathy. And when he had finally asked to court her, she'd been over the moon with delight and the envy of many other young women in the village. The violence towards her didn't happen overnight either. It was so gradual and insidious that it crept up like a cat stalking a mouse, and then taking it unawares, going in for the kill.

Looking back, it all began on their wedding night. She'd been a virgin so pure and chaste, but he'd taken her with no thought for her pleasure. He'd been rough too, and it had been painful. She'd found herself weeping bucketsful afterwards while he'd snored like a drunken pig beside her, then acted like nothing had happened the following day. But after a time she'd got used to it, and it hadn't hurt as much, and she guessed that's what married life was like for most women. You just had to grin and bear it.

Morgan had wanted a child as soon as possible. He was older than her and his brothers and their wives already had children, but when after six months she hadn't conceived, that was when she began to see the back of his hand.

Well, a year had now passed and there was still no sign of a baby. Someone in the village had told her to speak to Anwen Llewellyn who lived in a farmhouse on the mountainside. They reckoned she had secret potions and spells that could induce fertility. But she wasn't about to tell her mam and sister she was after anything like that — they both knew the woman but didn't discuss such matters. What they did think, though, was it was just as well she hadn't conceived to an evil brute like Morgan James and wished her rid of him altogether.

'Come on,' Mam said sympathetically, breaking into her thoughts. 'I'll make us all a cup of tea and we'll have a little chat . . . '

Seren nodded. She knew what one of Mam's chats were like, they were more lectures of why and how she could leave Morgan, with her sister chipping in support from time to time. Sometimes it felt as though they were both ganging up on her, though she realised they both only had her best interests at heart.

* * *

It was a long climb up the mountainside, but for once today the sun was shining and the sky was a pure azure blue. A light breeze ruffled Seren's fair hair as she paused, puffing, for a break. Resting her wicker basket on the mossy ground, she turned to stare at the small village down below with its small mineworkers' cottages and narrow streets. Up here, she felt like she was away from it all. Oh, what a view Anwen must see each and every day just gazing out of her farmhouse window. The old woman had lived alone for the past twenty years since her husband Gwynfor had passed away and most of her livestock had been sold off to meet her crippling debts. All that remained were a few chickens and goats and her trusty horse that pulled a cart behind him. Seren wondered how the woman managed to survive at all. She rarely ventured out to the shops in the village as there were so many rumours circulating. If Anwen Llewellyn wasn't being referred to as an eccentric old woman then she was being labelled 'a wizened old witch'! That shocked Seren as her family had known the woman for years, and all she seemed to be guilty of was helping alleviate their ailments with lotions and potions she made from things like nettles, herbs and spices. She achieved good results too. But people didn't understand that kind of thing. After all, why go to see an old witch when you have kindly Doctor Owen living in the village? He was well trained, a professional, while Anwen was into experimenting with all sorts of plants. Bunkum, some called it, and even hocus-pocus, but Doctor Owen himself never ran the woman down and was a regular caller at her home for a cup of tea and a chat.

As far as Seren could see, the elderly woman didn't charge for her services either, though people often left her gifts for her help and advice, and today Seren had baked her some *teisen lap* and a few Welsh cakes for her assistance.

Just think . . . her life could change for the better if she bore Morgan a son. Then he'd be happy and wouldn't drink any more, nor would he lay a finger on her. She was sure of it. Sighing heavily, she lifted her wicker basket and carried on walking up the mountainside, convinced that her luck was about to change for the better.

2

From her scullery window, Anwen Llewellyn squinted to see who was headed her way. Her rheumy eyes weren't as good as they used to be. Visitors weren't always welcome as they didn't always have the right intentions, but today she could see it was Seren James who was coming a-calling. She was such a lovely young woman, and Anwen had known the family for years.

Relieved, she set the kettle to boil on the hob and went to answer the front door. Her old hips weren't as bad this afternoon as the weather was getting warmer, and so her usual painful movements were far less stiff than usual.

'Hello, Mrs Llewellyn!' Seren shouted through the half-open farmhouse door.

'I'm just on my way, *cariad*,' Anwen said softly. 'Come in dear, you're very welcome.'

Seren stepped over the threshold, stooping to kiss her cheek.

What was it about the young woman today? Anwen hadn't seen her for a few months, not since she'd especially climbed the mountain with a pair of leather boots her husband had affixed new soles to. That had been very thoughtful of her. Back then, she seemed chirpy but today, although her tone sounded sweet to the ears, Anwen detected a slight break in her voice.

'My, my, Seren. Have you lost weight since we last spoke to one another?' She stood back, appraising the young woman's appearance.

Seren removed her cape and hung it on a peg on the wall behind her. 'Not that I'm aware of, Mrs Llewellyn.'

Anwen clucked her teeth as she often did when she felt someone wasn't telling the truth, but there would be time to get to the crux of the matter later. 'Never mind all that then, sit down, dear, I've put the kettle on to boil.'

'Oh, I'm forgetting, I've baked you some cakes, Mrs Llewellyn.' Seren handed the basket over to Anwen, who lifted it, her gnarled fingers roughened by all the work she did around the farm.

'Thank you, *cariad*.' She removed the covering cloth and her lips curved into a smile. 'Very nice they look and all. We'll have some of these Welsh cakes with our tea, shall we?'

Seren nodded eagerly. But Anwen felt perhaps the woman had no appetite. As well as looking frail, she noticed the light had long since gone out of her eyes. What could be troubling her so?

After pouring the brew into two mismatched cups, the women settled themselves by the table. 'Mind if I do?' Anwen said, her eyes lighting up like those of a mischievous young child just about to do something wicked.

Seren smiled. 'No, go ahead, Mrs Llewellyn. I won't be eating any, I'm not hungry.'

That young woman is troubled, I can see it in her eyes, but I'll not probe. I'll wait for her to tell me what it is that's on her mind. Anwen took a Welsh cake from the basket and nibbled on it. Not quite as good as her own but passable nevertheless.

'Did you know that Mr Gruffudd is leaving the chapel?' Seren said suddenly.

Anwen swallowed. No, she did not know. 'I haven't heard anything about that, but when are people likely to tell me, anyhow? I'm the last person they'd want to tell as they think I'm a witch!' And she cackled purposely which made Seren chuckle. By now Anwen realised the young woman was used to her antics.

'Not all of us think you're a witch, Mrs Llewellyn,' Seren said kindly. 'I, for one, know you're a healer.'

'Well, you and your family know that, *cariad*, but there's folk in the village who think I'm up to all sorts, casting spells, slaughtering cattle and dancing naked by moonlight!'

Seren giggled. 'But seriously, I'm going to miss Mr Gruffudd.'

'Aye, me and all. I expect we'll get some green as grass new minister who'll want to change things here in Abercanaid. Remember that one who stood in for him when he was ill a couple of years back?'

Seren nodded. 'He had some funny ideas . . . '

'Funny ideas? The man was a fool! I think, between you and me, he'd invented his own form of religion! I wouldn't mind betting he's gone off with the Saints to Utah!'

'Aw, that's a bit unfair . . . ' Anwen saw the girl's eyes flash. 'I know a couple of people who have joined the Mormon religion and they're good people, not the Saints of Satan that some Welsh Baptists call them!'

Anwen, realising she had caused a bit of upset,

said softly, 'No, you're right, *bach*. I, of all people, who have been condemned by so many, shouldn't poke fun. I mean no harm by it. Don't take any notice of the ramblings of an old woman. But you have to admit that young minister was barmy!'

Seren smiled. 'Yes, he was a little unusual.'

'I hope he won't be coming back here?'

'No. Apparently we're getting a young minister called Elwyn Evans, he's from Pontypridd.'

Anwen sniffed loudly. 'That's all right then!' She stared at Seren. 'Now then, young lady, what brought you here today?'

There was no use hiding anything from the likes of Anwen Llewellyn. Seren swallowed a lump in her throat. 'It's been almost a year now and I still haven't conceived, Mrs Llewellyn . . . '

Anwen smiled and shook her head. 'Well, it's still early days. Maybe you're not having marital relations at the right time?'

Seren knew that wasn't the case at all as Morgan forced himself upon her most nights, but she didn't want to tell Anwen that. 'It's just that it's causing a little bit of upset between me and my husband as he badly wants a son.'

Anwen drummed her fingers on the table. 'Oh, does he now!'

Seren nodded. 'Is there anything you can give me to help me conceive? I'd be most grateful to you . . . '

Anwen raised her straggly silver eyebrows. 'I think as you're young and fit you'd be better off letting nature take its course.'

Tears began to fill her eyes. 'Please, Mrs

Llewellyn . . . a herbal drink, a potion, anything?'

'There's desperate you sound, Seren.' Anwen's eyes narrowed. 'I'm thinking there's more to this than you're letting on.' It was then her eyes were drawn to the bruising on Seren's forearms. 'Has that husband of yours been hitting you around?'

Seren swallowed. She couldn't lie. 'Y . . . yes. But only now and then, he reckons I ask for it most of the time and I need the wilfulness knocked out of me.'

The old woman spoke softly to her as she shook her head. 'But those bruises on your wrists? No woman deserves to be treated like that. You must leave him. Why do you stay? Do you have nowhere to go?'

'I do, yes. My mam's always offering for me to stay with her, but I know he will come after me causing all sorts of trouble.'

'What is it you really fear, then? That he'll drag you back home and give you an even bigger thrashing for leaving him in the first place?'

Anwen's words hit home. 'Can't you cast a spell to make him nicer to me?'

There was pity in the woman's eyes as she smiled, then shook her head. 'I don't do that kind of thing, no matter what the villagers say. I only collect wild herbs and make lotions and potions to heal folk. Look, I've made an ointment you can use on that bruising. It's made from elder leaf and daisies, *cariad*. It will get rid of that bruising in no time at all.'

Seren nodded, severely disappointed that Anwen didn't have something in her apothecary cabinet to help her conceive.

As if reading her thoughts, Anwen said, 'Look, there is a potion I could make up for you to encourage a pregnancy, but that wouldn't solve your problem. Believe me, there's no magic cure to tame a beast who beats his wife! And having a new babe to contend with as well as a six-foot-tall brute isn't going to solve your problems!'

Seren felt the grief rise up like a wave of despair and she began to sob profusely. Anwen was right, why was she putting up with such behaviour from her husband? But deep down she knew the answer to that. It was because she feared Morgan would bring trouble to her mother's door if she ever left him, and she didn't want that for her at her time of life. Her mother had been widowed after her father had died in the Gethin Pit explosion at the end of last year. Life hadn't been the same since then, and, come to think of it, hadn't Morgan suddenly become handy with his fists after her father's death as there was no man in the family to challenge him any more? Her father would have sorted him out, he'd been fit for his age and all, but she realised she mustn't dwell on it as there were others who'd lost menfolk in the village who were far worse off, other widows left behind with several young mouths to feed.

* * *

Anwen watched from her kitchen window until Seren was a dot on the landscape. Who knew what that poor girl had in store for her when she returned home? She'd warned her to leave early enough so Morgan wouldn't have got home from work himself yet, but according to Seren he often went straight to the pub anyhow. She wished there was more she could do to help her out, but other than offering her a place at the farm, what could she do? It could be an idea in an emergency, though, and as far as she knew, Seren didn't tell him about her visits to the farm.

It was at a time like this that she wished she *were* a bloody witch! Then she'd command all sorts of forces to rain down on the head of Morgan James to stop him from laying a finger on that lovely young wife of his.

What was it Seren had said about a new minister coming to the chapel? *God forgive me for thinking such things about the cruel-hearted cobbler, but I can't help it. If there is a new minister at the chapel then maybe I shall return to attend Sunday services*. Mr Gruffudd hadn't shown her any support when the villagers had turned against her, accusing her of sorcery and all sorts. But then again, she shouldn't be too surprised about that; he was an elderly frail man and maybe he'd feared that if he took her side, they would turn against him too. There were some in the village, like Maggie Shanklin, who had an evil tongue in her head, who'd smeared her name from Troedyrhiw to Trefechan.

At least she'd put some soothing balm on both of Seren's wrists before she'd departed and had given her a small jar to take home with her. Other than that, and warning her to leave the man, what else could she do?

* * *

Calon lân yn llawn daioni,
Tecach yw na'r lili dlos . . .

Seren heard the strains of her favourite Welsh hymn, 'Calon lân', as she passed the chapel on her way back home. The words were about someone who asked for a happy heart and not worldly treasures, which was exactly how she felt right now. She yearned for peace within herself. This wasn't the chapel she usually attended; this one was run by Evan Davies and his lovely wife Lily. No doubt they'd get to meet the new minister from her chapel soon enough. It sounded as if someone was practising their singing, and what a melodious voice she had too.

As she rounded the corner of her street, someone was there to greet her. 'Hello, Mrs James. What have you got in your basket there, might I ask? Something for your husband's tea?'

Seren held her breath. The gossiping old crone, Maggie Shanklin, was the last person she expected to see. Maggie was from Ireland. She'd arrived at the town with her family as a young girl when her father and brothers had sought work in the ironworks at Merthyr Tydfil.

'I've just been to visit someone, that's all, Mrs Shanklin . . . ' She made to move away but the woman blocked her path.

'I hope it's not Anwen Llewellyn you've been to see? 'Tisn't right the way you've befriended someone who by rights ought to be burnt at the stake!'

Filled with fury, Seren gritted her teeth. Maggie had a way of winding her up and she had to be careful now what she said in case it got back to Morgan that she'd paid the woman a visit. Even when he'd mended her boots, she had pretended they were for someone else in the village, else he'd never have done them. That's why she'd insisted on taking the boots to Anwen herself for fear she'd call to the shop to collect them. 'Mrs Shanklin . . . ' she said, breathing out to calm herself, 'where I go and what I do is none of your damn business!'

Maggie's eyes widened and for a moment she was speechless and then she said, 'Well, if you can't tell me what you've been up to then I'm guessing it's something or other your Morgan wouldn't be at all happy with!'

Oh no, this could turn out badly. She was going to have to tell an untruth. 'If you must know, I was visiting my aunt at Lewis Square. She's not been well. I took her some Welsh cakes.' She removed the covering cloth on her basket so that Maggie could see the empty plate.

Maggie's eyes narrowed. 'Ill, you say? Your Aunt Maud? I only saw her a couple of days ago in the shop.'

Seren shook her head. 'It all happened quite suddenly, she's feeling a bit better now, anyhow . . . ' She turned and made her way home. What a fine mess she was getting herself into, now she'd have to pay her aunt a visit before Maggie bumped into her. Otherwise, Maggie and her evil tongue would spread it all over the village like wildfire that she was lying to her husband and that simply wouldn't do. He'd beat a confession out of her if he found out.

As she opened her front door, she called out his name, but there was no reply. She heaved a sigh of relief and took the basket to the scullery, stacked the plate away and hid the basket out of sight. There was no need for him to find out about her jaunt to see Anwen.

That reminded her. She slipped her hand into her skirt pocket and extracted the small glass jar that contained the balm Anwen had made for her. Better not show him this either or he'd only ask questions. She slipped it behind a couple of jars of jam her auntie had made for her on the shelf in the pantry, reminding herself that out of sight was out of mind.

* * *

Morgan failed to return that evening and, fearing what state he would be in if left to his own devices, Seren wrapped her shawl around herself and went in search of him at the Llwyn-yr-Eos public house on the canal bank. The pub was very popular in the village with the colliers, ironworkers and other working men. Some drank there morning, noon and night.

As she entered the little pub the men's raucous voices drifted away. There was a very long silence which made her feel awkward.

'Well, where is he?' she asked with hands on hips. Heads turned away, voices mumbled, but only one man met her piercing gaze. He was not a coward at least. It was Tom, Maggie Shanklin's husband, who had the courage to speak out, for many men in the village feared Morgan James.

'He was here all right, Mrs James,' he explained. 'But he left about an hour since . . . ' It was evident that although he'd spoken up, he'd say no more on the matter.

'Thank you, Tom,' she said. 'At least you have the courage to say so, not like some of the spineless men who sup here day and night!' She was that angry she could spit.

Hearing the words, 'Left with a floozie . . . ' she turned towards a man she didn't recognise at the bar. He was short in stature but of a stocky build. 'Oh aye, your old fella left here with a fine-looking filly, love. Rumour has it you're barren because you're not performing your wifely duties at home. You can't expect a fit, healthy man like your Morgan to go without, can you?'

'Right tasty little number she was an' all!' a man in the crowd shouted. 'Bet she gives him a good seeing to, love. Pity you aren't able to do the same!'

Seren's cheeks flamed with humiliation as hot tears sprang to her eyes. If only these men, these accusers, knew the truth about how her husband forced himself on her day and night! She turned and fled from the scene. Surely Morgan wouldn't take up with a woman of questionable morals behind her back? She had him down as many things but not as a philanderer. But it would explain why he was away from home so much, and why he no longer wanted to spend the evenings with her when he returned from work. He was spending more time in the pub of an evening rather than at his comfortable home. When and how had things changed so much?

Swallowing down her sadness, she felt her heart sink. And to think only this afternoon she had walked all the way up the mountain in search of some silly magic potion to help her conceive, and all for his benefit, too! And all the while he was diverting his attentions elsewhere and flaunting a floozie around the place!

She hardly remembered her path back to the house as a sense of fury took over. Flinging random items into a carpet bag, she thought, *he can ruddy well come home to an empty house and hearth*. She hadn't banked the fire up so it was almost out, and neither had she prepared his supper. His fancy piece could do that.

She was about to unlock the door when she heard voices outside.

'Mrs James is usually home of an evening . . .' It was the quiet, almost soothing voice of Mr Gruffudd, but who was he speaking to? 'Yes, Mr Evans, I'm sure you'll feel most welcome in Abercanaid.'

Realisation dawned. He was with the new minister from Pontypridd. What could she do now? The back way! She'd leave that way. She couldn't face them right now, with a lump the size of a piece of small coal stuck in her throat. What would they think of her to see her as upset as this?

She made her way through the scullery towards the back door and, glancing along the path through the small window, saw Morgan staggering towards the house, with hands deep in his pockets. He hadn't even noticed her as yet. She felt caught between the Devil and the deep blue sea. And there were no prizes for guessing who the Devil might be!

* * *

Anwen hadn't been able to get that poor girl out of her head. Sometimes she received visions about things, almost like a dream, except she was wide awake, and this vision now told her Seren was in serious trouble and needed her help.

She made her way down the mountainside in time to see the figure of a woman leaving the pub. It certainly looked like young Seren, but why was she marching off so purposefully like that? She decided to call at the house, Morgan or no Morgan. Dusk was fast approaching and she shivered. Even though it was September, the nights were drawing in and there was a nip in the air.

When she finally got to Seren's street, she found Mr Gruffudd standing on her doorstep with a smartly dressed young man beside him with a black book under his arm. Was this the new minister?

'Mr Gruffudd!' she called as she walked towards them. 'Have you seen Seren this evening?'

The minister shook his head. 'No, Mrs Llewellyn.' Dismissing her, he carried on knocking the door.

The young man looked at her quizzically. 'Hello. I'm Elwyn Evans, the new minister,' he introduced himself. 'We've been trying the door knocker for some time but there's been no answer.'

'I feel there's something badly wrong . . . ' She huffed out a breath. 'Mrs James came to see me earlier.'

Mr Gruffudd quirked a brow. 'Oh, and why was that?'

She bit her lip. She dare not tell him why for fear she got Seren into trouble with that husband of hers.

'She brought me a selection of cakes.' It was partly the truth so she didn't feel guilty saying so.

The young minister narrowed his eyes. 'So, what makes you think something is wrong with her, Mrs Llewellyn?'

'Because I just had another of my visions, warning me, like.'

Mr Gruffudd rolled his eyes. 'I've told you before and I'll tell you again, those visions are the Devil's own work. No wonder half the villagers have turned against you!'

'Hang on a moment, Mr Gruffudd,' Elwyn Evans intervened. 'This lady might have the gift of biblical prophecy . . . we should listen to what she has to say.'

Mr Gruffudd scowled. She could tell he was angered the way his top lip twitched. 'The only thing this woman practises is witchcraft! Come along, I don't know what they're teaching you at bible college these days.'

Elwyn shrugged and smiled at Anwen. 'Nice to meet you,' he said, then he turned and followed Mr Gruffudd.

* * *

There were no two ways about it, Seren would have to leave through the front door. She lifted the lace net curtain and was relieved to find the ministers had already departed but there, standing in the street, was Anwen. She opened the front door. 'How? Why?' she asked the woman, blinking several times.

'No time to ask questions,' Anwen said, glancing at the carpet bag in Seren's hand. 'You're in trouble, come back to the farm with me right now!'

Seren nodded. 'We'd better be quick, Morgan has just come in through the back gate, it won't be long before he'll come after me.'

'Well, it's almost dark and he'll never guess that you're with me at the farm.' But then a sudden thought occurred to her. Mr Gruffudd had just seen her, would he put two and two together? Hopefully not.

By the time they arrived at Anwen's farmhouse, it was dark and the moon had appeared from beneath a silver cloud, helping to illuminate their path.

'You're doing the right thing, *cariad*,' Anwen puffed. They were nearly at the top of the hill.

Was she doing the right thing, though? If Morgan were to catch her she dreaded to think what he might do to her.

Somewhere in front of her, an owl hooted, causing the hairs on Seren's neck to stand on end.

'What's the matter?' Anwen asked.

'I just don't recognise this place in the dark, it's making me fearful . . . '

Anwen laughed. 'We're taking the same route you took yourself to get to my house this afternoon. Don't worry, you shall be all right with me. I know this area like the back of my hand.'

That was something at least, she supposed. Seren had no doubts that as Anwen had lived on the mountain almost all of her life she knew it so well, but nevertheless, it was pretty spooky up here. She'd never walked here at night before. In the little village down below, she could see the gas lights twinkling and candles and lanterns illuminating people's windows and she wondered what Morgan was doing right now.

In the distance to the left, she could see the Cyfarthfa Iron-works and to her right, the Plymouth Ironworks, both lighting up the sky with every colour of the rainbow. Oh, but it was a spectacular sight to behold. So many folk from the town worked there and died there too.

Children as young as six years old crawled on their bellies for hours a day working alongside parents who needed every penny for their sprawling families. And she felt for the poor babies, sometimes left home alone for hours after being dosed up with syrup of poppies for them to slumber the sleep of the dead while their parents toiled in molten, melting conditions for the Crawshay family to live in that fine Cyfarthfa Castle on the hill. The family had a reputation for being hard task masters, and they also owned the Gethin Pit where the explosion had occurred.

Some poor young mites never awoke again after being overdosed on that medicine. How tragic was that when she, a woman who badly yearned for a baby, was denied one, while those poor babies and infants were killed at the hands of their own parents for needing to work?

Suffer the little ones to come unto me.

* * *

Seren spent a sleepless night tossing and turning in Anwen's spare bedroom and when it was time to wake up, it was then she felt ready for sleep.

The elderly lady tapped on the door. 'Are you decent, *cariad*?'

'Yes, Mrs Llewellyn . . . ' Anwen entered carrying a tray containing a couple of rounds of toast and a cup of tea.

'You really shouldn't have gone to so much trouble, you know . . . ' Seren pulled herself up in bed and settled on her haunches.

Anwen smiled, her rheumy eyes kindly but knowledgeable. 'I know, child, but I feel if anyone deserves special treatment right now, it's you.'

'Thank you. I shall work my keep here until I find a new home of my own. Now what can I do today for you?'

Anwen sat on the bed beside her and patted her hand. 'Don't fret, I've been up a couple of hours since, feeding the livestock. But if you'd really like to help me today then perhaps you could help me with the washing and ironing.'

Seren nodded, pleased she could be of some assistance to the old woman, but when Anwen had left the draughty room, her stomach lurched at the thought of what Morgan was thinking right now. He must be flaming furious!

* * *

Morgan's head ached as he opened his eyes. He'd had a right skinful last night, make no bones about it, but Seren would see him right. A nice cooked breakfast of sausage, bacon and eggs would set him right for a day ahead at the shop. But there was no sound of her clattering about in the kitchen and no smell of any food being cooked either. He reached out for her side of the bed: it was cold to the touch. Where on earth was she? The light filtering in through the window was a bit too much for him to bear until he'd had his first cup of tea of the day.

'Woman!' he bellowed down the stairs, half expecting her to rush up them to attend to his needs. She always put him first in whatever she did, and in some ways, he despised her for it.

He pulled himself out of bed, still dressed in last night's shirt and trousers which were wrinkled to high heaven as he'd been sleeping in them. He'd got so drunk that all he remembered of getting himself to bed was falling heavily on top of the covers like a sack of spuds. He ran his hand across his stubbled chin and felt a trickle of spittle. He must have been drooling in his sleep. He sniffed and wiped it with the back of his hand. Now he needed to get himself ready for work. He prided himself on the fact that no matter how much he drank, he was still able to do a day's work. How many could say that? Not many for sure.

He poured some cold water from the earthenware jug on the cabinet into the matching bowl and, hoisting his trouser braces over his shoulders so they dangled below his waist, he removed his shirt so he could have a good scrub. Seren usually boiled the kettle so he could wash in hot water. She really was neglecting him this morning, but she'd pay for it later.

When he'd finished, he wiped his face on the coarse towel that was hanging on a hook on the wall, then caught sight of himself in the wardrobe mirror and cringed. His skin looked sallow and his cheeks puffy. But at least his face was clean.

Opening the wardrobe door, he scanned its interior. Spotting a clean cotton shirt, he put it on. Fair play, Seren always kept his clothes clean and tidy and the house was spotless. She was a fine homemaker but as barren as the Sahara Desert. Now Mari, last night, she was insatiable, couldn't get enough of him, and she liked it rough and all, but with Seren, she always looked so defeated afterwards. Hurt like a little puppy with such sad eyes. If only she was like his Mari. A fine figure of a woman, a trifle buxom, but he loved that. Pity, though; Mari, who was a widow who worked at the wash house, was getting a bit old to bear kids. But then again, she had a bad reputation and he wanted the mother of his children to be respectable.

He lumbered down the stairs and headed for the privy. There was still no sign of Seren. Maybe she'd popped over to the shop? That would be it. She'd forgotten to get the eggs or something for his breakfast. She'd be back by the time he'd finished his business. He picked up a newspaper to take with him. He always read when he was going to be on the job for a long time. She'd be back before he knew it.

An image of Mari and her voluptuous breasts spilling out of her dress came to mind. How he'd loved tweaking them as he'd listened to her squealing with delight. And the things she could do with her tongue. Seren wouldn't have said it was decent, but he'd enjoyed it, something he'd never experienced before, only bad girls up in the notorious China district of the town did things like that, or so he thought. That woman couldn't get enough of him and him enough of her, which gave him an idea. Why not move Mari into the house? He'd have the respectability of having Seren as his wife and he'd pretend that Mari was a lodger, only he'd be in her bedroom at night warming her bed. It was something worth thinking about, that was for sure.

He was just finishing off in the privy when he heard the back gate creak open. That was Seren, back to cook his breakfast. He rushed out about to say something to find he was faced with the old crone, Maggie Shanklin.

'Where's your Seren?' she asked, her eyes shiny and inquisitive.

'None of your business, you nosy old cow!' he growled, slipping his leather trouser braces on to his shoulders.

'Well, it is my business when my Tom gets asked at the pub where you were last night!'

Morgan felt as if the stuffing had been knocked out of him. 'What do you mean?'

'She knows about your floozie, Morgan James. 'Tisn't right, if you ask me. You should never leave a heap of excrement on your own doorstep! She walked into the pub and asked if anyone had seen you and someone told her about that Mari one you've been knocking around with.'

A feeling of dread washed over him. He hadn't set eyes on Seren this morning, the bed was cold; she hadn't slept at home last night. A sense of fury overtook him as he pushed the woman out of his way and marched back to the house with his newspaper tucked under his arm.

Maggie Shanklin stood there shaking her head. ''Twill all come to a head, you see if it doesn't, Morgan James! You're bringing the tone of this street down, running after common whores!'

Angrily, he slammed the back door behind him, then raised his fist and punched the wall.

That bitch is going to pay for leaving me, but first I need to find her!

3

Word had been sent via a letter to Seren's mother saying she was safe at the farm with Anwen and informing her not to tell anyone except the family for time being. A young lad called Sam, who helped on the farm, had taken the letter with instructions not to tell anyone he'd delivered it. Sam was a good lad whose mother didn't want him going down the pit as there had been two explosions over the past few years. One in 1862 with the loss of forty-seven lives and the other in 1865 with the loss of thirty-four. A lot of young lads in the area, even as young as eleven years old, had followed their fathers underground. Sadly, one of those men lost in the last pit accident was Sam's own father.

The lad didn't earn a lot from Anwen as she didn't have the money to pay him a decent wage, but he was allowed to take home cabbages, potatoes and carrots from her market garden, as she called it, and that was a big help for his family. She had tried to sell to the village shops but, as people imagined her to be involved in sorcery, they wouldn't even consider it. And it didn't help with someone like Mrs Shanklin going around stirring the pot.

One morning Seren was hanging out washing on the line when she spotted someone walking up the hill. At first she feared it was Morgan, but this man didn't have Morgan's broad shoulders and appeared well dressed. There was something familiar about him, though, so not taking any chances, she dropped the wicker laundry basket on the ground and fled inside to be met by a very amused Anwen, who for once had her feet up by the hearth taking a well-earned break.

'Where's the fire, Seren?' she asked, looking up from her rocking chair.

'Th . . . there's a man walking up the hill, looks like he's headed here . . . ' she gasped.

Seren had never seen Anwen move so quickly in her life as she shot out of the chair to peer out of the kitchen window. Relaxing her stance, she turned to Seren. 'It's all right, it's only that new minister, Elwyn Evans. Go and hide in the bedroom and I'll keep him occupied.'

Seren did as instructed, hoping that Anwen was going to be able to get rid of him, but he had walked a long way to get here. She was sure that the old minister would have told him to keep well away from the place, so she assumed he was going out of his way to make a visit to the farm.

As Seren hid, snuggled under the covers of her bed, she heard some polite conversation and, oh no, Anwen was inviting him to stay for a cup of tea! She listened further to the minister's pleasing voice. He didn't sound threatened by Anwen at all, not like Mr Gruffudd and most of the villagers.

There was a sudden bumping noise beside her. Oh no! She held her breath. Had he heard it too? She lifted the covers to see that the book she'd been reading the previous night, which had been on top of the covers, must have slipped off the bed on to the floor.

The conversation in the other room continued, and she wondered how much time had passed as she badly needed to use the privy. Almost as if Anwen had realised this, she heard the woman winding up the conversation. 'It was good to meet you, Mr Evans. If circumstances were different with regards to the villagers, I would definitely attend your services at the chapel.'

The voices were drawing closer. 'You're welcome any time at all, Mrs Llewellyn. It can't be easy for you living somewhere as remote as this without any family.'

'Aye. I'm more than used to it by now, but just because I no longer attend chapel, doesn't mean to say I don't read my bible nor pray.'

'Glad to hear it. Good day to you.'

Seren heard the door click shut, then Anwen entered the room. 'That was a close one. He's very nice, that young minister. Very modern and forward-thinking, unlike Mr Gruffudd who's all fire and brimstone!' She chuckled.

Seren set about tidying the bed where she had messed it up. In some ways she'd have loved to have met the man herself, but then it might get back to the ears of Mr Gruffudd, who undoubtedly would inform Morgan.

Anwen smiled. 'You look like you've had a tremendous shock, *cariad*. Let's have a nice cup of tea, shall we?'

Seren nodded. A cup of tea seemed to be a panacea for all ailments, and right now she felt as though she could badly do with one. 'You sit yourself down and I'll just finish pegging out that washing, then I'll make it.'

Anwen let out a long breath of relief. She'd been up at the crack of dawn seeing to the animals; she was such a hard worker. Seren had no idea how old she was but she seemed fitter than some who were probably half her age.

* * *

Morgan pounded both his fists on Seren's mother's door. Normally, her door was left unlocked and he'd already tried to open it. There was no fooling him, Mabel Edwards knew something. And she was a very wily mother-in-law, unlike her naïve daughter, who he'd reckoned he could fool as easy as pie.

Feeling he might as well give up and go back to the Llwyn-yr-Eos, he noticed a curtain twitch in the house next door. He glared at the elderly woman looking out and raised a fist. This was so unlike him to show this side of himself to the ladies of the village, but he no longer cared. He hadn't even bothered to open up his cobbler shop today. They could all ruddy well wait for their old boots to be tapped! What did he care?

As he trudged over to the canal bank back to the pub, he dug his hands deep in his pockets. Someone was going to pay for this, by damn they were! As he entered the pub, the men turned their heads away as the conversation ceased. No one dared to make eye contact with him. 'Cat got your tongues?' he growled, then, turning to the landlord, shouted, 'Another pint of ale.'

The landlord, who did not dare to refuse, poured his foaming pint in his favourite battered pewter tankard and, shaking slightly, handed it over to him.

Morgan nodded and drank it over his head. Wiping the beery foam from his lips with the back of his hand, he gasped loudly and said, 'I'll have a glass of whisky next, my good man!'

Someone muttered behind him, but they knew better than to raise their voices to Morgan James.

* * *

Seren's mother and sister were regular visitors to the farmhouse over the next few days.

'I think you've done the right thing, my girl,' her mam said, crossing her hands at the kitchen table while Gwendolyn nodded and Anwen set about preparing to make cups of tea for them all. 'Despite that Maggie Shanklin one spreading it around the village that Morgan has dumped you in favour of a brazen hussy!'

At the mention of her husband's name, Seren's heart pounded profusely. 'Well, the old crone can spread it about like butter as far as I am concerned because it's all true anyhow!'

Anwen, who was stood behind Seren, placed a reassuring hand on her shoulder. 'Aye, you're well rid of the big bully, but I don't believe he'll let you go without a fight — he's not that sort.'

Mam nodded. 'Well, he has no choice, he's been to our house several times and I've given him short shrift each time and sent him away. If your father was still alive, he'd sort him out. Although, he doesn't dare try any of his tricks with me, and he's gone away like a dog with a tail between its legs.'

'And we all know what dogs are capable of doing . . . ' Seren raised her voice, 'biting!'

Her mother's eyes widened. 'He daren't touch another hair on your head, *cariad*! It was all very well when you were living under his roof, I couldn't be there to keep an eye on you, but now you've escaped, you stay away, my girl! In any case, he hasn't returned to our door since I had words with him!'

'I wouldn't put it past him to beat me again, Mam. It's only now my last lot of bruises are beginning to fade.' She subconsciously rubbed her wrist as if it would somehow erase the bruising.

'But things will have changed now you are no longer under the same roof; he can no longer exert his control over you.'

Anwen shot Seren's mother a worried glance. 'Men like Morgan James never change, Mabel — they will use their fists at any given opportunity. And the problem is, most men in the village are too afraid to give him a taste of his own medicine as he's strong and able enough to thrash the living daylights out of them, too!' Anwen raised a fist. Seren had never seen her exhibit any anger before, she was usually quite placid by nature.

'The main thing is that Morgan doesn't find out where my sister is . . . ' Gwendolyn said in a worried tone of voice as both Mam and Anwen mumbled their agreement.

Seren wasn't so sure, though, that they'd be able to keep her hiding place a secret for much longer.

* * *

From the corner of a darkened room, Morgan rolled over and groaned. Where was he? He could see various shapes moving around; sometimes they were large and seemed to tower over him as he lay prone on the bed, then they became smaller and drifted away, but he just didn't care, he felt so chilled and at peace. Every last bit of anger seemed to have evaporated into the ether. She was here somewhere in the room, his Mari. He could hear her voice as she sang softly and smoothed his forehead, and he also heard the voices of many others he didn't recognise. Where was he and what was he doing here?

It was then he remembered they were in the China district of Merthyr where Mari worked. The flowery, other-worldly, overpowering smell reminded him he was in an opium den. But why was he here in the first place? He didn't really want to remember what he was so desperately trying to forget.

* * *

Seren awoke as the first light of dawn filtered in through the curtained window. The one thing she noticed about being on the mountain was the quietness of it all. Back home she'd hear the sounds of Morgan banging around the place, dropping his hobnail boots on the hardwood bedroom floorboards as he got ready for work, and outside in the street, the rumble of cart-wheels and the mumble of voices. Here, all she could hear was birdsong and the distant babble of the brook. Living in Merthyr Tydfil was like living in both the town and the countryside at the same time. The rolling green hills that had previously been mainly farmland until the industrial revolution took over were partially ruined by the sight of the pits and ironworks as sulphurous smoke spewed out from within and ashen smoke piped out of chimneys in the streets below.

Anwen drew her water from the brook, and today, as Seren was awake earlier than usual, she decided to help the woman by fetching the day's supply of water for her. She got herself washed and dressed and made her way to the brook as she swung a wooden pail in either hand. Humming softly to herself, she stepped through the dew-glistening grass and over the wooden stile until she reached the brook which was shielded by an overgrowth of bushes and trees. Pushing some branches out of the way, she was startled to see a man in front of her on his knees as if in prayer. She was about to turn to leave when the man spotted her. It was then she recognised him as Elwyn Evans, the new minister.

He smiled and pulled himself to his feet and made his way over to her. What could she do now? It would look rude if she suddenly dropped the buckets and ran off. She waited as he approached, hoping he wouldn't hear the internal drum-beat that was thudding in her ears.

'Hello there,' he said. The dark hair framing his face suited his swarthy colouring and she felt her cheeks flame at their sudden encounter.

She nodded shyly, noticing for the first time his emerald-green eyes. 'Hello.'

'And you are?' His eyes were questioning.

Should she tell him the truth? 'I'm Mrs James.'

'Ah.' Recognition dawned on him. 'So, you're the Mrs James who Mr Gruffudd was so keen for me to meet?'

'Yes, that's me. He wanted me to welcome you to the village and help you if necessary, but please don't tell anyone you saw me here . . . ' She lowered her head.

'Why ever not?'

'Because I have left my husband. I know it's a sin, but you see, he was cruel to me.' Should she trust him or not?

'I'm sorry to hear that and don't worry, I half guessed there was someone staying at Anwen's cottage the last time I called there . . . '

'Oh?'

'Yes, I heard something fall in the bedroom, and to be honest, I noticed a figure which looked too young to be Mrs Llewellyn hanging out the washing, then she disappeared . . . '

'Yes, that was me.'

'Now I know why, you no longer have to fear me. What are you doing here anyhow?'

'I could be asking you the same thing?' Her chin jutted out.

'I was praying.'

'You came all this way to do that?'

'Not especially, I planned on visiting Anwen again, but came here first as I thought it seemed private. Well, it did so at the time.' He chuckled, which caused her to smile.

'I'm sorry about that. I just came to fill up with water. This is fresh mountain water.'

'I know,' he said. 'Here, let me.' He took the pails from her grasp and filled them with the crystal-clear water.

Seren and the new minister chatted quite amicably on their way back to the farmhouse as he carried the full pails for her until he paused a moment, and then, looking at her in earnest, said, 'But why did you marry such a man if he's a brute?'

The direct question took her aback, so much so that she was at a loss for words for a few moments. 'I suppose it was because he seemed kind and loving to begin with . . .'

'Then he changed?' His green eyes darkened.

'Yes. It was a few months after we were wed, when he discovered I'd not yet become pregnant by him. That's when he began slapping me around, calling me the most vile, disgusting names. Once he even . . . ' There was a catch in her voice as the memory flooded back like a great big tidal wave that engulfed her entire being.

'He even what?'

She swallowed hard. 'H . . . he even tried pushing me down the stairs. I clung for dear life to the bannister and I think he would have done and all had it not been for a caller at the door which brought him to his senses.'

'But didn't you take that as a warning sign that you should pack your bags and leave?'

It was easy for a stranger to remark at what she should or could have done at that time, but he wasn't her, where she feared that even by leaving the man she would suffer for it too, and so might her family. He'd warned her often enough how he could seduce her sister and how she'd love it and all, and Gwen would bear him the child he so badly wanted as she was younger and fresher than she who had lost her bloom. Or how he could follow her mother one night in the dark and push her into the canal, and she'd have no clue who had done it to her either.

She looked at the minister, her chin jutting out in determination. 'I was ruled by a rod of fear, Mr Evans . . . I can see that now I am away from him. Unless you've been in that sort of circumstance, how can you possibly understand? For all your biblical training in Cardiff, you have little understanding of what makes people do what they do. So, I suggest you stay put here and find out! We in Abercanaid weren't brought up in the lap of luxury, oh no! Most of the men around here don't have clean fingernails like yourself because they're caked in coal dust! Else they're coughing up their lungs, plagued with respiratory diseases!'

She watched as a cloud of uncertainty passed over his face. Why was she turning her anger on to him? He was only trying to help, he hadn't asked for any of this. 'Please forgive me, Mr Evans . . . ' She released a composing breath.

He smiled. 'It's quite all right, I can see you've been through such a lot, Mrs James, you are bound to get angry sometimes.'

'Seren, please. My name is Seren.'

'What a lovely name. Doesn't it mean 'star' in Welsh?'

She nodded.

'Please call me Elwyn when we're alone together, drop the formality!'

She guessed he must feel so dreadfully alone in Abercanaid what with not having a wife or family in the area, and now she felt so ashamed of herself for losing her temper like that, and him being so forgiving and all.

He set the pails of water down on the grass for a moment. 'Do you know, I really feel it's so peaceful up here. If you didn't look at the village below, you'd never realise it existed.'

She nodded. 'But of course, the pits around here remind us of where we are; they're a blight on the landscape with their pit wheels and black grime. But as they say, where there's muck there's money.'

He nodded. 'I was watching the sky lit up by the ironworks last night from my bedroom window. It really was a spectacular sight to behold.'

'It is and all, but the Crawshay family are such hard task masters. Do you know there have been a couple of disasters at the Gethin Pit in the village? The Crawshays own it. Robert Thompson Crawshay didn't even turn out for the men's funerals. I say men, but there were boys injured and killed too. One was only eleven years old . . . ' She caught a breath.

He gasped. 'That's dreadful. I shouldn't want that for a son of mine.'

'Mine neither, but people living in this area have little choice, it's either the pit or the ironworks. It's hard for most living in Merthyr, unless they have money. While the Crawshays are lording it up with their fancy balls at the castle, many in this town are living in dire poverty where their only options are the street or the workhouse. My father died in that pit disaster last year . . . ' she said, lowering her head.

He touched her shoulder, causing her to look at his face. 'I am so sorry,' he said sincerely.

She nodded her thanks. It was something maybe she'd never fully get over. Feeling that she wanted to make up for her earlier unexpected outburst, she decided to offer the minister a cup of tea. She intended brewing up anyhow, as she hadn't yet had her first cup of the day. That was always the best in her book.

Not only did he stay for a cup of tea, he accepted another fresh brew as Anwen burst in through the kitchen door, her face ruddied, huffing and puffing, with a pile of sticks in her arms.

Immediately Elwyn leapt out of his chair to help the woman carry them to the grate. 'Any time you want sticks cutting, Mrs Llewellyn, I'm your man!' he said enthusiastically.

Anwen chuckled. 'Aye, maybe, lad, but I dare say I've chopped more sticks than you've had hot dinners and I'd be far quicker at it an' all.' She flexed her arm to show how muscular it was, which was unusual for a woman of her age. Even though most of the women Seren knew were hard workers in the home for their families, not many did the shifting and carrying that their menfolk did like Anwen. She guessed the woman had little choice since her husband passed away. If the villagers weren't so hostile towards her maybe she'd have left the farm and settled down in the village by now, living a less harsh life. But then again, who was happiest? Anwen with her livestock for companions and the odd visitor, or Maggie Shanklin, who seemed so bitter and twisted she felt it was expected of her to spread gossip to her so-called friends?

Seren reckoned Anwen would be right that she'd chop sticks quickest, she was very efficient around the farm. Elwyn caught Seren's gaze and she found herself turning away in embarrassment.

When he'd left to return to The Manse, Anwen looked at Seren and said, 'My, my, you pair looked sort of cosy there, *bach*!'

Seren shook her head. 'Oh, I don't know about that. I only bumped into him near the brook this morning . . .'

Anwen wrinkled her nose. 'What on earth was he doing there?'

'He was praying, by all accounts. I feel a little guilty as I disturbed him as I went to fetch water.'

'I don't expect he'd have minded. Doesn't seem that sort to me.'

'I think you're right.'

'I can well understand him going there as it's so peaceful. God's in his heaven and all's right with the world.'

'That's exactly what Elwyn told me about it being peaceful.'

'Oh, it's Elwyn now, is it?' Anwen chuckled.

Seren's cheeks flamed. 'That's what he told me to call him when we're alone.'

'So, he intends getting you alone now, does he?'

Seren smiled at the mischievous twinkle in Anwen's eyes and she realised it was the first time she'd felt happy in a long while.

* * *

Morgan had by now shot out of his reverie and was hopping mad when he fully awoke from his other-worldly haze to discover all his money was missing from his trouser pockets and Mari had gone too. There was now no one else in the room, just some grubby stained pallets on the floor and the odour of unwashed bodies tinged with some sort of flowery, pungent aroma. Opium! A memory of how he'd puffed away on some long sort of pipe came back at him along with all the grinning faces surrounding him. He was in the China district of the town but had little memory of how he'd come to be here apart from the fact he'd known Mari worked at the wash house. He remembered now. The wash house was next door and this was the upstairs room of an inn owned by one of the most feared men in China — Twm Sion Watkin.

Fear gripped him as he realised he couldn't remember the last time he'd opened the shop. He'd let a lot of people down and now maybe word had got around Abercanaid that he was a wife beater and all.

Was this the life he really wanted for himself? Out of his brain on a mind-altering substance?

In these parts it was more usual for the ironworkers and colliers to drink alcohol, which had been the ruin of many a good man as he'd pissed his wages up against the wall. But puffing an opium pipe was a different thing altogether. How had he ended up in China with the dregs of society? No sir, this life wasn't for him. He was going to clean up his act, ditch Mari, who was little more than a prostitute for having sex with him and pilfering his hard-earned wages, and then he might be able to get his wife back.

4

Anwen had persuaded Seren to help Elwyn at the chapel to take her mind off her situation. If she was careful to get there by not passing either the Llwyn-yr-Eos pub or their home, then likely Morgan wouldn't see her. So it was with a glad heart she set out with a basket laden with a jam and cream sponge cake she'd baked especially for him and a selection of books Anwen thought he might enjoy.

It must be so lonely for him being in a strange working-class area when it's so obvious he's been brought up well, maybe in a middle-class home.

It was mid-afternoon when she set off down the mountain with her woollen shawl wrapped around her shoulders and her long hair blowing in the breeze. It was such a fresh day, a day of new beginnings, maybe. She knew she'd find him at the chapel as he'd told her he wrote his sermon there on a Wednesday morning ready for Sunday, and of course, due to her leaving Morgan, she'd missed his first sermon last weekend.

The chapel door was open when she arrived and the street deserted which was just as well. The sound of the church organ piping the strains of 'Thine be the Glory' pulled her up sharply. He wasn't alone then as she'd hoped, but she had come all this way and even if she couldn't stay for a chat, she could leave the cake and books. As she approached and looked past the long wooden pews to where the organ stood, she blinked several times. For it wasn't the usual organist seated there, who was more often than not Enid Williams who played on Sundays, and when she wasn't available then Leighton Pugh stepped into her shoes — this was Elwyn himself. Speechless, she stood there for a moment enthralled. She hadn't realised he was so talented and he seemed totally absorbed in the music. When he finished, she found herself clapping in appreciation.

He turned and smiled, then rising from his seat, walked towards her to greet her. 'Hello, Seren. What brings you here today?'

'Never mind that. I didn't know you were musical, Elwyn?'

He nodded. 'Yes, my parents tell me I had picked up a few tunes on the piano forte by the time I was four years old! I'm just keeping my hand in as it were, with some practice.'

She cleared her throat. 'I came today to bring you these . . . ' She drew back the covering cloth on the basket to reveal the cake and books.

'My, my, you have been busy, Seren.'

'I love baking, but the books are a gift from Anwen.'

'Please thank her for me, will you?'

She nodded. 'Of course. Where shall I put these?'

'Bring them through to my office out the back, if you please.'

Seren followed the minister to his small office which was located down a dimly lit corridor that smelled strongly of musty damp and didn't look as if it had seen a flick of a duster in months. Taking the basket from her, he set it down on the desk in front of him.

'Please forgive the appearance of this room. Mrs Shanklin used to clean here according to Mr Gruffudd, but apparently she stopped working here when she fell out with some of the congregation . . . '

'And why was that?'

'It was all over Anwen Llewellyn.'

'Yes, Maggie Shanklin dislikes Anwen with a great intensity, I'm afraid. She sees her as some sort of sorcerer — a witch who should be ducked in the village pond or burnt at the stake, which is a bit rich as Mrs Shanklin often reads the tea leaves for folk! I'm telling you it's all untrue, Anwen is a healer, that's all — knows the right plants to mix together to make potions and lotions.'

Elwyn looked at her with avid interest. 'You mean an herbalist?'

'Yes, that's correct. She has one of those apothecary cabinets — you know, the sort that has lots of little drawers. She crushes seeds and leaves with a pestle and mortar. She's no more a witch than you are an alcoholic!'

Elwyn nodded. 'I understand. It's my intention to get both women to return to this chapel and put their feud behind them.' He paused for a moment as if he had some matter or another on his mind. 'Please seat yourself, Seren. There's something I wish to speak to you about.'

This sounds serious, what has he to say to me?

'It's about Morgan.'

She huffed out a breath. 'Oh, yes . . . ' She sat herself opposite him, with the desk between them.

'I've been informed by someone that he's been associating with a woman of questionable morals, who is known as Mari.'

Her spine stiffened and she felt the hairs on the back of her neck bristle. So that was the woman's name. It was pretty too. But the picture of her husband being with someone by that name made it more real somehow. Feeling incensed that people were talking, she pursed her lips. 'What business is it of theirs? It is ours and ours alone!'

'So, you are saying it's untrue?'

'No, I have heard the rumours, of course I have, but I shouldn't wish to save the marriage in any case.'

He gazed at her as if about to say something she might not care to hear. 'But what about if your husband were to clean himself up?'

'Pardon?'

'To stop drinking alcohol and leave the woman alone and turn back towards your marriage, what then?'

She thought for a moment. 'It's of no use, as he can even be violent towards me when he hasn't drunk any beer or spirits, and as for the woman . . . ' she scoffed, 'she's more than welcome to him and she's done me a favour!' Her chin jutted out in defiance. Why was he asking her such questions?

He steepled his fingers as if deep in thought,

then let out a long breath. 'I don't know how to tell you this, but Morgan called here to see me yesterday morning. I wasn't going to tell you as you have enough on your plate.'

'But why should he want to see you, Elwyn? He hasn't set a foot inside the chapel since the day we were wed!' She thought back to the wedding day itself. She had felt happy then and maybe they both were, so why had it all gone so wrong?

'He said he needed to speak to someone.'

She frowned. 'I'm sorry but you should have refused.'

He shook his head and let out a long breath. 'I couldn't, I'm a man of the cloth and if a parishioner calls to see me, then it's my duty to speak to them. I turn no one away from the House of God.'

She nodded. 'Yes, I understand that. I was surprised, that's all. So, how was he?'

'In a bad way; he didn't look as if he'd seen soap and water for days. Mind you, he said he intended cleaning himself up, as I told you.'

'They're only words.'

'He seemed sincere.'

'But you can't possibly be serious?' Seren could hardly believe her ears.

Elwyn tapped the large black family-size bible in front of him on his desk. 'How long have you been married?'

'Not yet a full year. It will be a year next month.'

He cleared his throat. 'It says here in this bible, 'What therefore God hath joined together, let no man put asunder . . . ' From the gospel of Mark, chapter 10, verse 9.'

She swallowed hard. 'I know that verse well enough as I heard it uttered by Mr Gruffudd on our wedding day and I've heard it at plenty of weddings, but where does it say what a wife is to do if her husband treats her in a cruel fashion after they are wed? Go on, tell me that!'

Elwyn smiled. 'No, it does not say that, Seren. But what it does say is, 'Husbands, love your wives, even as Christ also loved the church, and gave himself for it . . . ' You'll find that in Ephesians, chapter 5 . . .'

She shook her head. 'You don't need to keep preaching to me, Mr Evans, I know my bible very well indeed. And you don't need to try to convince me that my husband is a changed man and to give him another chance because he's had every chance he's going to get from me!'

Elwyn frowned. 'But if you'd seen the humble, contrite man before me yesterday, you'd understand how he was prepared to put aside his wrongdoings to make you happy, Seren . . . '

She snorted in disgust. 'Believe me, I've heard it all before. He sure knows how to lay on the charm, especially to other people. He loves to make a good impression.'

The minister shook his head sadly. 'Look, he knows he has wronged you and wishes to make amends. You have some teething troubles in your marriage, that's all. Mr Gruffudd told me . . . '

She felt her hackles rise and she balled her hands into fists. 'Mr Gruffudd told you what?'

'That he understands you are somewhat wilful

and you need to submit more to your husband as he is, after all, head of the home.'

She let out a long groan of despair. If only people realised that she'd already done that. What about the times when he'd taken her by force to satisfy his lustful urges? Or when he'd woken her out of their bed, drunk, when he'd come home in the early hours of the morning, demanding she make him something to eat because his evening meal was now cold and shrivelled up? Wasn't that submission? Painful tears pricked the back of her eyes as she studied the painting hanging on the wall behind him. It was of Jesus in the Garden of Gethsemane. It depicted a time when the good Lord was about to be betrayed by Judas. The calm before the storm. Her cross to bear in life was her husband's cruel, tormenting behaviour towards her.

'I can't believe I'm hearing this, Mr Evans!' She took a deep composing breath to prevent herself from breaking down into tears. 'You're a new minister in this village, and as far as I'm concerned, out of touch with real life here.'

He looked at her with questioning eyes. 'All I'm asking is that you think things over, that's all. I would hardly be doing my job here as new minister if I were to ignore the pleas of one of my congregation. Morgan told me that this is the chapel where you both wed. All he's asking for is another chance.'

A sudden thought occurred to her. 'Y . . . you haven't . . . oh no . . . you haven't told him where I'm staying, have you?'

'I'm afraid he has found out, but not from me. He said Mrs Shanklin told him where you were.'

Seren blinked several times. 'But how on earth could that gossiping old crone have known that?'

Elwyn's face flushed. 'I mentioned it to Mr Gruffudd as he was here when your husband called yesterday. He came to collect a few personal belongings and to have a word with me.'

As Elwyn's eyes darkened she knew he realised he had made a grave mistake. Now she knew a little of how her Lord felt by such a betrayal. What right did that man have to tell Mrs Shanklin of her whereabouts?

As if reading her mind, he added, 'To be fair to Mr Gruffudd, I don't think he realised what he was doing. He's very fond of Mrs Shanklin. He thought it was just a lovers' tiff between the two of you.'

She leaned across the desk with her knuckles white as she balled them into fists, glaring at him. 'A lovers' tiff? It is far more than that. Not only does my husband get involved with a whore from a wash house in China, but he beats me amongst doing other horrific things! You and Mr Gruffudd have quite no idea what you've both done!'

A sudden thought occurred to her. She pushed back her chair to get away from the desk, making a hard scraping sound on the flagstone floor. 'I must return to Anwen to warn her my husband will come to find me. I need to go elsewhere, somewhere safe now!' She glared at Elwyn who now could no longer look her in the eye.

Shame, that was. And so he should be ashamed

too, after letting the cat out of the bag like that. He had known Morgan had been violent in the marriage towards her, though she hadn't filled him in on the worst details.

It was a man's world all right where sometimes women were expected to have their hides tanned like a piece of old shoe leather.

* * *

All was quiet when Seren arrived back at the farmhouse, huffing and puffing in her haste. Sam was outside scattering corn for the chickens. 'Where's Mrs Llewellyn?' she asked.

'She's gone for a lie down.' He angled his head curiously. 'She seems tired a lot lately . . . '

She nodded and smiled nervously. She just couldn't relax now. She had gone to the chapel earlier feeling hopeful and returned with a feeling of dread welling up inside her. She decided to brew a pot of tea and explain the situation to Anwen, then she'd pack her things and head off for her auntie's house at Lewis Square. She did not intend bringing trouble to Anwen's door. It wouldn't be fair on the elderly lady.

When Seren entered the bedroom with a cup of tea in her hand, she was dismayed to find it in semi-darkness. The curtains were still drawn and the silhouetted woman lay slumped to the side of the bed with her head lowered. Seren quickly drew back the curtains to get a better look at her.

'Oh, Anwen, what's the matter? Are you feeling unwell?'

'I'm not too sure . . . ' She let out a groan. 'My old bones are playing me up something rotten. I think I might have over-done things working on the farm today.'

How could she think of leaving the woman at a time like this? Anwen needed her help.

'Let's sit you up and you sip that nice cup of tea, you hear?' Anwen nodded gratefully. 'What you need is complete rest. Me and young Sam can manage the farm for a few days.'

Seren helped the woman to sit up and propped plenty of pillows behind her. 'Now, as well as rest, is there anything I can get for you from the apothecary cabinet? Something you'd advise for someone who felt as you do?'

Anwen smiled. 'There's good you are to me, *bach*. There's a potion I made up I've been taking for the past few days and it does help, I forgot to take it yesterday. It's not in the cabinet, it's in the dark in the pantry on the top shelf. If you could fetch that for me with a spoon, that would be wonderful.' She patted Seren's hand. 'You're becoming like the daughter I never had.'

Seren sat on a chair that was positioned near the bed. 'You never had any children then, Anwen?'

'No, and it was not for the want of trying either.' She chuckled. 'Gwynfor and I really longed for children but it was never to be. I even tried my own potions. That's why I was reluctant to give you one that time you asked me. Not because I don't think it would help with your fertility, but I sensed there was trouble with that husband of yours.' Her eyes darkened and Seren wondered if she should tell the woman right now what Elwyn had told her. She watched as Anwen slowly sipped her tea. 'What's the matter, *cariad*? You've been staring at me as if you've seen a ghost. Got something on your mind?'

'It's Morgan . . .' She bit her bottom lip.

'Oh yes?'

'When I called to the chapel earlier, Elwyn told me he'd been there saying he's going to sort himself out to win me back. Reckons he's a reformed character and it sounds as if both ministers have fallen for it!'

Anwen slowly shook her head and tutted. 'Aye, well, they don't know him like you do.'

'True. Anyhow, I said my piece to Elwyn and I think, or at least hope, he understands. But apparently Maggie Shanklin has informed Morgan that I'm staying with you. And Anwen, it was not my intention to bring my troubles to your door.'

'I know that and you can stay here as long as you like. But how does that woman know your business?'

'She's found out from Mr Gruffudd. Elwyn had told him.'

Anwen shook her head. 'For goodness' sakes, what a pair of do-gooders who have caused some trouble for you, Seren!'

'To be fair, I don't think either of them intended to. Apparently, they'd got it into their heads that Morgan and myself have 'teething troubles' in the marriage. This was even though I confided in Elwyn that Morgan was violent.'

'You know what it is, though?'

She shook her head, having no clue what the

woman was speaking of. 'No?'

'We're living in a world where it seems it's a husband's right to discipline his own wife. Sad, but true. You take my Gwynfor though . . . he'd never have laid a finger on me, but I've seen many a woman in this village with a black eye or bruised arms. Of course, they claim it all happened by accident. 'I walked into a lamppost!' or 'I fell down the stairs!' They've come here a time or two and all looking for some sort of potion to clear up their bruising. I usually give them witch hazel for it, or that ointment I gave you.'

Seren looked at Anwen blankly. 'It makes me so sad.'

'At least you know you're not the only one. The women keep silent about it as they don't see it in their best interests to speak out. And if they leave their husbands, often they have a brood of children to support as well, so they put up and shut up.'

In Seren's book, having a taste of it herself, she knew how wrong it really was. And she thanked her lucky stars that although she longed for a baby, Morgan hadn't got her pregnant as yet.

* * *

'Pregnant? But you can't be!' Morgan scratched his head as he allowed Mari into his house. He looked up and down the street but thankfully he couldn't see anyone out as it was early.

'Well, I'm telling you I am. So, what are you going to do about it?'

He should have been overjoyed that there was a baby on the way, only he didn't want one with Mari, the neighbours would talk. They'd say it wasn't decent.

He stood there a moment.

'Aren't you going to ask me to sit down?'

He nodded, not really caring whether she did or not. He was going to need to get rid of her fast in case one of those ministers came knocking on his door, after all he'd told them and all. He'd meant every word. He wanted his wife back, not this whore standing bold as brass in front of him. Looking at her in amazement, he said, 'Yes, sit down.'

She smiled and sat in the armchair, her eyes darting around the room. 'Nice house, this! That wife of yours, she's still away then?'

He nodded. He could just imagine her mind ticking over. Wife away, now I can move in. Well, he wasn't bloody having it, he needed to get shot of her fast. 'How much do you want?'

'Pardon?'

'How much do you ruddy want to leave me alone?'

She opened her mouth and closed it again as if she was catching flies. 'I haven't come here for that. I thought now I'm pregnant and your wife has gone, you'd offer me and the baby a home here.'

His eyes narrowed. 'Oh, you did, did you?'

'Yes,' she said firmly, thrusting out her chin.

He lifted it between his thumb and forefinger as he gazed into her eyes. Although part of him felt like taking her to the bedroom, for she was very attractive, he realised he couldn't. 'Look, will a few bob do for now? Go and buy yourself a pretty dress or something. I can give you a shilling a week when the baby's born for its upkeep as long as you promise to leave me alone.' Dropping his hand to his side, he turned away from her.

A sense of fury overtook him as she leapt out of the armchair and pulled him around to face her, bringing her hand ready to slap his face. Before she could, he grabbed hold of it and twisted her arm behind her back.

'Ow, you're hurting me, Morgan!' She'd never seen this side of him before because he had deliberately withheld it from her, but now what did he have to lose?

'Good!' he sneered. 'Now get away from here before I hurt you even more, you dirty bitch! I don't even know that baby you're carrying is mine anyhow!'

He released her arm. She was close to tears and he feared she might spill her guts outside in the street once she left. It would only take the likes of Maggie Shanklin to find out and it would be spread around the village like wildfire, damaging his reputation for good.

Lowering his voice a notch, he reached into his pocket and handed her a florin. 'I'll give you more next week,' he said. 'But you're not to tell anyone, you hear?' He wagged a finger in her face.

She nodded and he realised he'd knocked the stuffing out of her. She was scared, that was for sure. Trembling, she whispered, 'It is your baby though, Morgan, whatever you think . . .'

Deep down he realised it was, as Mari only had eyes for him no matter how tarty she acted. He smiled. 'In future, keep away from the village. I'll come to you, that's the best way.'

She nodded, then she turned around and left.

She could remain his guilty secret if he didn't flaunt her around the place. He could have his cake and eat it and people would think he had a respectable marriage. An idea began to play on his mind. Maybe he could get the kid for himself and Seren and bring it up as their own. Now that was a thought.

5

Seren and Sam were busy at the farm the following few days helping out with the chores that Anwen would normally have done for herself. It was hard work but worth it to see the woman recovering. There was a bloom back in her cheeks and the anxious look she'd earlier exhibited seemed to have disappeared altogether.

One morning, Sam failed to show up for work, which troubled Seren as he was so trustworthy. 'Something must be wrong,' she told Anwen. 'That lad is normally so dependable.'

Anwen clucked her teeth. 'It's not like him at all. You're right. I had a dream last night of a black cloud sweeping over the village. I had the same dream when his father was killed in the last pit explosion . . .'

Seren hoped that the woman was wrong and that there wouldn't be another pit accident or anything that caused a cloak of death to sweep over the village once again. Grabbing her shawl, she made her way out of the door, not caring whether she bumped into Morgan at all. That boy's welfare was more important to her.

Sam lived in Nightingale Street, which was a long street of small houses. She knocked on the door but there was no answer, so she pushed it open, gasping at the state of disarray there. The place smelled of damp and something rotten. Thinking there was no one there, she was about to call out when she heard a weak groan emanating from the corner. Her eyes were drawn to a bed, where someone lay. As she approached, she could see it was Sam's mother.

'What's happened, Mrs Williams?' she asked, noticing the woman's sallow appearance. She looked much thinner than she last remembered, her eyes sunken in her head and her cheeks hollow.

'It's too late for me. Take my baby girl . . . '

For the first time, she noticed the baby lying in a wooden drawer wrapped in a woollen blanket. The child's body seemed lifeless. Oh no. Was the poor mite dead?

'Where's Sam?' she asked with a note of concern in her voice.

'He's gone to fetch Doctor Owen . . . ' Mrs Williams said breathlessly. 'I gave him all the money I have left to pay him but I know in my heart it's too late . . . '

'Don't say that,' Seren said, then she lifted the baby from her makeshift bed, who thankfully, to her surprise, let out a little mewl. Seren nursed the baby in her arms. The baby opened her eyes and, staring up at Seren, appeared to smile. 'She's absolutely gorgeous,' she said, cooing at the young child.

'Please,' the woman implored, 'if there's nothing that can be done for me, take care of her and Sam.'

Unable to think what to say, Seren nodded. Hearing the door open from behind her she turned to see Sam and Doctor Owen enter the house. The doctor's face bore a look of extreme concern.

'I came as soon as I could . . . ' The doctor huffed out a breath and nodded at Seren. 'What's been the matter with her?'

'I'm not sure, Doctor. I've only just got here myself. I noticed young Sam hadn't shown up to work on Anwen's farm this morning, so I came to see him here, and found Mrs Williams looking like this. She appears to be very weak. The baby seems all right though.'

'Well, I'll examine them both, just in case,' the doctor said, turning to Sam. 'Could you boil some water, young man?'

Sam, who stood there staring at his mother, appeared to be in some sort of stupor. 'Come on, I'll help you,' Seren urged, then she laid the baby down gently in her makeshift cot.

She found the tap in the scullery and filled the kettle, putting it to boil on the hob. Then she turned behind her to look at the lad. His weary-looking face seemed full of anxiety and his eyes were hooded with despair. 'What happened, Sam?'

He shook his head. 'I don't rightly know. I got up for work this morning and found Mam slumped on the couch. She hasn't had much energy for days, so I thought it best for me to stay with her, then I told her I'd get the doctor. She didn't really want me to go as it will cost money we don't have. But how could I leave her like this?'

Seren had heard rumours that the woman hadn't been right since her Bertie had died in the pit explosion at the end of last year. She'd been pregnant at the time too. All of that must have taken its toll on the woman's health, she reckoned.

Seren draped her arm around Sam's shoulders. 'Hopefully the doctor can give your mam something to make her better,' she said, hoping she sounded more confident than she felt. She had no idea what the doctor wanted the hot water for and guessed it might be to wash his hands after examining Mrs Williams.

Bending over, she ruffled Sam's hair. 'All will be well, you'll see,' she said comfortingly as she looked around the small scullery, which was bare save for an old pine table and a few pots and pans.

'But I don't know what we'll do if anything happens to Mam, we could end up in the workhouse . . . ' His eyes had a hollow, haunted look about them, as if it was something he'd considered a lot. Many feared that place with its high walls and strict regime.

The boy spoke the truth, that much was evident. Entering the workhouse was a possibility for the family, but hopefully his mam would get well again.

After giving the doctor plenty of time to examine the woman and baby, Seren went and hovered around near the doorway of the front room, causing Doctor Owen to turn and face her. 'It's a severe case of melancholia,' he said. 'Nothing too much to worry about. She needs to be well fed, she's been neglecting herself. I had worried as there are rumours of cholera visiting the town again . . . ' He turned to Sam. 'Make sure you boil all water before using it, lad. I'm putting you in charge of that.' Sam nodded, with tears in his eyes. It was obvious the lad had been under a lot of stress from worrying about his mother's health.

'And Mrs James, if you could help out to ensure the woman eats well and assist with the baby, that would be a great help.'

How could she refuse, even though she was already helping Anwen? She knew it would wear her out caring for two invalids, but she found herself nodding, agreeing to the doctor's request. 'Did you want the hot water to wash your hands, Doctor?' she asked.

'Heavens no, there's no sign of any infection here,' he replied. 'I thought we'd all have a cup of tea.'

As they took tea together and Seren waited for Mrs Williams's cup to cool down before giving it to her so she didn't tip it all over herself, she was that weak and shaky, the doctor went on to explain something. He looked at Seren with a grave expression on his face. 'Not only has Mrs Williams been coping with grief after her husband's sad demise, but she's gone through the trauma of pregnancy too at a time when her body didn't feel up to it. I know for a fact she was eating very well. Some women suffer from melancholia following childbirth in any case.' Seren felt glad again she hadn't got pregnant.

'I see . . .' she said, staring down into her teacup as if it might hold some vital answer to the situation. If only she had Maggie's gift for reading the tea leaves, but then again, would it be wise to know what was lined up for everyone?

Doctor Owen shook his head. He was a kindly man with grey hair and large bushy sideburns that suited his square-jawed face. 'I fear for Mrs Williams. Does she have any relatives living in the area?'

Seren shook her head. 'None that I'm aware of. The family came here from farming stock in Carmarthen like many others have done before them . . .' It wasn't uncommon for people to come to Merthyr from rural farming communities, seeking work either in the coal mines or the ironworks.

What did Doctor Owen fear? She hadn't liked to ask him such a thing and it concerned her greatly.

* * *

Seren sent word via Sam to Anwen that she would be staying with his mother to care for her until someone else could be found to take over. Anwen was now back on her feet but she'd told Sam to go and help her for time being. He was more than happy to, and she guessed he was glad to be away from the home for a while — it must have been hard on the lad the past few weeks. Why hadn't he told someone instead of trying to put a brave face on it?

Doctor Owen had explained to her he'd seen other widows and mothers in the village who'd lost their menfolk in the pit succumb to melancholia too. After all, there'd been two recent disasters at the same pit within a few years of one another. Was the village of

Abercanaid ever going to be left alone? It had troubled Seren greatly when Anwen had told her she'd had that dream of impending doom. Not another pit disaster, surely?

By the end of the day, Seren had got plenty of fluids down Mrs Williams and now she was trying a little drop of cawl. Thankfully, Sam had used his sense to get some food in from the shop as the doctor had waived his fee. He'd also stocked up on plenty of vegetables from Anwen's farm in the larder, so Seren had been able to make the nourishing soup for the woman.

'What's your Christian name, Mrs Williams?' she asked. It didn't feel right addressing the woman so formally when she wasn't much older than herself.

'Mary.' The woman managed a weak smile as she carried on eating the cawl. 'This is delicious. Thank you.' She glanced at the baby in the wooden drawer beside her. 'I'm afraid my milk for Betsan has all but dried up. I've been trying her with milk sop.' Seren had seen several mothers trying to wean their infants on it as it was cheap and easy for little ones to digest and was only bread soaked in milk, which their mothers would sometimes sprinkle with sugar as a treat. It was often eaten from a cup and a way of introducing young children to solids.

'She's a few months old so would be weaned before too long anyhow, though if you like, I know of a woman in the village who's recently had a baby. Maybe she'd feed your baby for you for a few days just to build her up.'

Now Mary's smile widened. 'Oh, could you

ask? I would feel happier if she would.'

'Of course I will. Meanwhile, there's a little oatmeal left in the larder, I'll mix a little with some warm milk for her.'

'There's kind you are to me . . . ' Mary said. 'And me being almost a stranger to you and all.'

'You're not a stranger, Mary, you're Sam's mother and I'm going to get you well again.'

It gladdened her heart to know that she could do something to help. Her mother had often said she was born to care for folk, and if she hadn't ended up marrying that brute with his own cobbler shop, she could have been a nurse or even a teacher.

* * *

When Elwyn learned that Seren was having to divide her time between helping Mary and her baby and Anwen, he vowed to help.

'But I can't expect you to do that,' Seren said, shaking her head, one afternoon when they were both on their way walking up the mountain to see Anwen.

He smiled. 'I don't see why not. To be truthful, it will give me something else to think about. And, if the villagers weren't so hostile towards Mrs Llewellyn, she would be classed as one of my parishioners anyhow, so I'd be duty bound to call at the farmhouse. And do you know, considering that most are calling her a witch, it is Anwen herself who has shown me most Christian charity in this village. Not the likes of Mrs Shanklin, who is too full of her own pious importance to realise right from wrong and that our good Lord is all about love, compassion and forgiveness!'

Seren had never seen Elwyn fired up so much before and she tended to agree with him. The villagers had hardly given Anwen a chance to redeem herself because as soon as she tried to, she got shot down in flames by a poison-tongued harridan.

'So, how are you coping between both homes?' he asked, stopping to take her heavy wicker basket from her arms. 'You look like you've been run ragged. What have you got in this basket, anyhow? Two tonnes of potatoes?' He grinned.

'Just some provisions from the corner shop for Anwen. She has plenty to eat at the farm but I like to ensure if she's unwell, she has something to fall back on.' She paused to rub her aching back. 'I am tired, to be honest with you. Baby Betsan was awake most of the night screaming in pain with colic and her mother is in no fit state to attend to her.' Although she was near exhaustion, just the feel of holding that beautiful little girl in her arms had brought home to her the deep longing inside herself to be a mother.

He looked into her eyes. 'Has anyone ever told you what an angel you are, Seren James?'

She smiled shyly and looked away as she felt the colour rise to her cheeks. Why was he having this effect on her, making her feel as though she were a young girl again? When she was in his company, she felt without abandon and free to be who she really was.

'I thought you were going to move in at your

aunt's house at Lewis Square?'

'Yes, I had planned that as I don't want to bring trouble to Anwen's door, but once I could see she was poorly, how could I possibly have left her to her own devices? It just wouldn't seem right walking out on her when she needs me most.'

He nodded in understanding. 'That's all very admirable of you, but who will look after you?'

This time she really did find herself blushing and wished Elwyn would change the subject, if only for a short while. But he waited for an answer to his question.

'My mother and my sister, Gwen, both look out for me. But it's difficult as they can't always be around and — ' She paused. 'I do fear my husband will come to claim me shortly.'

Elwyn swallowed. He met her gaze with honesty in his eyes. 'I am sorry that I told Mr Gruffudd what you'd passed on to me in confidence, Seren. I thought I was doing the right thing.'

'The truth is, if my husband is of a mind to find me, then he will. Someone in this village would have eventually told him my whereabouts, anyhow.'

What was truly worrying Seren, though, was why hadn't Morgan come for her as yet? Was he biding his time, seeking the right moment to strike? And was this the calm before the eventual storm?

6

When Seren and Elwyn arrived at the farmhouse there was little sign of any life there. Although Anwen had been ill, she'd still managed to peg her washing on the line or get up to feed the livestock and perform small tasks around the place. But now there was no smoke coming from the chimney either, no sounds of Anwen clattering around in the kitchen or singing to herself as she went about her daily duties. Seren's gut clenched as she experienced a sense of foreboding. Looking at Elwyn, she said, 'There's something wrong, I just know it . . .' The words caught in her throat and she wished she had Anwen's ability to see things ahead of time, then she'd know what was truly wrong.

'You stay here, I'll go inside,' he warned her, tapping her hand in reassurance, obviously not wanting her to find something she shouldn't. Although Anwen was a decent age she had, up until now, been fit as a flea from all her clean living, hard work and knowledge of the healing properties of various plants and herbs. She'd even been improving from her recent illness, so this seemed most odd to Seren.

It seemed an age before Elwyn returned to her side. 'The place is empty!' he said with a puzzled expression on his face. 'Maybe she's taken the horse and cart and gone to Merthyr.'

Seren sincerely doubted that. 'Let's go and

check the stable,' she suggested. But the horse was still there munching on a bale of hay, though his water trough was low.

'When did you last see Mrs Llewellyn?' Elwyn's eyes widened with concern.

Seren fought to think back to how long ago that would possibly have been. 'It would have been a couple of days ago, I think. I didn't call to the farm yesterday as I was busy with the baby, but Sam called to see if she needed any help, so she must have been all right then or he'd have told me; he's a good boy who would have looked out for her but I think he had to go into Merthyr town for his mam today.'

'That means it's a short period of time she's gone missing for then, but I don't think she'd have left the horse without much water nor the livestock unfed. We'll carry on looking nearby and then I'll return and feed and water all the animals.'

A shiver of apprehension skittered along Seren's spine and she dragged her shawl closer around her shoulders as if it would somehow afford protection against the feeling of impending doom.

They made their way through a nearby field, but there was no sign of Anwen there. Seren tried to think where else to search for the woman as they returned to the farmhouse. 'I suppose she might have gone to the village . . . ' she said hopefully, chewing her lip, although really, she doubted it. Then a thought occurred to her. 'The brook!' she said. 'If the horse didn't have enough water, maybe she went to collect some.' That would make sense.

Elwyn nodded. 'That's possible, come on!' he said with a note of excitement to his voice, and he headed off with extreme purpose.

Seren deposited her basket by the farmhouse door and, lifting her skirts, followed after Elwyn who was taking great big strides to get to the brook. A pang of fear took over Seren. What if the worst thing had happened? She couldn't possibly imagine life without Anwen. She was like a second mother to her. The woman was so warm and understanding and had given her sanctuary when she needed it, and for that she would always be extremely grateful.

As they approached the heavily wooded area, Elwyn warned, 'Remain where you are for your own sake.'

Seren nodded. It would be more than she could bear if anything happened to the woman.

Elwyn vaulted over a wooden stile and she watched as he neared the brook. It felt like an age before he returned and she felt her heartbeat thudding like a drum in her ears. Her mouth was dry with apprehension.

'Elwyn!' she cried out. What was going on? She could hardly bear the wait.

There was a long pause before he replied in a shaky voice. 'Please don't come any further. Go back to the house and fetch a warm blanket and a wet cold compress. Mrs Llewellyn has fallen, probably when she was fetching some water from the brook. Only bring previously boiled water though,' he warned, 'remember what Doctor Owen has said about boiling it.'

Seren had a sickening feeling in the pit of her

stomach. She lifted her skirts and ran as quickly as she could in the direction of the farmhouse. Her hands were trembling so much once she got inside that she could hardly hold anything in them, and her mind was racing. She should never have left the woman to her own devices, she simply wasn't well enough.

She managed to rummage in the cupboard in Anwen's bedroom and located a thick woollen blanket on her bed, then soaked a flannel in a small bowl of water to take to the woman. When she reached the brook, Elwyn had come to the stile as if he wanted her to remain where she was, but she was having none of it. What did he think she was? Some little helpless woman who couldn't cope with life? She was sure she'd seen and experienced a lot worse at the hands of her own husband.

'I'm coming with you,' she said firmly.

He knew better than to object, so he took the blanket and the bowl from her outstretched hands. Then she hoisted her skirts as he helped her over the stile. There was no time to worry about her modesty right now.

She took a deep breath as her eyes searched the wooded area until she spotted the clearing where the brook was to see Anwen lying sprawled out on the ground. Seren gasped as she approached; the woman's body seemed lifeless.

'I'm afraid she seems to be unconscious, feels a little cold too,' Elwyn said with deep concern to his voice.

'Hurry, please! We need to keep her warm . . . '

When they got to Anwen, Seren snatched the blanket off Elwyn and draped it over the woman. She looked so pale and her eyes were closed.

Seren knelt beside her and, softly touching the woman's cheek, said, 'Anwen, it's me, Seren. Are you all right?'

There was no response, so Seren tapped her face, causing the woman to slowly open her eyes and Seren to breathe a sigh of relief. She didn't want to admit it, even to herself, that she'd feared Anwen was dead.

'I'm all right, *cariad* . . . but where am I?'

'Sssh,' Seren soothed, 'you're near the brook. It looks like you've had a nasty fall. Can you remember what happened to you?'

Anwen shook her head.

'Help me to sit her up a little, would you, Mr Evans?'

Elwyn nodded and helped her into a sitting position as he knelt at her side. Then Seren began to gently cleanse a small wound on the woman's forehead.

'It's only a superficial graze I think, but it seems as if you took quite a tumble there. As soon as you feel well enough, we'll try to get you back to the house, all right?'

Anwen nodded gratefully. 'There's silly I feel, *bach*. Causing you both all this trouble.'

'It's no trouble at all, Mrs Llewellyn,' Elwyn said kindly. 'Now take your time there until you get your sea legs. It might be an idea if we can give you some water to drink. I'll go back to the house if you like and fetch a cup of water.'

Seren shook her head. 'There's no need — the

water in this bowl is still clean.' She looked at Anwen. 'Can you manage a sip or two?'

Anwen nodded. 'I'm parched. I've no idea how long I've been out here for.'

'For some time by the look of it.' Elwyn regarded her with a great deal of sympathy in his eyes. 'You felt very cold when I got here.'

Seren held the small bowl to the woman's lips and she took several sips until well satisfied. 'B . . . but what time is it?'

'It's about three o'clock,' said Elwyn.

'Yes, that would be about right.' Seren smoothed back the woman's hair from her face as it had got messed up by the fall. 'I would guess you might have been here from breakfast time as that's about the time you collect the water, isn't it?'

Anwen nodded slowly and put her hand to her bruised temple. 'You're right, but I can't even remember if I've fed the animals yet . . . oh the poor things.'

Elwyn gently touched her shoulder. 'Don't go bothering yourself. When we arrived we noticed they needed attending to but we needed to find you first. I'll feed them for you, but first we need to get you inside the house to warm you up. Do you think you can stand?'

She nodded. 'I'll try if you can both help me?'

'That goes without saying.' Seren smiled, then glanced at Elwyn who nodded at her.

They both rose to their feet, then taking one of Anwen's arms each, pulled to get her up from the stony ground. She felt a dead weight to Seren even though she was a small woman, but they managed to get her into a standing position. She swayed a little at first but Seren guessed that was because she'd been without food for so long. 'When we get you back home, I'm going to warm up some stew I brought for you in my basket with some nice crusty bread, then Elwyn will sort out the livestock for you. Then after that, I'm putting you to bed. All right?'

Anwen nodded gratefully as she took small steps, holding on tightly to both their arms, puffing and panting as she went as if it was all too much for her.

If only I'd never had to leave her, then maybe this would never have happened because I'd have been the one collecting water instead. Living on a farm is hard work and particularly for someone as elderly as Anwen.

Back at the house, Seren helped Anwen into her favourite armchair by the fireplace while Elwyn banked up the fire which had almost gone out. Fortunately, it was still in when they got there so it was just a case of raking the coals and covering with kindle wood and stoking it up to get a little air into it. Within minutes, it was crackling and spitting as the flames danced before their eyes, making Seren wonder if maybe Elwyn had watched someone at work who was good at lighting fires in the past. Even though he'd come from a more privileged background than herself, where they probably had a maid or two when he was growing up, he seemed very handy at times. Seren placed the blanket over Anwen's knees, then went to fetch another from the bedroom to place around her shoulders.

'While I'm warming the stew, you can have a nice cup of tea to warm you up, and Elwyn, as soon as you return from the barn, there'll be one for you too.'

He nodded.

'All the animals' food is in a cupboard by the side of the barn,' Anwen added. 'Make sure they've got plenty of water as well, won't you?'

'Sssh now,' Elwyn said in almost a whisper, 'it will all be sorted, never fear.'

She smiled, safe in the knowledge all would be well, and by the time Seren had filled the kettle and put it on to boil, the woman had nodded off.

Seren chewed her bottom lip. *I better not let her sleep though. As soon as I've made this tea I'll wake her, just to ensure she's all right. There'll be time for her to sleep later once she's had some nourishing food inside her, and it wouldn't hurt to get Doctor Owen here neither.*

Once Anwen had eaten her fill and Elwyn had gone in search of the doctor, Seren sat in the rocking chair reflecting on the flames of the fire. She hadn't been expecting this today on top of everything that had happened lately and she felt worn out, but she decided she'd better keep Anwen going until the doctor arrived, so chatted in general about things at the Williams household and how much stronger Mary was becoming, which was true.

By the time Doctor Owen had arrived, having come the long way by taking his horse and cart along the old Parish Road, Seren was almost asleep herself.

She heard the front door click and Elwyn

stood there with the man in his wake.

'How's the invalid?' Doctor Owen asked in a bright and breezy fashion.

Seren rose from her chair and went to greet him so that Anwen was out of earshot and whispered, 'She managed to eat some stew, Doctor, and drink a little too.'

Doctor Owen removed his bowler hat, then nodded as he set both his hat and bag down on the kitchen table. Then looking into Seren's eyes, he said, 'Does Mrs Llewellyn seem very with it to you? Mr Evans has filled me in on all the details.'

'Yes, she seems of sound mind, Doctor, though she can't remember the events leading up to the fall.'

He nodded, then he opened his leather Gladstone bag, removed his stethoscope and turning to Seren asked, 'Could you fetch me a lit candle perhaps?'

Puzzled, Seren went to fetch one from the windowsill. What did he want one of those for?

'It's to test her pupil reaction, you see. Because she's had a fall. If I shine the light in her eyes her pupils should go smaller and enlarge when I remove the light.'

Seren had never heard of that before but decided the doctor knew what he was doing. He'd done a lot to help Mary Williams.

Following a thorough examination where the doctor listened to Anwen's respirations and felt her pulse, he asked her several questions to check if she understood where she was and what day of the week it was. Then he asked to see

Seren and Elwyn in private.

'I don't think the fall has done her much harm, to be honest with you,' he said quietly, 'but maybe it's just as well it has happened.'

Elwyn raised a brow. 'Sorry, Doctor, I don't understand.'

'Well, it's like this, you see. Because you called me here, as a matter of course I listened to her chest and I have to admit it's not good at the moment. I fear she might come down with a case of pneumonia if she is left to her own devices. She needs someone to take care of her. Now, Seren, I know you have been busy lately with Mary Williams but I think your priority now needs to be at the farm.'

Seren nodded. 'I understand, Doctor.'

He smiled. 'She needs good nourishing food, no more chopping sticks or walks to the brook to bring back heavy pails of water. Does she have any family close by?'

'No,' Seren said, 'none that I am aware of.'

'Well, I can help you,' Elwyn said eagerly. 'I can come here for an hour a day and chop the sticks and fetch water, and feed the livestock as well.'

That made Seren feel better but it still didn't solve her own problem. She clenched her hands. 'My fear, Doctor Owen, is that my husband will come here and create trouble. You have heard I've left him, I suppose?'

Doctor Owen's face flushed as he lifted his hat from the table and, putting it on his head, said, 'Yes, I had heard something about it from Mrs Shanklin.'

'Don't worry,' Elwyn said, placing his hand gently on Seren's shoulder. 'I won't allow anything to happen to you.'

'Nor will any of the other men in the village, Seren,' Doctor Owen said kindly. 'You're well thought of. Mrs Llewellyn needs you right now. You're the nearest thing she has to a daughter.'

Then he lifted his bag and bade them both a good evening with a promise to visit the following day to see how things were.

Seren had some money to pay him on Anwen's insistence, but he waved her hand away.

When the doctor had gone and the woman was safely tucked up in bed, Seren and Elwyn both sat at opposite ends of the fire in companionable silence, sipping cups of cocoa.

'You know, I meant what I said.' Elwyn looked into her eyes and, although she knew she should look away, she felt strangely drawn to him and she didn't know why that was. 'I'll never let anyone hurt you, Seren.'

She nodded and smiled, then rose from her chair. 'I'll make us some more cocoa, shall I?' she said brightly, breaking the intensity between them. If she was a free woman maybe she'd enjoy the moment, but she was not. She was married even if she wasn't living with Morgan, and she knew the trouble she could get into if she allowed her feelings to overtake her.

7

It was late the previous night when Elwyn had finally said goodbye to Seren. At his departure he'd held her hand a little too long by the kitchen door, but she was comforted by the fact he would be returning to the farm to help out the following day.

Anwen had slept well overnight and was sitting up in bed, having eaten most of her breakfast of porridge and a round of toast with her usual cup of tea. 'I really don't know what all the fuss is about,' she said, tutting.

Seren sat on the bed to explain things. 'Doctor Owen was quite concerned last night; he said you need plenty of rest for now and that you've been overdoing things. So, I am going to carry on staying here for a while and Elwyn will help around the farm for one hour a day.'

Anwen frowned. 'But what about Mary Williams? Won't she still need you?'

Seren smiled. 'She's a lot better now, thank you. Elwyn will call there on his way to the farm to see if she needs anything and to explain the situation. I dread to think what might have happened to you though, if we hadn't found you when we did yesterday. It might have been days until you received any other callers to the farm, and even then, they might not have thought to look for you at the brook.'

Anwen shook her head and closed her eyes.

'I'm not afraid of dying though, *bach*. It will come to us all in good time.'

Seren touched the old woman's crepe-like hand. 'I know, but you could have a lot of life left in you yet, Anwen Llewellyn, if you looked after yourself a little more and rested up.'

Anwen smiled. 'Aye, I know that and all, and you only have my best interests at heart, but I'm worried about you because something tells me you were going to leave here but you're now staying to help me.'

Seren shook her head. 'No, no, of course not.'

'You seem to forget I know these things, *cariad*. You're frightened to death of Morgan. I can see it in your eyes sometimes when you mention his name. It's good you have the local minister watching out for you but be careful . . .'

'What do you mean?'

'People will talk. They'll say it's wrong for a married woman to be so friendly with a single man, even if he is a man of the cloth.'

She laughed nervously. 'But we're not up to any shenanigans!'

'I know that and you know that, but others don't. It will only inflame Morgan if he discovers the man is calling here regularly. I think I should pay a big strong lad to help here as well as Sam. He's a bit young to do any back-breaking work.'

'Please don't worry about it, Anwen. Elwyn is more than happy to help here free of charge.'

'It will all end in tears though, my girl. You wait and see . . .'

Seren said nothing, but took the tray of food

from the bed and silently left the old woman's bedroom.

* * *

Seren pondered on what Anwen had said to her. Would people really gossip about her and the handsome young minister? Surely not! He was a man of God. How could people even think such a thing? Yet, deep down she realised his tender touches and the way he looked so deep into her eyes with understanding in them, told her a different story. He was a man, wasn't he? And most men had needs. And what if . . . Her hands flew to her face. What if people were to think the worst because Morgan couldn't give her the child they both so desperately longed for? Oh yes, he'd called her a 'bloody barren bitch!' more times than she cared to remember, but what if it were him? What if there was something wrong with his seed? Maybe people in the village were already thinking that much about the man. Maybe a few had said it to him and all. Those that might be brave enough to incur his wrath, like Tom or Maggie Shanklin.

Maybe that's why he's knocked me around so much as he feels somehow emasculated by their comments?

Stop this now! None of this is any of your fault. Even if you were barren it would never excuse a man hitting a woman.

And at that realisation, she broke down and wept painful, bitter tears as she realised the truth of those words.

Oh, it wasn't a big booming voice that had said so much to her, but rather a soft gentle one. Was that her inner voice that spoke, or the voice of God? She wondered. If it was her heavenly Father then he was only looking out for her, and she sank to her knees and uttered a silent prayer of gratitude for her understanding of the situation.

When Elwyn arrived at the farm later that morning, she told him about what had happened — about the voice, but not about the idea that Anwen had planted in her mind.

He smiled and said, ''Be still and know that I am God . . . ' It says that in Psalm 46, verse 10, if my memory proves correct.'

She nodded. It was a comfort to hear him say those words. She was aware the verse lay somewhere in the bible, but she hadn't for the life of her remembered where it was she'd read it. But now that she did know, she would ask Anwen if she might read her family bible later. It had been in the woman's family for years and at the front of it were recordings of people's births, deaths and marriages.

'You know, I've been thinking things over and I've had an idea,' Elwyn said, smiling. 'I'd like to start a bible class at the chapel. At the moment there is nothing there like it. Oh, we have our normal three Sunday services, Sunday School itself and two short services during the week, but I'd like to hold a proper bible study group a couple of times a week for people so they can ask questions. I'd like *you* to run it for me. I don't mean right now, but when Anwen is up on her feet again . . . ' He scratched his chin.

'Me?' Seren blinked. 'But why me?'

'Because I think you have a good understanding of the bible, Seren. Well, would you like to start one?'

She took a deep breath and let it out again. He was putting a lot of trust into her, but then he'd obviously seen something in her she hadn't even seen in herself. 'If you think I can then I will. There are a lot of lonely women in the village since their menfolk were killed in the pit disasters. People like Mary Williams might like to attend and make friends with the other women, as she seems so isolated right now.'

'A splendid idea!' Elwyn said. 'I knew I could rely on you.'

'There's one other thing . . . ' Seren said, wondering how Elwyn would react to her suggestion.

He angled his head to one side, curiously. 'Yes? Go on?'

'It's Anwen. I'd like to take her to the chapel when she feels up to it. Maybe start her off quietly one Sunday.'

'Do you think that's wise, considering how the villagers feel towards the woman?' He stroked his chin. 'I had considered it myself but then I thought as Anwen has been unwell, she could do without the animosity.'

She had considered that of course and was all for keeping away from conflict, but not when a wrong hadn't been righted in her book. 'Absolutely, I think it's the right thing to do, Elwyn. It's those hard-hearted villagers who are keeping her away from worship. They are the heathens, not Anwen. She has done nothing wrong whatsoever.'

And so it was decided, as soon as the woman was well enough, they were taking her to chapel.

* * *

The following week, when Anwen was back on her feet and had made a full recovery, Elwyn arrived at the farm to accompany her to chapel on the horse and cart with Seren and Sam walking behind them.

Anwen had protested that she was well enough to take the reins but to Seren's relief, Elwyn had been firm with her: there was no use her straining herself, she was still in recovery. As they arrived at the chapel and Elwyn dashed inside to get changed into his robes in the vestry, Seren became aware of how late they were. They'd misjudged how long it would take to go around the long way using the Parish Road. She looked up and down Chapel Street. The street was quiet, no sign of any last-minute stragglers heading towards the chapel, which gave her a sinking feeling in the pit of her stomach. Oh dear, now all eyes would be on them. This wasn't what Seren had planned. She'd hoped they could slip in quietly. All was quiet outside, so that meant the last of the congregation had disappeared in through the double doors and were seated inside.

To Seren's dismay, she noticed by the bobbing of heads from the pews how packed the chapel was that morning. She wondered if it was because Elwyn was a far more charismatic preacher than Mr Gruffudd had ever been — his services had sometimes bordered on being boring, though he'd held a healthy amount of respect in the village, particularly amongst the elderly members of the community.

Heads turned to stare at them and whispers circulated as several sets of eyes glanced in their direction. Were those stares of pity or compassion? Or were they ones of hostility? There was no way of knowing as she felt unable to maintain her gaze. The only available pew left to sit on was right at the front. Taking a deep breath, Seren led Anwen by the arm and guided her down the main aisle. She felt the hairs on the back of her neck prickle as she thought she heard someone whisper 'witch' as they passed. The only person who turned and smiled at them was Mary Williams, and even then, Seren wondered was that smile meant for her son Sam, as he trailed in behind them with his flat cap clutched firmly in his hand.

The muttering died away as Elwyn Evans took to the pulpit, pausing to allow them to be seated before he spoke a greeting to his congregation and then his face looked serious as his eyes darkened.

'It has come to my attention,' he said in a grave tone of voice, 'that there are some folk in this village who have been acting in a most uncharitable and unchristian like fashion.' The muttering started up again and heads turned to glance at one another, as if they were wondering who the minister might be speaking of, eyes wide with surprise. Then the congregation hushed as Elwyn carried on. To Seren's astonishment, he raised his voice a notch. 'I shall name no names for time being,' he said, his fingers curling tightly around the big black bible before him, his knuckles now white. 'But if things do not change then the gossipmongers amongst you shall be ousted from this chapel!' His echoing voice sent a shiver down Seren's spine. There was a deadly silence. Seren turned to Anwen who was staring straight ahead as if she wore blinkers, her only focus being on the minister himself. Did she realise that he was addressing those folks who had admonished her, Seren wondered? Something caught the corner of her eye and she swallowed as she noticed Maggie Shanklin seated in a pew beside her husband. When had she started back at the chapel? And today of all days.

Nothing more was mentioned during the service and several rousing hymns were sung with gusto before and after Elwyn's sermon about love and forgiveness, but he had made his feelings known to all. After the service, Seren was delighted to see several people came over to speak to them, some passing on their good wishes after hearing that Anwen had been ill. But Maggie Shanklin and her cronies kept well away, and for that, Seren was extremely grateful.

* * *

'There we are, I told you all would go well in the end!' Elwyn enthused, rubbing his hands together in anticipation of the meal they were about to eat. They were all seated around a large dining table at The Manse, where Elwyn's housekeeper had cooked a Sunday roast dinner for them of beef, roast potatoes and seasonal vegetables. The aroma was simply divine, causing Seren's stomach to growl with hunger. She hadn't eaten much all morning as she'd feared what would happen when Anwen arrived at the chapel, but the stoning and cat-calling she'd been expecting simply hadn't arrived. What had she really expected though? That the villagers would run after the woman with pitchforks and toss her on top of a bonfire? Or duck her in the village pond? She realised she had a vivid imagination, but she had heard of these things happening in the past to old Welsh witches who may have been as innocent as Anwen Llewellyn.

'I have to admit though,' said Seren, as she watched Mrs Johnson dishing up the meals, 'that I did fear someone would say something derogatory.'

'They wouldn't have dared,' chuckled Anwen, 'not after what our caring minister had to say.'

'Did you see the face on Maggie Shanklin though?' Sam laughed. He, his mother, and the baby, had all been invited. Mary dined whilst the little one was fast asleep in an old wooden drawer that Mrs Johnson the housekeeper had lined with soft blankets.

'I didn't notice,' Anwen said stiffly. 'She's the least of my worries. I'm more concerned with things getting back to normal at the farm.'

'Well, you've got some good help with my Sam,' Mary said proudly, as Seren gently patted the woman's hand.

What a difference in the woman since the first

time she'd met her. Her cheeks had roses in them and now she seemed more positive about things. Seren took the opportunity to ask her something. 'Mr Evans has asked me to set up a bible study group, Mary. Would you be interested in joining us?'

Mary's eyes sparkled. 'Yes, I would, but could I bring the baby along, please?'

'Yes, that's fine, but I bet Sam wouldn't mind watching her for an hour or two a week for you, would you, Sam?'

'No, Mam. You go along. She likes me,' Sam said, with a big beaming smile on his face.

'That's true,' said Mary. 'She loves the way you sing lullabies to her to get her to sleep.'

He smiled at his mother. It was lovely to see the family settled at last.

When Mrs Johnson had finished plating up the meals and stepped away from the table, Elwyn uttered a few words of thanks to God for the meal before them as Sam placed his hands together and squeezed his eyes shut, but the temptation to peek got too much for him, causing Seren to smile.

'There's one other thing . . . ' Elwyn waited until Mrs Johnson had left the room. 'There's been some talk about Morgan . . . do you mind me discussing such things in front of the others?'

'Oh, no, we're in trusted company here.' Seren sat forward in her chair to hear what Elwyn had to say.

'It was hinted at to me that your husband has taken a woman to live with him at your home . . . '

Suddenly, Seren felt nauseous. The thought of him with *that woman*, was it that image that was making her feel so sick?

'Excuse me,' she said, pushing herself back from the table and standing to leave the room. She dashed to the hallway where she found Mrs Johnson.

'Is it the toilet that you're needing?' she asked.

Seren nodded with her hands over her mouth as Mrs Johnson directed her outside to the garden. She only just made it in time as she expelled the contents of her stomach inside the porcelain bowl.

She just couldn't understand it. She was glad to be away from the man, so why should she feel sick like this? Not unless . . . no, she couldn't be, could she? It was a few weeks since her husband had carnal knowledge of her and even then, he had taken her by force. She couldn't get pregnant, she was barren, wasn't she?

Once back inside the house, she managed to wash her hands and face at the kitchen sink under the watchful eyes of Mrs Johnson.

'Everything all right, dearie?' The elderly lady's eyes were full of concern.

Seren nodded. 'Yes, thanks. Must have been something I ate this morning.'

'I can make up a smaller plate for you if you like?'

'No, thank you. I'll be fine now; in fact now I feel rather hungry.' And she did too, she had noticed lately she had a better appetite than usual, though it was the first time she'd felt nauseous when she didn't actually feel ill.

There was plenty of conversation as she returned to the table and thankfully, no one questioned her regarding her sudden absence, but she caught Elwyn gazing at her across the table several times. What was he thinking, she wondered?

Considering she'd just vomited, she ate very well, and after the dinner they sat around the fireside chatting as Mrs Johnson brought them a pot of coffee on a tray with thick slices of fruit cake.

'You might as well all stay here for the evening service,' Elwyn suggested. 'No rest for the wicked,' he joked.

Later, when the others were leaving to return to the chapel, he caught her arm in the hallway. 'Is everything all right? I was worried in case I'd upset you when I mentioned to you about Morgan and that woman . . . '

'Yes, all is well,' she said too quickly and too brightly. There was no fooling him though — even as he nodded, she could see the questions in his eyes.

'Later,' he said.

* * *

The evening service passed far more smoothly now the ice had been broken. There was no sign of Tom and Maggie Shanklin and Seren wondered after Elwyn's warning if the woman had purposely decided to stay away in silent protest.

Following the service, after the chapel had been locked up and they'd said farewell to Mary, the baby and Sam, Elwyn drove them back to the farm on the horse and cart.

Anwen hadn't mentioned anything regarding Seren's sudden departure from the dinner table, until now. She'd chosen her moment well. 'Do you have something to tell us both, Seren?' she asked as soon as they entered the farmhouse and seated themselves by the fire.

'N . . . no, not really.'

Elwyn cleared his throat. 'Look, you're amongst friends here. What is it?'

Seren ran a hand across her brow. All of a sudden, she felt so weary and she had guessed why. 'I think I must be p . . . pregnant,' she said. 'That's why I left the dining room suddenly like that as I felt nauseous.' Then to her horror her shoulders shuddered as she burst into tears before them, realising her period hadn't arrived as yet. Usually she was regular as clockwork.

Anwen's hand stretched out to her in silent reassurance as she patted Seren's shoulder. 'We must let her cry it out,' she advised Elwyn.

Finally, Seren looked at the pair through glassy eyes and asked the question that so far she hadn't even asked herself: 'What am I going to do?'

⋆ ⋆ ⋆

'Wake up, Seren! Are you all right?'

Seren's eyes flicked open and she blinked as the sun filtered in through a chink in the curtains. Who was calling her? A swift pang of nausea caused her to groan loudly.

'It's all right, you rest up, *cariad* . . . It's the

morning sickness you have,' Anwen said brightly. 'I've brought you a cup of ginger tea, it's good for keeping sickness at bay.'

Seren smiled and sat up in the bed. It was like a complete role reversal. It wasn't so long ago she was the one doing the fetching and carrying whilst Anwen was in bed. Still, it was nice to see her up and about and more her usual self — maybe going to chapel yesterday might have had something to do with it. Mr Gruffudd hadn't done much to help matters when Mrs Shanklin and her friends had turned on the woman, labelling her a witch. Elwyn, on the other hand, sought amicable means to resolve differences. She did feel guilty though for putting the woman to any trouble.

Anwen smiled and, handing the tea over, left the bedroom and Seren to her thoughts. It was troubling her that she'd heard nothing whatsoever from Morgan. It was definitely unlike him, but if he had that other woman and was blatantly flaunting her to all and sundry, maybe he had moved on and it would be the best solution for all.

After finishing the ginger tea and washing and dressing to find the nausea had indeed abated, she was ready to face a couple of rounds of toast which Anwen had prepared. As they sat by the fire — the mornings were now getting nippy with autumn on the horizon — she stared out of the window on to the rugged mountainside. It was so peaceful here.

'A penny for them?' Anwen said curiously.

'I don't know if they're even worth that much.'

Seren gave a hollow laugh.

'Aw come on, *cariad*, a trouble shared is a trouble halved . . . '

Seren looked at the woman and then nodded. 'It's Morgan.'

'What about him? You mean what Mr Evans said yesterday about him and that woman?'

'No, it's not that. It's just I'd have expected him to come after me by now. It's so unlike him to leave me alone!'

'Don't tell me you miss that swine, Seren? Not after all he's done to you! You sound disappointed.' Anwen shook her head.

'No, no, you are reading things wrong!' She surprised herself with the tone of her voice.

'Now don't go upsetting yourself, it's bad for the baby. I'm sorry, I shouldn't pry.'

'It's not that. What I meant was, every time I've tried to leave him in the past, he's come after me and dragged me back home, but not this time. He's been too quiet and it unnerves me somewhat.'

Anwen shrugged her shoulders. 'Could it be that he's lost interest? In my opinion, when a man has another woman on his mind, he becomes short-sighted. Men tend to live in the moment and as long as their needs are being met, they don't much care.'

Seren nodded thoughtfully. 'Yes, maybe you're right. And if that's the case, it's a blessed relief.' She let out a long composing breath.

Anwen stood and, patting Seren's knee, said, 'Now, you need to stop worrying yourself and worry more about the baby. What do you think you should do next?'

'Get the pregnancy confirmed by Doctor Owen, I suppose.'

'That would be a good idea. Anyhow, there's plenty of room here for a new baby; he or she will bring some new life around here.' Anwen smiled as if the thought of a new life in her home would bring them all a bit of happiness.

8

Seren stood outside Doctor Owen's home and swallowed hard at the thought of entering the building and of being told what in her heart she already knew to be true. The doctor's house was much larger and more imposing than the small terraced dwellings that housed the working folk of Abercanaid. He was wealthy enough to employ a housekeeper and one or two other staff to do his bidding, but for the work he did for the community, no one would have begrudged him that — after all, the villagers viewed the great man as one of their own.

There were already a few people seated on wooden chairs in the surgery when she arrived, misery etched into one or two faces as they waited patiently to be seen. Seren wondered if that was due to pain or perplexity. She made polite conversation with the elderly woman sitting beside her, who must have told her all her own ailments as well as those of her husband, though thankfully she did not ask Seren what was wrong with her — that would have been too much for her to cope with in public, and she'd have hated the thought of lying to the woman, so she breathed out a silent sigh of relief.

Finally, it was her turn to be called in to see the doctor. 'And what can I do for you today, Seren?' Doctor Owen asked, as he closed the door behind her then gestured for her to take a seat opposite him in front of his large wooden desk. 'Nothing the matter with Mrs Llewellyn, is there?' He raised his straggly brows.

She shook her head. 'No, she's doing well, thankfully, Doctor.' She paused. 'It's about myself why I'm here.'

His eyes clouded over with concern. 'Nothing wrong, is there?' He looked her up and down as if somehow assessing the situation, though of course he couldn't possibly know what was wrong until she told him so, no matter how good a doctor he happened to be.

'No, nothing like that, but I think I might be pregnant . . . ' Now she'd uttered those words, it felt more real to her somehow.

If he was surprised, he didn't show it.

'What makes you think so?' He tilted his head in curiosity.

'Lately, I'd been feeling very tired, Doctor.'

'That's not surprising though as you've been helping both Anwen and Mary Williams out.'

'No, I know it's not just that, and there's something else . . . ' She twisted her cotton handkerchief in her hands.

'Go ahead, my dear.'

'I've been feeling nauseous, especially in the mornings.'

'I see. In that case, I'd better examine you then. If you could go behind the screen and lie on the bed for me . . . '

She did as told and waited for a while for him to attend to her. He handed her a small blanket. 'You're going to have to remove your skirt and cover yourself with this blanket.'

Finally, he was able to palpate her stomach with his fingers and listen using his stethoscope, then he told her to get dressed and sit back at the desk when she was ready.

She watched his face to see if she could gauge one way or the other whether she was with child or not. But his face gave nothing away and she guessed it was because in his profession he had to be careful not to give too much away at times.

Eventually, he said, 'Yes, you are correct, Seren.'

She took a deep breath and let it out again. At least her mind wasn't playing tricks on her. 'Any idea how far gone I am, Doctor?'

He nodded. 'I should say about three months, no more than four months' gestation.'

They discussed things further about how she would cope and just before she left, he said, 'I think I should warn you that I've received some information from Doctor Dyke, the medical officer of health in Merthyr Tydfil. I mentioned my concerns to you a while back, and now I'm afraid cholera is definitely revisiting our town — I fear there might currently be an outbreak in Lewis Square where your aunt lives.'

'Oh no.' She stood up momentarily, but reseated herself with the shock of it all as suddenly she felt a little light-headed.

'I'm telling you this to advise you to stay away from the area and to warn your family. The house involved isn't your aunt's, but I have instructed people living there to disinfect everything and to boil their water.'

'Have there been any deaths yet, Doctor?'

He shook his head. 'No, but they are imminent. It all seems to centre around one small house where there are a lot of people crammed in such small living quarters.'

'Is that what causes it, Doctor?' Seren felt a sudden cause for alarm.

He nodded. 'Put it this way: it certainly doesn't help matters, but it's not the cause. It's thought this time it somehow entered the country at a sea port in Bristol or Liverpool and has spread across the country. It's a water-borne disease and unfortunately, in Abercanaid, we are both near a river and a canal. Lewis Square, as you know, is very near the canal. The lady in question where the outbreak has occurred, had taken in some lodgers and the house is in a filthy state as the woman is ill. It makes it an ideal breeding ground for germs.'

Seren had never seen Doctor Owen looking so sombre. He wiped his brow as if he couldn't take in the thought of it himself, but then she guessed he'd witnessed enough at the last outbreak twelve years previously, where hundreds had died in the town and no doubt some had survived but suffered seriously as a result.

'I'll go straight from here and tell my mother about this . . . ' She bit her bottom lip.

'Warn her to keep away from your aunt's house though, Seren. They've lime-washed the outside of the house in question and told people to keep away.'

She nodded, though she doubted her mother would; she was very close to her only sister and would only want to help. 'Are there any outbreaks elsewhere, Doctor?'

'Yes, in Dowlais and there's been mention of Quarry Row in the Georgetown area, too. I'm hoping it won't be as severe as the last outbreak, mind you, as we have learned lessons. Years ago, people were being told to use cold water only to wash and what a load of bunkum that was! They thought that the cold water would kill the disease. Unfortunately, this town is overcrowded in general as people flood here from outside the area to find work in the ironworks as if it's a gold rush town! So, consequently, when there are more people living cheek to jowl in deplorable conditions, it makes the incidence of disease more likely.'

'Let's hope it won't be so bad this time.' She drew her shawl around her shoulders as if it would somehow afford her protection against the terrible disease.

'Sorry, I hate to be the bearer of bad news, but I thought it best to warn you,' he said gravely. 'Now before you go, don't go worrying. It's not as if you are having a baby out of wedlock. I'd get that husband of yours to cough up towards its keep!'

Morgan! She didn't want him to know about the baby. She shook her head. 'Oh no, I couldn't possibly . . . '

Noticing the look of alarm on her face, the doctor said, 'Look, Morgan has a right to know and if you don't tell him, in time, others will notice you're in confinement and tell him themselves. It would be far better coming from yourself.'

'But you don't understand, Doctor, he has been heavy with his fists in the past. I couldn't bear it if he hurt me with this poor innocent soul inside me.'

'I know that, Seren, but I doubt he would.'

It was all very well Doctor Owen saying that, he didn't know him like she did, and she wasn't willing to take that chance.

* * *

'Cholera's revisiting Merthyr? Oh my goodness! I thought we'd seen the last of that!' Anwen had her hands in the mixing bowl in the kitchen at the farmhouse. She placed the round of dough down on the wooden counter and began pounding at it as if her life depended on it.

Seren nodded. 'Doctor Owen says I should keep well away from my aunt's house at Lewis Square as there's a neighbouring house where a lady's been taking in lodgers and that appears to be the house where the problem lies. He's expecting some deaths there by the sound of it!'

'It's just as well you didn't move in with your aunt as you'd planned to do, Seren.'

Seren huffed out a breath. 'Yes, someone was looking out for me!' She looked heavenward.

'Well, what did the doctor say, are you pregnant?'

She nodded. 'Yes, he thinks I might be three or four months pregnant. But he also says I should tell Morgan.'

Anwen slammed the dough down hard on the counter. 'You'll do no such thing! Not until you're ready anyhow! It's all right for Doctor Owen, he hasn't had to live with the brute. I'd keep it quiet for now, if I were you.'

'I think you're right, Anwen. But I won't be able to keep it quiet forever, my pregnancy will start to show soon.'

'I think you'd best go and tell your mother and sister though.'

Seren chewed on her bottom lip, realising her mother had enough on her plate. To be told now there would be a new baby in the family and that her own sister was now living in an area where cholera was rife, would it be too much for her to take? Realising the sense of Anwen's words, she said, 'I'll call there later today. I did call earlier but there was no one in.'

'The sooner you do it the better, before she goes anywhere near Lewis Square. Meanwhile, Elwyn has been here and he wondered if you could start the bible study group this Wednesday?'

Her eyes were drawn to two cups and saucers on the table; he'd obviously had tea with Anwen. Her heart sank, how disappointed she felt to have missed him.

Seeing the expression on her face, Anwen set down the dough and wiped her floury hands on her pinafore. Then, stepping forward, she said, 'You're getting too close to that young minister for my liking, Seren.'

Seren's chin jutted forward. 'But you're close to him yourself, Anwen.'

'Ah, but that's not the same thing at all . . . ' She sat at the table as Seren followed suit. 'I'm an elderly woman, the gossips won't speak of me and him in the same breath, but they will with you. You're an attractive young woman, and to all intents and purposes you shouldn't really be alone together. He's a handsome single man. In some ways it would be easier for you if he were married.'

Married? She felt a sharp pang of disappointment at the thought of Elwyn having a wife, someone close to him that wasn't her. Maybe Anwen was right and she was developing feelings for the man.

'I'm right, aren't I?' Anwen said sagely.

'Yes.' Seren lowered her head and stared at the cake crumbs on the plate before her.

'Look me in the eye.' She brought her gaze to meet with Anwen's. 'I knew it!' the elderly woman said excitedly. 'You're in love with him, aren't you?'

She nodded silently, not even realising it until now.

'Maybe it would be better if you didn't run that bible class, *bach*. Or at least ask someone like Mary Williams to help you.'

'Perhaps you are right. You usually are.' Then, changing the subject before Anwen could say anything else that might expose her true feelings, she said, 'How about a fresh cup of tea?'

'Aye, that would be wonderful, but think on about what I said.'

She'd think on all right — apart from the baby, she could think of nothing else.

* * *

The thought of new life inside her brought a smile to Seren's face as she walked purposefully towards her mother's home, but as she neared the canal bank she noticed a familiar figure headed towards her. Maggie Shanklin! The woman's hooked nose and beady eyes reminded her of a wicked witch, yet it was she who had the cheek to call Anwen one!

'Hello, Mrs James.' She greeted Seren in what sounded like an amicable fashion, yet her lips were set in a grim line.

'Hello, Mrs Shanklin.' She made to carry on walking before the woman had the chance to say anything further that might inflame her emotions, but Maggie carried on speaking, causing Seren to turn and face her again out of politeness.

'And how is *your* Morgan?'

Seren felt her hackles rise; the woman had a way of getting to her by the use of words.

'Mrs Shanklin, I'd be very surprised if *you* of all people in this village, didn't realise that my husband and I are no longer living together?'

A gleam appeared in Maggie's green eyes as she continued, 'Been keeping a lot of company with the new minister, I notice? Didn't he invite you to Sunday dinner at The Manse?'

Seren stuck her chin out in defiance. 'Yes, he did, but there were others present at the time.' Why should she have to explain herself to the nosy old crone?

'He's a single man, so I'd take care if I were you. If Morgan should discover you're getting so close, I doubt he'd like it and, as you know, he has a terrible temper, been known to punch a hole in the wall at the pub when he's had a few and flown into a rage!'

Seren gritted her teeth. 'And what about my husband's friendship with another woman then, Maggie?' As soon as the words left her lips she regretted them as she had played right into the woman's hands.

Maggie smiled knowingly as if she had one up on Seren. 'Oh, yes, I've noticed the woman calling to your home since you've abandoned your Morgan. Very loved up they look together and all, but then he's a man and a man has needs. He won't get a bad reputation like you will!'

Fuming, Seren turned her back on the woman and walked away as quickly as possible with her fists clenched at her sides.

Lord help me! Otherwise I'll say something I might regret.

What was it about that woman and her mouth? God only knew for only *He* could love someone like her. Then a sense of guilt overtook her for thinking that way about a fellow human being, but the woman was forever stirring the pot. It was her fault that some of the villagers had turned against Anwen.

By the time Seren turned up at her mother's door she must have been visibly shaking as her mother led her inside to the living room. 'Whatever's the matter?' she asked. 'Is it Morgan again?'

'No, Mam,' Seren said, removing her cloak and bonnet. 'It's that Mrs Shanklin, she goaded me on the canal bank just now.'

'That bloody woman! Please excuse my language. She needs a scold's bridle to fill her gob!'

Seren furrowed her brow. 'What's that, Mam?'

'It's part of a bridle used by a horse. It was said that in the old days they made gossips wear them to still their wagging tongues!'

Seren chuckled. 'I'd love to see Mrs Shanklin wear one of those!'

'Now then, what brought you here today? You haven't called for a while.'

'Sorry, Mam. I've been that busy helping Anwen and Mary Williams.'

'I know that, I just wondered if anything was wrong?'

'Yes and no.'

Her mother angled her head to one side in puzzlement. 'Go on? Give me the bad news first.'

'I've had it confirmed by Doctor Owen that cholera is back in Abercanaid.'

Her mother's hands flew to her face. 'Not again, surely?'

Seren nodded. 'I'm afraid so, and unfortunately, it's at a house in Lewis Square so you'd better not visit Aunt Maud.'

'But I have to warn her!' The alarm in her mother's voice was evident.

'She'll already know about it, it's such a small place. The doctor told me they've lime-washed the outside of the house and told people to keep away.'

Her mother shook her head and now there were tears of desperation in her eyes. 'But if I go to see her maybe I can bring her to live with me and our Gwen? She'll be safe here.'

'I wouldn't advise it, Mam, you don't want to spread it to the rest of the family and this end of the village, do you?'

'I suppose not. Oh dearie me . . . ' She sniffed, then, taking a handkerchief from her pinafore pocket, dabbed at her eyes. 'This is dreadful. It can't be common news around here yet as I was in the shop earlier and no one mentioned it.'

Seren laid a hand on her mother's shoulder. 'I doubt they know, I only found out as Doctor Owen told me earlier. He's only recently been informed himself.'

Her mother blinked. 'But why were you speaking to him, was he at the farm visiting Anwen?'

'No. I went to see him.' There was no other way than to come out with it. 'Mam, I was there at the surgery as I thought I might have been pregnant, and now the doctor's confirmed it!'

Suddenly, she found herself in her mother's arms. 'Oh Seren, I'm so pleased for you as it's what you've always wanted, but the timing doesn't seem to be right, not now after you've got away from that thuggish brute.'

Seren's shoulders wracked as her whole body convulsed and she wept as her mother stroked her hair like she did when she was a child. Then after a minute or two she said, eyes moist with tears, 'I've thought about it long and hard and it must be God's will for me to have this child.'

'Then if you are accepting of the situation, so am I,' her mother said stoically. 'For there's nothing that can change things anyhow, but I fear what will happen once that man finds out he is to be the father.'

Seren shook her head. 'I had feared he'd come after me, Mam, but this time he hasn't.'

Seren's mother chewed on her bottom lip. 'But I think that's because he's distracted by that floozie. While a man is getting all his needs met he won't chase after you, you mark my words. But when he tires of his tart, he'll return like a bad smell. The best thing you can do is get away from here. You could go to stay with your aunt and uncle in Swansea for a while.'

'Oh, no, Mam. I'm needed here, particularly at the farm. I couldn't leave Mrs Llewellyn, she's been very kind to me, and in any case the minister has asked me to run a bible study group at the chapel, particularly for those widowed women from the recent pit accidents. He thinks it will be a good way to keep their morale up and get them out of the house.'

Mam nodded. 'Well, that sounds a real good thing to do, Seren. But I do fear for your safety sometimes.'

'Don't worry, Mam. I'm a big girl now, I can look after myself.'

Seren could see in her mother's eyes that she very much doubted that but wasn't about to say so.

* * *

The bible study group began the following week in the chapel hall. Initially only a few women turned up, including Mary Williams, who Seren was delighted to see, but by the following week, numbers had swelled as word had got around and even a couple of men joined the group too.

Another couple of weeks and Seren realised that she wouldn't be able to hide the pregnancy, but at least this child wouldn't be born out of wedlock even if its parents no longer lived together. People in the community would be well aware of that, or so she thought.

''Tisn't right you teaching bible classes in your condition!' Seren turned to see it was Maggie Shanklin behind her as she collected up the bibles ready to put away in the cupboard. Everyone had departed apart from Mary Williams, who was in a corner of the room placing the used teacups and saucers on a tray.

Maggie was the last person Seren was expecting to see. 'Can I help you, Mrs Shanklin?' Seren asked, determined the woman wasn't going to goad her on this occasion.

'You're obviously ignoring what I just said to you, *Mrs James*, but any fool can see how you're in the family way!'

'And how would they know that, pray tell?'

Keep a cool head, the woman knows nothing whatsoever! Mam would never tell her, nor Anwen nor the doctor . . . unless Elwyn had betrayed her trust again? He wouldn't, surely?

'Because I can tell your face looks a bit plumper than usual. Oh, your dress might be hiding the signs for time being, but I can see there's a definite bloom about your demeanour.'

How on earth the woman could tell what she'd hardly told anyone herself was beyond her.

To her way of thinking, it was far more likely Maggie was a witch than poor old Anwen. She wondered how she might answer, when she was saved from doing so as Elwyn entered the room. His eyes widened in surprise to see Maggie when she'd been keeping well away from the chapel after that ticking off he'd given her and her cronies in his sermon that time.

'Ah, Mrs Shanklin,' he said brightly. 'Come to enquire about the bible study group, have we?'

She shook her head. 'No fear, not with half the heathens that come to it.' Seren guessed she was referring to Anwen, who in her opinion was the most God-fearing woman she'd ever met.

'Then what can we do for you?'

Her face reddened, which was unusual for Maggie. 'I'd like to speak to you alone if I may, Mr Evans . . . ' She lowered her voice and averted her gaze as if there was something she didn't want Seren or Mary to know. Whatever it was, it was for Elwyn's ears only, that much was evident.

Elwyn nodded. 'Then you'd best come through to my office.' He glanced at Seren. 'Carry on, Mrs James. I shan't be long.'

Mary had already washed the cups and saucers, so left for home as she didn't want to leave the baby with Sam for too long. Seren wondered what Mrs Shanklin had to say to the minister that was keeping him for this long. He had promised to walk her back to the farm as it was getting dark.

Finally, he returned to the hall looking a bit flustered. 'I'm sorry, Seren. Can you hang on a bit longer for me, something's come up. I should be about another half hour. Mrs Shanklin is very distressed about a decision Tom's just made. I can't leave her like this.'

'It's all right, Mr Evans.' She decided to address him formally for fear Maggie was eavesdropping by the door. It just wouldn't do to give her any ammunition. If the woman knew for sure she was pregnant and was friendly with the minister, she might put all sorts around the village with that sharp tongue of hers. 'I'll walk home, you can lock up here if you like.'

'You'll do no such thing!' he warned, but there was mirth behind his eyes. 'Make yourself a cup of tea and by the time you've finished and washed your cup and saucer, I promise, I'll be back.' For one moment she thought he was going to plant a kiss on her forehead like a protective husband might do to his wife but, not waiting for her answer, he turned on his heel and left the hall.

She put the kettle on to boil and set out two cups and saucers in case he returned and wanted one himself. All the while, she marvelled at how caring Elwyn was to everyone, not just herself. Even the likes of Mrs Shanklin was worthy of his time and attention, and she hadn't even attended chapel this past couple of weeks.

Seating herself on a wooden chair, she rubbed her aching back, realising she needed that cuppa; right parched she was after all that talking tonight. The questions had come fast and furiously as people took great interest in discussing Jesus's parables. Why did he speak that way? What was the meaning behind them? The questions were endless, but Seren had enjoyed them so.

If only someone could explain the parable of the cobbler who was cruel to his wife, that would be enough to satisfy her. The meaning behind her having had to endure such a life, which thankfully now was over for her.

She set down her teacup on the table as she heard footsteps in the corridor outside. The door opened a fraction. Elwyn had returned.

'You're earlier than I thought you'd b . . . ' She didn't get to finish her sentence as striding purposely towards her was Morgan and his face was red with anger, his eyes seeming to bulge out of his head.

'So, this is where you've been hiding, you bitch!' he shouted as spittle sprayed from his mouth.

Quickly, she rose to her feet. 'Please, Morgan, not in the house of God,' she protested. But her pleas fell on deaf ears as he grabbed her roughly by the elbow and led her away.

'You're hurting me! Please let me go!' she wailed, but there was no one around to hear.

9

Anwen stood at the back door of the farm swinging a lantern in her hand. My word, Seren was late returning home tonight. She heard footsteps and was about to cross the yard to meet the girl, when she spied the silhouette of a man. Realising it was Elwyn but that there was no sign of Seren, her heart sank.

'Mrs Llewellyn,' he gasped as if he'd been rushing up the mountainside. 'Is Seren back yet?'

'No, *bach*, I thought she'd be with you.'

He shook his head. 'I told her to stay put at the chapel hall and make herself a cup of tea. I had to go with Mrs Shanklin on some urgent business. I said I'd be less than half an hour, which I was, but when I returned, there was no sign of her. There were signs she'd made herself a cup of tea though, but why wouldn't she wait?'

'That's not like her at all!' Anwen shook her head. 'Look, you'd better come in before you keel over and we'll discuss this. Hopefully, meantime, she'll turn up.' Anwen tried to keep the concern out of her voice so as not to alarm the minister, but she had a bad feeling about this.

Elwyn nodded, obviously pleased the woman had invited him to rest inside. But it was so unlike Seren to just go off somewhere like that and she feared that Morgan James might have had something to do with it.

After waiting for one hour, there was still no

sign of Seren. 'I think my worst fear has been realised,' said Anwen, sombrely. 'And that's she's been taken by Morgan.'

'Then I must go and check their house,' Elwyn said, leaping out of the chair. 'I've been wasting time sitting here when I should have been out looking for her!'

'Take someone with you,' Anwen advised. 'You'll be no match for that man. Ask Tom Shanklin, he's not afraid to stand up to him.'

'I'm sorry to say the Shanklins have enough problems of their own at the moment. I shall go alone and try to reason with the man, if indeed he does have her. We don't know that for sure, do we?'

Although Anwen shook her head, in her heart she knew that's who had hold of her, but to be clear, she said, 'Go and check her mother's house first, just in case.'

He nodded, then went to leave through the back door. 'Here, take this lantern with you. I have another. And don't go doing anything silly. I know you have feelings for the woman,' she said with a sympathetic smile.

As Anwen touched the minister's back in reassurance, she felt him stiffen. It was almost as though he didn't want to admit his feelings for Seren, but Anwen wasn't daft — she knew how the pair of them felt about one another. At another time and in another place, they would be the perfect couple, but not in this imperfect world where Seren was married to someone else.

Elwyn turned to take the lantern from Anwen's outstretched hand. 'Thank you, Mrs

Llewellyn. I won't do anything foolish, you can be sure of that. Please pray for Seren's safety, won't you?'

'Now that I can do,' Anwen said brightly.

* * *

As Morgan dragged Seren up the back path of their garden, he growled, 'You'll pay for what you've put me through, you whore! You'll get the buckle end of my belt tonight good and proper and you'll perform your wifely duties too, whether you want to or not! You've paid more attention to that minister than to your own husband of late!'

She bit her lip. *Dear Lord, what is he thinking? That there'd been something between her and Elwyn? Surely not? But why then had he called her a whore? If she was to save herself and the new life inside her, then she was going to have to tell him about her circumstance.*

He shoved open the scullery door. The room was dimly lit by an oil lamp that had been left burning on the windowsill. She recoiled as she realised once inside closed doors anything could happen to her. He pushed her roughly inside so she went flying on to the hard, cold flagstone floor. In pain, touching her stomach in the semi-darkness, she saw him looming above her like a great Goliath, a silhouette of his shadow cast against the wall. She had no slingshot to fire at him, all she had to fire were her words, but somehow, they wouldn't come: she was frozen with fear.

Then she saw the steel toe cap of his boot

come flying towards her head.

Seren's hands flew to her face to protect herself from the blows raining down on her body.

Tell him! For pity's sake, tell him now before he kills you and the baby!

Her voice was frozen inside her but knowing she needed to protect the innocent life within, she whispered: 'I'm pregnant . . .' then louder, 'I'm pregnant,' then even louder, 'I'm having a child!' The voice emerging didn't sound like her own but it was strong and loud enough for him to hear.

Help me, Lord!

Then, with all her might, a voice arose within her, stirred up from something beyond her own understanding. 'Stop! Stop it now! I'm having *your* baby!'

'What?' He stood, backing away with his hands raised, palm outwards, almost in defence at the horror of his actions. Then he was on his knees to her. 'Sssh, don't say anything . . .' She was drifting off into unconsciousness as she felt him stroking her head.

There was another voice. A female one. She didn't recognise it and she couldn't understand what was being said. Swirls of colour danced before her eyes, then everything went black.

* * *

Anwen had a bad feeling and she couldn't let it rest. She opened the door and followed him to his cart. 'Take me with you, Elwyn!' she commanded. 'If you intend to find Seren, I need to come along, and forget about going to Seren's mother's home, we need to get to Seren's house, now, fast!'

He turned to face her and nodded soberly, knowing better than to challenge the woman. She watched as he harnessed the horse and attached it to the cart, and they set off towards the village. The bad feeling grew stronger and she closed her eyes as the cart clattered along over old stones and uneven ground on the Parish Road.

'Mrs Llewellyn, are you all right?' Elwyn asked with a note of concern in his voice.

'I'm getting one of my visions, but you won't want to hear about that. You'll claim it's wicked witchcraft like Mr Gruffudd does.'

'You'd better tell me what you see . . . '

She let out a long breath before saying, 'All right then. I see Seren lying on a cold flagstone floor in fear . . . '

'Of her life?'

'More for her unborn child. And I feel something else too. Pain. A deep emotional pain and a physical one too. I can feel pain to my head, it's muzzy. Drive the horse faster, please, and let's hope we're not too late — I see the angel of death hovering over her lifeless body . . . '

* * *

There was a strange kind of singing going on.

'I was only a farmer's daughter, only a lowly lass, but the day I slipped in pigs' swill, I landed on me ass! Singing too ra, too ra, Henry, you are

the lad for me, you'll take me behind the cow shed and shaft me against the tree!' A deep throaty chuckle emerged from the woman's throat.

Then, 'Mari! Mari! She's waking up, see!' from another woman.

Seren opened one eye and then the other. Why did her face feel so sore? She let out a little whimper of pain. 'W . . . where am I?'

'Sssh now, darlin', 'tis in the wash house at China you are, my dear.' The woman had a soft Irish inflection to her voice, all sing-song like, but this wasn't Maggie Shanklin's voice, but somebody else's.

China? That bloody hell hole!

What was she doing here?

'Take yer time now,' the woman who'd been singing said, 'he's gone and given you some right shiners to your eyes, make no bones about it. I thought it was only me he got so angry with!'

'Aye, and you wanted to live with the man, Mari, you must have been mad!'

Mari? Wasn't that the name of the woman who Morgan had been visiting at night when he should have been home?

Seren's eyes began to focus and she realised she was lying on an old mattress pallet while the two women were stood near a large stone wash basin in front of a grimy window-pane. The air was warm and moist and she noticed steam arising from the basin.

So, this was what the wash house looked like! She'd heard plenty of tales about this place, about how a lot of the women who worked here had fallen on hard times as it was used as a front for the brothel next door. Indeed, there was one young woman from Abercanaid whose husband had left her and her two kiddies to fend for themselves. She'd worked here and ended up hitting the gin bottle. In the end the children's grandmother had to look after them. It wasn't reputed to be a nice place at all.

She stared intently at the two women. The Irish one looked middle-aged and as if she had suffered hard times, going by her heavily lined face. She had flaming red hair drawn away from her face and she wore a white mobcap and grubby pinafore. The younger of the two was buxom to say the least. Her breasts were spilling out of the bodice of her dress. Her dirty-looking blonde hair fell into waves upon her shoulders. If she were not so coarse in her manner and words, she'd be very attractive indeed. She walked over to Seren. 'Stay where you are, *cariad*, I brought you here for your own safety. That Morgan James has been cruel to us both, and both of us were carrying his child . . .'

'Were?' Seren sat up abruptly, even though every bone in her body ached. Immediately, her hands flew to her stomach.

'You're all right, darlin', you've still got your baby inside you. I miscarried mine just a few days ago, Morgan kicked the little mite out of me. Course, he didn't intend to do that, he just got carried away with his anger . . . '

'He did an' all,' the Irish woman agreed. 'I'm Connie, love. I've known Mari here for some time. She didn't go out of her way to steal yer husband. He was a regular visitor here and at

The House of Blazes next door. It's a local inn where there's a lot of shenanigans going on upstairs, if you get my drift . . .' She tapped the side of her nose and Seren reckoned that must be the brothel that people spoke of.

Seren frowned.

'It's a knocking shop, that's what it is. Local men have needs, don't they? Can't say I'm proud of it but even at my age I've serviced a few; well, the working-class ones. Mari here is luckier; as she's younger she gets to service some of the bosses from the ironworks and they tip her well for her time an' all!' Connie leaned over and inspected Seren closely. Lifting up a lock of her hair, she said, 'You're a fine-looking woman, I'll say that much for ye. You could easily earn a bob or two next door . . .'

Seren almost gagged as she inhaled the familiar fumes of alcohol that reminded her so much of her husband. What kind of life did this pair have? Connie had obviously seen better days and her rough, calloused hands were immersed in soapy water most of the day or else she was lying on her back for a few bob next door. No wonder Mari had viewed Morgan as a lucky escape from where she worked, but in reality it hadn't been one at all, it had been a hard road to hell. It all came at a high cost — the cost of the life of her unborn child. She'd even excused Morgan for his behaviour by claiming it was she who had made him angry and that's why he'd turned on her.

'I need to get out of here,' Seren said finally.

Mari's chin jutted out. 'I'm sorry but you just

can't. Morgan has paid me good money to hang on to you.' She stood looming over Seren as though she had her under some sort of arrest.

Seren blinked, feeling confused. 'But why?'

'Because he doesn't want the villagers to see he's given you a good hiding, see. He told me that he'd never have touched you if he'd known you were with child!'

'But he did the same to you and he murdered yours!' She spat out the words in disgust. Somehow, she had to get through to the woman. It was obvious to Seren she was in some sort of denial. And for the first time, she realised what it was. Mari was in love with Morgan. It should have caused her some pain, but it didn't. All she felt was revulsion that this woman she saw before her could prostitute herself for a man who had no heart or soul.

Mari's features softened. 'Aye, I know, but he didn't mean to kill our child. He thought the baby was someone else's, see. I lied to him to wind him up one night. So, we can't blame him for flying into a rage, really, can we?'

Seren finally found the strength to drag herself from the mattress, and shakily she stood, holding on to a chair and looking into Mari's eyes. 'Mari, I know you and I ought to be enemies, but really I don't feel that way about you at all. You are as much a victim as I was. Please don't waste your time and energy on a man who can never really love you back . . . ' She maintained eye contact with the woman for a few seconds and noticed tears forming in the woman's eyes. Mari was breaking down but Seren knew she had to escape this place, and to do that she had to overcome Mari's loyalty to Morgan. She turned in the other direction.

'Connie,' she said gently. 'You understand, don't you?'

Connie nodded. 'Aye, I do.'

'Then take care of her. She knows not what she says and she needs nurturing. If you can, keep her away from that brute.'

Connie's eyes were full of concern. 'I'll try my best but she's that besotted with him.'

Then Mari's shoulders began to wrack as she yelled out a guttural cry from somewhere deep inside her. And Seren just knew it was for the baby she'd lost. But she now had her own child to think of.

'I'm going home,' she said with determination, realising as she had no money she'd have to walk.

As if reading her mind, Connie said, 'Tain't right what's happened to you. Here, take this . . .' She squeezed a shilling into Seren's palm. 'Go and get a hansom from the High Street.'

'But don't you need that money?' She gazed into the woman's eyes and only saw kindness there. A moment since and she'd thought the woman to be a hard-hearted harridan, but it simply wasn't true. 'I'll borrow the money then. I will be back to repay you soon.' Connie nodded. Then turning towards Mari, Seren whispered, 'Take care of yourself . . .'

Mari seemed in a world of her own, but this was Seren's chance to get away and she realised that at least for time being, she might need to get away from her hometown too.

'Hang on a minute, love,' Connie said. Seren turned as the woman lowered her voice. 'Be careful you don't get caught up with any of the sorts round 'ere, especially that inn next door. The girls who work there are on the rob from the men — they get the men plastered with booze, lead them upstairs and when they fall asleep, pick their pockets. You don't want to get mixed up in any of that.'

Seren smiled at the woman and touching her hand, nodded, then turned to leave. She opened the door to be met with a group of gaggling women and girls with their backs towards her. Some were scrubbing clothing on metal washboards, whereas others had their arms immersed elbows-deep in soapy, suddy water. One was singing and two women were folding up starched white sheets. This looked like the heart of the wash house.

From the corner of the room, one of the women turned as if she sensed she was being watched. Her brown eyes were big and beady, while her limbs were thin and spindle-like, reminding Seren of a sparrow. She narrowed her eyes. 'What-cha looking at?' she snapped at Seren.

Although Seren felt like replying, 'Nothing much at the moment, darling!' at her, she kept her cool and her mouth firmly shut as she averted her eyes elsewhere in search of a door to escape through. The woman, though, seemed annoyed that there was no answer forthcoming from Seren. She raised her voice as she strode towards her, making the others turn and stare.

'I asked you whatcha looking at?' She jabbed her index finger in Seren's face, causing her to take a step back. Her mouth felt parched and her head began to spin. She couldn't even remember when she'd last had something to eat or drink and all she longed to do was get out of the hot, stifling environment into the cool air outside. Her heartbeat quickened. What could she do?

'I'm sorry. I shouldn't be here, it's all a mistake,' she replied meekly.

'It's all a mistake!' the woman mocked, with her hands on her hips as several of the girls laughed. She tossed back her chestnut curls. 'I'm a lady, that's what I am!'

'Leave that lady alone, Nellie!'

Seren's head whipped around in the direction of the loud, booming voice, which caused her to shudder. All of a sudden, the girl's cockiness disappeared faster than a rat up a drainpipe and she returned to the big stone bosh to resume her duties with her head bowed low. And for the first time, Seren noticed a woman emerging from a small closet room beside the main wash room.

'I'm Mrs Gowerton and I'm in authority here,' she said, addressing Seren with a fixed stare as if wondering why she was in her wash room. She was dressed differently to the others; this lady wore a long black dress with white collar and cuffs. 'I'm in charge of the ladies here, though I think on this occasion they have acted more like a load of savages. What are you doing here, might I ask?'

Oh dear, this was going to prove awkward. Perhaps she should tell the truth but with ten sets of prying eyes on her, she really didn't feel she could.

* * *

Mrs Gowerton guided Seren past the women and girls back to her small room, then, being watched by them all, she closed the door in their faces. How Seren longed to escape. It was so confining and claustrophobic, but once inside the woman was kindness itself, her voice taking on a softer tone than that used in front of her workforce. She gestured for Seren to sit in front of her desk, whilst she seated herself behind it.

She clasped her hands together in front of her as if she meant business, causing Seren to swallow hard before she'd even said anything. There was a long pause as if Mrs Gowerton was mentally appraising her. 'Right, now, I'd like to know your name, please, and why you're really here?'

Seren hesitated before speaking. Her head was feeling muzzy and a feeling of weakness took over. As if sensing this, Mrs Gowerton poured her a glass of water from a pitcher on the desk. 'It gets so hot in here,' she explained. 'I always have to keep a jug of water to hand.'

Seren gratefully accepted the water before taking a few sips. Then she set the glass down on the desk before her.

'I'm Seren James,' she began, her thirst now quenched. 'One moment I was in Abercanaid where I live and the next thing I knew I was being beaten up by my husband, but I awoke here and I've no idea how I came to be here . . . ' The memory lapse concerned her greatly.

Mrs Gowerton got up from her chair and

approached Seren. Then gently, she examined Seren's face in her hands. 'I did notice the bruising and swelling to your face but had no mind to mention it to you as so many who work here turn up for a day's toil looking like you do. If it's not their husbands who have taken to the drink and turned on them, then it's the customers from the inn next door. Some of the women and girls work there too to supplement their earnings. Can't say I like it myself, but needs must. It's part and parcel of life around these parts of China and sadly, it's considered quite normal . . . ' She paused a moment. 'But in your case, I'm guessing something has gone badly wrong? You don't look like you belong here.' She released Seren's face from her hands, smiled and reseated herself behind her desk.

Seren nodded slowly. There was a lump in her throat that threatened to choke her. She took another couple of sips of water before setting her glass down again. 'My husband is a cobbler in Abercanaid. Up until recently he was hard-working and well respected in the community. We've only been married for about a year. At first, we were happy, but as time went on and there was no sign of me bearing him a child, he began to get angry with me and took to the drink.'

Mrs Gowerton's wise old eyes held a sense of knowing about them. 'And I'm guessing he got involved in all the things that go along with the temptation of alcohol? Womanising and gambling?'

'Yes.'

'I've seen it often enough with the women who work here, how they've suffered at the hands of their menfolk.'

Seren wondered if she should tell the woman about Mari's part in all of this but thought better of it; she didn't want to be the cause of the woman losing her job. Then she would have lost everything, as Seren realised in her heart that Morgan wouldn't stand by the woman, no matter how much she loved him.

'But what I don't understand,' said Mrs Gowerton, her eyes narrowing in suspicion, 'is how you came to wake up here in my wash house? Don't get me wrong, some of the women have a little kip on the straw pallets in the back room from time to time and that's allowed if they're overly tired, as I feel they could be a danger to themselves otherwise, with all that boiling water and those hot irons around. I allow them to rest as an act of kindness . . . '

It was no use, Seren was going to have to come clean.

'I think it was Mari who brought me here. When I was being beaten, I sensed another presence somewhere in the house, and thought I heard a female voice. One I didn't recognise. Then I must have passed out and I found myself here.'

Mrs Gowerton's eyebrows knitted together curiously. 'Mari, eh? Now it's starting to make sense. Is your husband a tall, handsome chap, well built, wide shoulders? Looks like he could handle himself in a fight?'

'Yes, that sounds like him. Dark hair, brown

eyes. He often wears a leather waistcoat . . . '

A knowing look swept over Mrs Gowerton's face. 'I've seen him hanging around here at the back door a time or two waiting for Mari to finish her shift and at The House of Blazes next door.' There was a long silence that seemed never-ending and Seren wondered what the woman was thinking.

Finally, she drew a breath and said, 'What is it you would like me to do with Mari Morris? Dismiss her?'

Seren's hands flew to her face in horror. 'Oh no, Mrs Gowerton, I wouldn't like that at all! Two wrongs don't make a right, particularly not now . . . Not now after what's happened to her.' She feared she'd gone too far with that revelation but it was too late to stop, the cat was already out of the bag. 'She lost a baby a few days ago and it was my husband's fault.'

Mrs Gowerton nodded as she took Seren's hands in her own across the desk to comfort her. 'Don't you worry, I don't believe in kicking someone whilst they are down,' she said quietly, which made Seren remember how Morgan had kicked and punched her whilst she lay defenceless on the floor. She really hadn't stood a chance.

'I'm pregnant by him myself,' she found herself confiding in the woman.

'Then that's all the more reason you must not return to the man. And poor Mari, I had no idea she'd miscarried, and to think she's been working during that time too. The physical pain and mental anguish she must be going through.'

She closed her eyes as if trying to imagine it all, then her eyes flicked open and she looked at Seren. 'You need to keep well away from him.'

'I had managed to get away from him. I was living with an elderly lady at her farmhouse on the mountainside, but he found me on my own at the chapel hall last night and dragged me back to the marital home.'

Mrs Gowerton shook her head. 'I'll send for a pot of tea and some biscuits, my dear. Then I'll sort you out with a cab to get you safely back to the farmhouse.'

It was only then that Seren felt able to break down in tears as she was overwhelmed by the kindness shown towards her.

* * *

Anwen Llewellyn was banging on Morgan James's door using both her fists. 'I know you're in there, Morgan. Come out and speak to us!'

'Calm yourself down, Mrs Llewellyn,' Elwyn said soothingly. 'It won't do to get yourself upset, you're only recently making a recovery from that turn you had.'

She stopped what she was doing and glanced at him. Then, letting out a long, ragged breath, said, 'You're right. Let's creep up on the enemy instead.'

'Pardon?'

'We'll go via the back entrance . . . '

He nodded.

It was a plan of sorts, she supposed, and she hoped they wouldn't arrive too late. Glancing up and down the deserted street, she hoped no one had seen them arrive to alert the man, but they might have heard her furious banging on the door of course.

As they neared the back door of the property, the hairs on the back of Anwen's neck prickled. That was never a good sign, she just knew that something bad had taken place here.

'Stay where you are,' Elwyn warned. 'I'll go inside.'

'Mr James!' he called out through the half-open door, but his voice seemed to echo into nothingness and, tentatively, he stepped inside.

Anwen rushed in behind him and before he had a chance to chastise her, they both stared at the flagstone floor.

Could that be blood on it? The table and chairs were over-turned. Elwyn rushed through the scullery door into the main part of the house, all the while calling out Seren's name. Meanwhile Anwen closed her eyes and clasped her hands together as if in prayer.

Yes, something bad has occurred here. He's hit her. I can see her on the floor and she's raising her arms to protect her face and then her stomach to protect her unborn child. But wait . . . there's someone else here too, another woman!

Within moments, Elwyn had returned to her side. 'I've checked the whole house but there's no sign of anyone. What's the matter, Anwen?'

'I've just had one of my visions but you'll think it's the Devil's own work like Mr Gruffudd does . . .'

'No, I won't. I know you're a godly woman, Anwen. It's probably divine prophecy you're experiencing. A message from above, if you like.'

She shook her head. 'It's not good, I'm afraid. I fear for Seren and that new life inside her and . . . '

'And?' His eyes were full of concern, she knew just how much he thought of Seren.

'And, if what I'm experiencing is true, she was lying on this floor with her hands to her face and then her stomach as that bastard laid into her. Oh, I'm so sorry, Mr Evans, I didn't mean to swear.' She began to tremble as she sensed the feelings of horror and revulsion that Seren must have endured.

'That's all right, Mrs Llewellyn, it's perfectly understandable that you should feel so angry. I feel angry myself.' But this wasn't just anger she was feeling right now: it was laced with fear, a fear that if they didn't find Seren soon it might very well be too late.

She shook her head. 'I hope this blood isn't a bad sign. There's not a lot of it, but what if she was losing the baby?'

His face became a blank canvas as his lips set in a fine line. It was unusual to see the young minister like this. She noticed him ball his fists at his sides, flexing and unflexing his fingers from time to time as if to abate his anger.

They remained where they were for several moments before he said, 'I think we ought to pray, don't you?'

'Yes, because it says in the Good Book, 'For where two or three are gathered together in my name, there am I in the midst of them . . .''

'Matthew, chapter 18, verse 20,' he smiled, as he laid his hand on Anwen's shoulder.

They both closed their eyes and bowed their heads as Elwyn uttered a simple prayer. 'Dear Lord, we implore you to help us find our sister, Seren, as we fear she is in grave danger right now. Please keep her safe wherever she might be, protect her from any wrongdoing and bring her home to us. Amen.'

'Amen,' concurred Anwen. Then she immediately began reciting The Lord's Prayer in Welsh, '*Ein Tad, yr hwn wyt yn y nefoedd . . .* ' praying like she'd never prayed before. Elwyn said 'Amen' at the end, too. She realised he wasn't a Welsh speaker like herself, but he would have heard the prayer uttered in Welsh enough times over the years to recognise and understand it. Whenever she felt stressed or anxious, she returned to her native tongue, which was a source of comfort to her.

Elwyn righted the table and chairs and they left via the back entrance of the house. Anwen realised she'd made enough of a commotion at the front that would have alerted folk, and now she was beginning to regret it as she held up her lantern to see Maggie Shanklin striding up the path to meet them with a very determined expression on her face.

'Well, what's happened then for you to be hammering on Morgan James's door?' she asked with a wicked gleam in her eye. 'And he didn't open his shop this morning neither!'

Anwen shook her head sadly. If she wasn't so

upset, she'd slap that old busybody across the chops.

'It's nothing to concern you, Mrs Shanklin,' the minister intervened. 'We're just looking for his wife, that's all.'

'Fine bloomin' wife she is to him and all, no wonder he brought that floozie to live here!'

'Have you seen Seren, Mrs Shanklin?' Anwen asked.

She shook her head. 'Contrary to popular belief, 'tisn't in my nature to poke my nose into people's business!'

Anwen could have laughed her socks off at that one. 'Well, have you seen Morgan then?'

'I just told you, didn't I? His shop is shut.'

This wasn't helping at all. Anwen was about to cuss at the woman when Elwyn said, 'When did you last see him?'

Maggie folded her arms. 'Early this morning, he was walking along the street here so I assumed he'd gone to open up the shop. I had a pair of our Tom's boots that needed tapping before he takes off; you know what I was telling you about when you came to see me earlier, Mr Evans?'

He nodded.

'So, I ran back to the house to get them and rushed to the shop but he wasn't there. And Tom needs those boots and all!'

It was no use, they were still none the wiser. Anwen clucked her teeth and walked away from the woman. If she stayed facing her head on, she feared she'd do her some serious damage.

When they returned to the cart and were

safely seated, she asked, 'Why did you have to go to see Mrs Shanklin earlier, Elwyn?'

His face reddened as he took the reins, then he let out a long breath and, looking at her, said, 'I'm not one for breaking a confidence but you'll find out soon enough. As Tom Shanklin has been laid off from the pit due to injury, he and some other men are taking off to London to look for work. As you can imagine, she's not best pleased about it.'

Anwen nodded. Although she despised the woman for how she'd treated her and how she'd circulated gossip in the village, she realised how close Tom and Maggie were. 'Well, to be truthful, it doesn't make all that much sense to me that he should go so far to seek work.'

'Yes, I know, there is plenty of work in this town and easy to find and all for able-bodied men, but since Tom badly injured his leg underground, it's left him with a bad limp. He can't find any employment here. There are so many new people flooding the town that the bosses can afford to pick and choose these days, from what Maggie's been telling me.'

Anwen shook her head. 'It's a shame, but I suppose if it's what he wants to do. So, what did you advise the Shanklins?'

'Nothing, really. Tom was in the pub and Maggie was in tears, so I just prayed with her. I don't make it my business to interfere in people's marriages!'

'Oh, don't you, Mr Evans? That's not what Seren told me.'

He frowned. 'And what has she been telling

you, Mrs Llewellyn?'

'That you once interfered by telling Mr Gruffudd something she told you in confidence.'

'Oh, that.' His face reddened again. 'Well, I do regret it. I didn't realise that Mr Gruffudd had loose lips. It was not intentional, I can assure you.'

Tell that to Seren James, Anwen thought to herself.

10

Seren was just finishing off her cup of tea when there was a hard knock on Mrs Gowerton's door.

'Enter!' the woman shouted.

One of the washerwomen popped her head around the door. 'Ma'am, it's Mr Watkin, he'd like a word with you.'

Mrs Gowerton's face paled. 'Not again,' she muttered under her breath, replacing her teacup on its saucer. She rose from her chair and went into the main wash room to meet with her caller.

Seren strained in her chair to hear what was being said through the partially open door. It was obvious that Mrs Gowerton was trying to keep her voice down but the man's voice was rising by the second and he sounded angry with the woman.

Then to her astonishment, she heard her husband's name being mentioned. 'The woman is to remain here at all costs, ma'am!' What woman was he talking about? Mari?

A thought struck her as a shiver travelled along her spine. *He means me!* Her husband would have known she'd been taken here. She had to get away. It sounded as if Mrs Gowerton was keeping the man at bay.

She looked for a means of escape but all she could see was a small window high up and she realised she was in the cellar of the building. The only way she could get up to that window was via the woman's desk, and even then it would be a hard squeeze to get through in her condition. But she had no more time to think further as the man burst into the small room, closely followed by Mrs Gowerton, whose hands had now flown to her face.

Mr Watkin was all dressed in black in a rumpled suit that had seen better days and a grubby white shirt. The tailcoat had probably been quite an attractive garment when new. His battered top hat was slightly askew on his head, and in his hand he held a wooden cane with a gold tip.

Seren trembled as he smiled. 'So, what do we have 'ere then?' He perused her with interest as if she were a cow at a cattle market as he walked around her chair, appraising her. She shivered as he lifted a strand of her hair and blew on the back of her neck, emitting a blast of alcohol. 'This one could prove a nice little earner at the inn next door, Mrs Gowerton. I'd have her on her back in no time, after I'd had the first go at her!' He laughed, throwing back his head. It was the sort of laugh that chilled Seren to the bone. She got out of her chair and turned to face him.

'Sir, I shall not be remaining here!' Her chin jutted out in defiance. 'I am on my way back home and wouldn't work next door if you paid me to!'

His eyes widened as if he was taken aback by her impudence, but he smiled. 'You've got spirit, I'll give you that much. I'm Twm Sion Watkin and I run the place next door. I didn't really have that line of work in mind for you, anyhow. Morgan tipped me the wink to look after you.' He touched her face with his filthy-looking hands, causing her to recoil. 'My, my, he's given you a right couple of shiners there, my dear . . .'

Mrs Gowerton looked on as if she didn't know how to react as her eyes darted all over the place and she twisted her hands.

'How much is my husband paying you to keep me here?' Seren demanded.

'Paying?' He narrowed his gaze and wiped his brow. 'No, you misunderstand, I'm doing this from the kindness of my heart, lovely girl. I owe Morgan a favour, big time. Now come along with me, and you shan't have to lie on your back, neither, much as I'd love you to.'

Mrs Gowerton stood there shaking her head over the man's shoulder and Seren realised there was little the woman could do. But then, quite unexpectedly, Mrs Gowerton spoke. 'Perhaps you could leave the lady to work here instead, Mr Watkin, as you own both places? She could do a little light washing and ironing for us.'

He glared at the woman as if he could hardly believe his ears. 'I'm well aware of what I own, ma'am, and if I say she's coming with me, then she's coming along with me!' he bellowed.

Mrs Gowerton lowered her head and then, mumbling something, walked away.

'I won't be coming with you!' Seren snapped. 'I'm having a baby so I shouldn't have to work hard for someone.'

Twm Sion Watkin frowned. 'And Morgan pasted you in your condition?'

'Yes, he did. He didn't know I was pregnant at the time, but that's no excuse. And now he's trying to hide the evidence from all and sundry.'

He stroked his chin. 'Well, if he has, then Morgan has gone down in my estimation. I've whacked a few whores around in my time but never a pregnant woman. As you must have been trying for a child, he would have realised there was a chance you could be pregnant.'

To Seren's astonishment the man seemed totally disgusted by her husband's behaviour.

'Well, I'll have to take you next door with me to keep to my side of the bargain, so he can see where you are later today, but if you were to escape unbeknownst to me tonight under the cover of darkness, I won't be making it known to anyone until first light next morning, if you get my drift.'

She thought she did get his drift very well indeed and smiled at him. For the first time he returned the smile, and this time, it was genuine. She had a feeling she was going to wrap the much-feared Twm Sion Watkin right around her little finger.

'You can call me Sioni,' he said, and she nodded, feeling more at ease with the man than she would with her own husband.

* * *

Sioni led her out of the building under the watchful eyes of Mrs Gowerton and the girls, no one daring to utter a word, though Seren guessed they'd have plenty to say after she'd departed. They ascended a stone staircase and then left via a door out into the alleyway outside, where dawn was just beginning to break. The cold air hit her, making her feel more awake and more alive than she had in a long while. She had been right, she'd been in a cellar of the building. How oppressive it had been too, those poor girls and women working for hours in that place. The only consolation for them was that Mrs Gowerton seemed a firm but fair sort to work for, and she was grateful to the woman for trying to help her at least.

'Here's my humble abode,' Sioni announced as she found herself outside a building that smelled strongly of alcohol.

'So, this is the infamous House of Blazes,' she muttered.

He nodded. 'It's a nickname for it, that's all. Its real name is The Forge and Hammer due to the fact that a lot of ironworkers used to come here, but it's hardly ever called that any more.'

He pushed open the heavy wooden door which was ajar. Even at this time of the morning, Seren could see some people inside swigging from pewter tankards and smoking pipes as the sounds of muffled voices and the odd bout of laughter drifted towards her. A strange odour permeated the air which she couldn't seem to identify; it definitely wasn't tobacco and it puzzled her.

A sudden hush fell over the room as Seren stood by Sioni's side. 'This 'ere lady is Seren James,' he introduced. 'She's Morgan the cobbler's wife, so be on your best behaviour, lads, else you'll have him to contend with!'

They looked her up and down, a couple of them nodding in her direction. It was obvious to Seren that those men respected her husband. He was well known in these parts and it made her feel saddened that on nights when he should have been by the fireside with her or tucked up next to her in their bed, he'd been here instead, enjoying the sins of alcohol and satisfying his lustful urges with whores, frittering their money away like shaking the feathers from a frayed pillow case.

For the first time, she noticed in the far corner of the room a couple of men and women. The women wore gaudy-coloured clothing, their breasts spilling over the top of their dresses as the men leered at them, stroking them intimately, it being obvious what was on their minds. So, these were the whores that Sioni had spoken of. One of them, who had long dark hair skimming her shoulders, glared at her. She looked like she had seen too much life, going by the hard look on her face, though Seren guessed she was probably only about twenty years of age. 'So, what's she doing here?' the girl asked Sioni.

'I've brought her 'ere, Rose, to be in charge of you and the other girls.' The girl was so surprised, her mouth opened and snapped shut again. 'It's about time someone took you all in hand.' She looked as if she was about to protest but then thought better of it.

Seren said nothing, just smiled at the girl with great amusement as she didn't intend hanging around all that long and would be out of the place before the cock crowed first thing in the morning.

Behind the bar stood a large-faced man with red hair and matching bushy sideburns. He was in the middle of filling up a couple of pewter tankards with beer, and had a towel draped over his shoulder. He winked at her. 'Pleased to meet you at long last, Mrs James,' he said.

'Thank you.' She smiled. 'I understand my husband was a regular here?'

He nodded, his face flushing before her eyes, then he turned away. No doubt he was embarrassed to be reminded that Morgan James had exercised his lustful urges with Mari and possibly others of her ilk upstairs at the inn. Seren felt no shame any more about it and was beginning to find it all so amusing. She realised with some sadness though, that if she now felt that way then she no longer loved her husband. He had kicked her love for him out of the window, like the night he'd kicked her with the toe of his boot as she lay helpless on the floor. What was happening to her? She was becoming hard as nails herself and she didn't much care for how it made her feel numb inside, as if her feelings had been sedated somehow.

'Come this way,' Twm Sion Watkin instructed as he led Seren up some narrow stone steps. As she reached the top she stood back a little as she was fearful of what she might see. As if realising this might be the case, he smiled. 'Don't worry, there's no action going on here at the moment. Apart from the two girls you saw downstairs, Rose and Deryl, the rest are sleeping it off, they had a busy night.' It was then Seren became aware of a gentle snoring sound arising from one of the bedrooms. 'And don't go concerning yourself about the men here either. The only ones on the premises are downstairs at the moment, supping their ale. I won't allow them to stay upstairs overnight. It's a rule of house. The girls entertain them downstairs beforehand then bring them up here . . . ' He stopped mid-sentence as if mulling things over, then he looked into her eyes. 'Pity you don't really want a job here. I could do with someone like you to oversee things.'

'Someone like me?'

'Soft and gentle and ladylike,' he said, gazing into her eyes. Then he stroked her face. She should have been horrified, but for some reason she found herself attracted to the man, though heaven knew why. He was obviously as dangerous as Morgan and feared by many, but the difference was she felt safe and protected by him and, from her understanding, he protected the girls who worked for him. The only reason he turned on them was if they betrayed him.

'I see,' she said finally. 'But I do need to get back to Abercanaid.'

'But why? Don't you want to keep away from Morgan if he's handy with his fists?'

'From him, yes. But I have friends there. I've been living with an elderly woman who has been like a mother to me. She'll be concerned for my welfare.'

He nodded. 'Look, there's an unoccupied room with a bed at the end of the landing. Use that to rest and I'll send the barmaid up with some food and drink for you. In your condition you need to take it easy.'

'Thank you. As long as the drink isn't alcohol, mind you.' She patted her tummy. 'I can't afford to drink alcohol in my condition.'

He nodded then left her to it, obviously having some other business to attend to.

She found the room as described at the end of the landing. Gingerly, she pushed open the door half expecting to find something that resembled a boudoir or some sort of bordello, but was cheered to discover it was just a simple room. There was a single bed against one wall, all made up and clean-looking, and against the other wall was a wardrobe and matching chest of drawers and between those a chair. The thick curtains were plain blue. She didn't know what she'd expected really. Maybe a four-poster bed, red plush curtains, fancy oil lamps, everything that could be associated with seduction, she supposed. It became obvious to her that whatever this room might be used for, it wasn't for that sort of thing. But she had noticed a strong whiff of perfume as she'd passed a couple of bedrooms on the way in.

She was just wondering if she should lie on the bed or get inside of it when there was a light tap on the door and a young maid entered, carrying a wooden tray. She couldn't have been much more than twelve years old. Her flame-red hair sprouted out at all angles beneath her mobcap and a speckling of freckles covered her face.

'Pardon me, missus,' she said, looking at

Seren. 'Mr Watkin has sent this for you. A glass of milk and a couple of rounds of bread and cheese.'

'Please tell Mr Watkin that I'm most grateful.' She smiled at the girl. 'What's your name?'

'Molly, miss. My father is the man behind the bar downstairs.' So that explained the girl's red hair!

'Well, I'm Mrs James, but you can call me Seren if you like,' she said kindly.

The girl smiled shyly.

'Can you do one thing for me, Molly?'

The girl nodded, then set the tray down on the bed.

'Do you know a man called Morgan James?'

Molly fought to think a moment as she chewed on her bottom lip.

'He's a tall, handsome man with dark hair and brown eyes. Works as a cobbler in Abercanaid.'

'Oh, I know.' Molly's eyes lit up. 'He is handsome and all, missus. Reminds me of Heathcliff from the book *Wuthering Heights*. My sister used to read me that at night.'

'Yes, that's him. Could you please let me know if he calls here, but whatever you do, don't let on you've seen me. It's to be a surprise.'

'Very well, missus. Anything else?'

'Oh, one more thing, where's the water closet?'

'There's a chamber pot under your bed, miss. I empty them at night and first thing in the morning, but if you need to do the other thing, if you wish to use it there's an outdoor privy. But be careful how you go as there's a stream of people's mess swilling out the back of here. It's not coming from this place, smells something rotten it does. It's some of the people around these parts, they dispose of their waste into the streets and it ends up washing down to the River Taff. It's a right health hazard, my mam says.'

Seren nodded. After Doctor Owen's warning about the return of cholera, she reckoned she'd better take care while staying at the inn. Perhaps the sooner she got out of here, the better for the sake of her unborn child. Even though the disease had reached Upper Abercanaid, Anwen's farm was isolated enough from the village and she rarely received regular callers except for Sam, the minister and the doctor.

'If you don't need anything else then, miss, I'll be off.' She curtsied which amused Seren greatly. At least the child had good manners.

'Thank you, Molly.' Seren smiled, wishing she had a few pennies to tip the girl, but she had no other money on her person except the shilling from Connie which she might need herself. When the maid had departed, she thought she'd make short work of the bread and cheese, but after a few mouthfuls, she found it hard to swallow even with a few sips of milk after each bite. There was nothing wrong with it either; the bread was freshly baked judging by the delicious smell and taste of it. It was just her. Last night when she'd been lying on the floor, she realised she'd never be able to return to her husband ever again and wondered why she'd put up with his savage treatment of her for so long — then a little voice answered her: *It was because you didn't have the responsibility of another life back then.*

She swallowed and wondered how she'd cope with it all. A new fear had taken over — fear for the future, of what lay ahead. Then she carefully laid the tray down on top of the chest of drawers, used the chamber pot, then removed her dress, placing it carefully on the chair. She clambered into bed and promptly drifted off to sleep.

* * *

Anwen felt she hadn't slept a wink all night worrying about Seren. In the end, they'd returned to Morgan's house and asked around the village about his whereabouts, but no one knew a thing. Elwyn had said to wait another day and if neither Seren nor Morgan turned up, then he would contact the police. Oh, she did fear for the girl, particularly in her condition. But she had a farm to run so she had to keep going as the livestock needed feeding.

Sam was due here too later, so at least she'd have some company. The thing that was concerning her the most was that Morgan might have murdered Seren and tried to hide her body. What if no one ever heard from her again?

Come on now, Anwen. Don't get carried away, there's no suggestion the man has done anything as extreme as that! You have to stay strong for Seren's sake.

Work on the farm was the best therapy for her for time being, she realised. She hefted herself out of her fireside armchair and made for the door. Time to feed the livestock and chop some firewood.

* * *

Seren was so tired that she went out like a light. Later, she became aware of muffled voices and giggles coming from one of the other bedrooms, so she guessed that it was probably afternoon time and the girls were entertaining customers. She rose from the bed and, noticing a key in the lock, safely locked the door. She didn't want anyone to barge into the room by mistake. She wondered whether she ought to try to find Sioni but then thought better of it; he would come to her in his own time, no doubt. She returned to the bed and drifted off again and was awoken by a tapping on the door.

'Who is it?' she called out, fearful there might be some stranger on the other side of the door.

'It's me, miss. Molly.'

Relief flooded through her. She rose from the bed and unlocked the door to see the girl there with a cup of tea in her hand. 'Mr Watkin thought you might like this,' she said.

'Thank you, Molly.'

'He says he'll be up to see you after you've drank that, miss.' Molly took the used tray stacked with crockery in her arms.

Seren nodded, then when the girl had left the room, she quickly dressed — there was no way she wanted Sioni to see her half-dressed. She sipped the hot sweet brew, truly grateful for it, and touched her face. Those bruises must have been coming out as her cheekbones felt so sore. Morgan's punches had just missed her eyes, thankfully.

Just as she was drinking the dregs of her tea, Sioni entered without knocking and she guessed that was his prerogative in this place.

'How are you feeling now?' he asked.

'More rested, thankfully. What time is it?'

'Half past three.'

'So as soon as it gets dark I can leave?'

He drew a breath and let it out again. 'I know what I said, but I don't think it's safe. Please remain here, only for a couple of days, then I can make plans to send you somewhere where your husband won't find you.'

Tears welled up in her eyes. This was all too much for her to bear, and finally she broke down crying.

'I'm not trying to trick you, Seren,' he said softly. 'It's Morgan. I've heard from one of the men downstairs, who is a trusted friend, that he has plans for you.'

'Plans?' She blinked several times.

'Yes, he plans to offload you to a butcher he knows from Cefn Coed and also to exchange shops with him.'

'Offload? I don't understand.'

'Sell you on to him, like.'

'You're lying to me.'

He held up the palms of his hands as if in defence. 'No, I'm not.'

'But why would he do that?'

'I don't know for sure, but I reckon it's because people in the village know what he's done to you and he wants you out of sight and out of mind. The butcher in question is a nice man. He lost his wife and baby daughter in childbirth last year by all accounts.'

Seren could not believe her ears. 'The butcher might be a nice man, he might be the nicest man in the whole of Merthyr Tydfil, but I do not want to marry him!' she cried out, then, standing, she rushed at him, pummelling at his chest, lashing out at him. But the anger she really felt was at Morgan, and as she wept, Sioni held her close to him and smoothed down her hair.

She pulled away. 'Well, I won't be a piece of meat in any butcher man's stew!' she said defiantly, feeling her emotions begin to rise.

He gazed at her for the longest time. 'Do you know, you're quite beautiful when you're angry like that? Despite those bruises. Your eyes flash dangerously, my dear. You must be sizzling inside like a piece of steak in the frying pan.'

His suggestion regarding her sensuality caused her to chuckle inwardly, but she didn't want to show him her mirth, so she turned away and pretended to make the bed, even though it was already quite tidy.

Suddenly, he grabbed hold of her hand and yanked her towards him, so they were facing one another and he was invading her space, bearing down on her, his masculinity powerful and omnipotent. He'd cleaned himself up since she'd last set eyes on him. The grime from his face had disappeared and his dirty fingernails now looked clean, and his shirt was clean this time. His lips hovered so close to hers that she felt her heart thud beneath the bodice of her dress. Surely, he must feel it too? This all-powerful attraction. Then when she felt as though he might pounce, pushing her on the bed, he released her and said, 'I mustn't dally with a pregnant woman. Though I would gladly pay your husband for just one night with you if it weren't so.'

She raised her hand and brought it hard across his cheek, causing him to recoil and touch it with his fingertips.

'There's not many I'd allow to get away with that!' he said. Now it was his turn for his eyes to flash. There was danger behind those vivid green eyes, but there was also something else — longing — he really wanted her badly, and for some reason that made her feel so good inside.

'Listen to me, Seren,' he said, taking her by the shoulders and looking intently into her eyes. 'I have a plan. Do you want to hear it or not? If not, then I'd let you go in a couple of hours when darkness falls.'

She huffed out an impatient breath. 'All right, what do you have in mind?'

He lowered his voice as if he feared being overheard. 'We'll show your husband that I'm keeping you here as planned to keep him sweet, and that your bruises are healing. But I'll also 'ave to show favour to the butcher, lead him on like, so he believes he's getting you from Morgan. But don't you worry as I can always sort him out with another wife — there's lots of women who have fallen on 'ard times what end up at the wash house. Some have been tidy women too in their time, but if they've been left widowed then times get tough for 'em. They 'ave to look for work and more often than not, hit the gin bottle. Find they need more money to finance their habit and ask me to give them work upstairs here. So, there'll be no shortage for me to offer to the man. But it'll mean you'll have to stay here a week or so until you look well again. Then I'll pretend to have sold you on to the butcher whilst offering him someone else as a wife to him. He'll not find out for some time as he won't have met you to know what you look like. Meanwhile, I'll help get you out of Merthyr for time being at least. I have some good friends living in Aberdare, a husband and wife, they'll take you in and look after you during your confinement.'

She nodded. 'That all sounds very good, but I can't believe Morgan would allow that Smedley fellow to take his child and all.'

Sioni's eyes widened. 'Oh, he's not allowing the child to be handed over to the butcher! Once the baby's born, he intends to keep him or her for himself. I expect he has plans for Mari to help bring up the child.'

'Over my dead body!' Seren yelled in outrage and she looked away, chewing her knuckle, as tears started to fall. What on earth was she to do now? Taking a deep, composing breath, she turned back to Sioni, looking at him through glazed eyes. 'You have got to get me out of here right now!' she said with conviction.

'All right. I'll see what I can do, but that will mean I'll make an enemy out of Morgan if he discovers what I've done.'

That was the least of her worries: her main concern was ensuring the safety and welfare of her unborn child.

* * *

Elwyn was on the verge of calling into the police station at Merthyr town, but he decided to take a detour one more time to find Morgan. He wasn't at home that morning, but was where he was expected to be at his cobbler shop. Elwyn pushed open the door that rang a little overhead bell to alert Morgan that a customer had entered his shop when he was in the back room. Elwyn inhaled the familiar smell of leather and shoe polish.

He found Morgan wearing a brown leather apron, bent over a boot on top of a last, absorbed in his work. He appeared to be tapping away at the sole with a small hammer and Elwyn wondered if those were Tom Shanklin's boots that Maggie had mentioned.

'Hello, Mr Evans!' Morgan said brightly as he looked up, leaving Elwyn feeling taken aback at how cheery the man was.

Elwyn cleared his throat. 'Hello, Morgan.'

'Brought a pair of shoes in for repair, have you?'

'No, not exactly. I'm here to find out what's happened to your wife.'

Morgan set down his small hammer on the wooden counter and, quirking a brow, stood to face him. 'Well, surely you'd know more about that than me, seeing as how pally you both are of late!' Morgan's face clouded over as he waited for Elwyn's response.

'Seren has only been helping me out at the chapel running a bible study group for the villagers, that's all.'

Morgan nodded and then narrowed his eyes, as if he didn't quite believe the man of cloth stood in front of him.

'Call it what you like, but from where I'm stood, I'd call it breaking one of the ten commandments, you know the one . . . *Thou shalt not commit adultery* and even that other one . . . *Thou shalt not covet thy neighbour's wife, house, ox nor ass!* Well, something like that! Might not be the exact words but you know where I'm coming from!'

Elwyn shook his head in disbelief. Did this man before him really think he'd been in a relationship with his wife? And had carnal knowledge of her? Surely not! And if Anwen's hunch proved correct, then maybe that's why he'd beaten Seren: to punish her for something he believed she'd done.

'Now hang on a moment, you've got the wrong end of the stick!' Elwyn held up his hands as if in defence.

'Keep your hands off my wife!' Morgan snarled at him.

'While we're on the subject of hands, then maybe you have blood on both of yours?' Elwyn said forcefully.

Morgan dashed out from behind the counter and glared at him, hovering inches away from his face. 'If you weren't a man of God I'd give you a right pasting right now!' He grabbed hold of the collar of Elwyn's jacket and pulled him close, so close that Elwyn could smell his beery breath. He'd obviously not kept his promise to keep himself clean, then.

'I'm not afraid of you, Morgan,' Elwyn said, 'not like some of the men in the village are. You can hit me all you like, but it won't help you make peace with your Maker nor yourself. You have wronged that young woman and well you know it!'

Morgan released his grip and stepped back from the minister.

'But I thought you were after my wife . . . ' he said, his eyes clouding over with confusion.

'Far from it! I would never do that to another man, it goes against every moral fibre of my very being!' Elwyn adjusted his collar.

'Aye, I suppose so,' Morgan said, nodding and lowering his voice. 'I just get so angry and jealous, see, then my fists start to fly.'

'One day that anger could cause you to kill someone!' Elwyn spat the words at him in fury.

Morgan held out his hands in front of him and Elwyn watched them tremble, unsure whether it was from fear or from the alcohol. He said, 'Now, please tell me, for pity's sake, where is Seren?'

Morgan's hands dropped to his sides. 'She's up in China! I got so angry with her I did something I'd never done before, though I admit I have knocked her around in the past . . . '

There were tears in his eyes as he spoke, but Elwyn guessed those were for himself, not what he'd done to his wife. 'I kicked her on the floor and you're right, I swear I'd have killed her but then she told me she was pregnant with my child.'

'Yes, that's right,' Elwyn said, keeping his cool. His head told him to remain calm but his heart told him to swing a punch at the man. 'So, what happened then?'

'Mari rushed into the scullery behind me, shocked she was, like, and I couldn't blame her. We decided to borrow Tom Shanklin's pony and trap to get Seren out of Abercanaid and took her to the wash house in China where Mari works. She said Seren could recover there and she'd keep an eye on her.'

'So, you sent her away so people couldn't see you'd laid your hands on her and almost left her for dead?'

'I'm afraid so. Twm Sion Watkin, one of the pimps up in China, knew about it; he owns the wash house and the inn next door where he runs the prostitutes.'

'Well, what did you intend doing after that?'

'After thinking she was seeing you, like, I was going to offload her.'

'Offload her! What do you mean?' Elwyn was careful to hold his clenched fists at his sides, not to show the man how angry he really was.

'There's a widowed man I know, a butcher from Cefn Coed, he said he'd take her off my hands in return for one of his shops. I thought of selling up here and moving up there, the only thing being that when the baby is born, he or she is returned to me and Mari to bring up as we lost our baby the other day.'

Elwyn could hardly believe his ears. 'So, you were prepared to sell your wife to another man?'

'Yes. It's happened before.'

'But hardly in this day and age. It's barbaric to treat your wife as if she were merely a chattel. What happened to those vows you made to Seren at the chapel just down the road? And while we're at it, if you thought Seren and I were having relations with one and other, why would you then assume the child would be yours?'

Morgan looked at him with a blank expression on his face. 'It all sounds so bloody daft now . . .'

'What's the name of that inn you mentioned?' Elwyn said sharply.

'What inn?'

'The one at China that Twm Sion Watkin owns!' he yelled at him in exasperation. Couldn't he see that Seren needed rescuing?

'The Forge and Hammer is its real name but the locals call it The House of Blazes.'

'I'm going there now to check on her welfare and I swear if you follow me then I shall call the police.'

Morgan nodded as mild-mannered as could be. It was true what they said, thought Elwyn, the best thing to do is stand up to a bully. He was going to check Seren was all right and warn her to keep well away from Abercanaid, but surely she realised that already.

11

As soon as darkness fell, Sioni was true to his word and arranged to take Seren to Aberdare on the back of a horse and cart owned by a friend.

'C'mon,' he said, taking her hand to help her aboard.

What on earth was she thinking of, going off with a stranger into the night? It was something she'd never have thought possible a couple of days ago, but the need to stay safe from her husband far outweighed any fear she might have of Twm Sion Watkin.

She clambered on to the cart beside him and he covered her legs with a thick blanket. 'Jim and Marged Hopkins are good folk,' he said. 'They've been like parents to me over the years . . .'

'I'm so grateful to you for taking me to a place of safety,' she said. 'How can I ever repay you, Sioni?'

He chuckled. 'I'll think of something . . . ' Then his voice took on a more serious tone. 'Seriously though, I'm just glad to be able to 'elp, like. I don't owe any man anything who beats up a pregnant woman!' He took the reins as they began their journey and Seren wondered where it might take her.

* * *

Elwyn practically ran all the way to Merthyr Tydfil, and though like most folk he feared the

China area of the town, his thoughts for Seren's safety spurred him on. Finally, he entered an archway where he spied several rag o' muffin sorts in bare feet. They were only young boys really, but he'd been warned of the child gangs operating here, so he ignored their pitiful cries as he passed as they begged for money. He knew if he stopped to talk then his pockets might well get picked over. So instead he avoided eye contact with the lads and waited until he found someone suitable to speak to to ask the way to the inn. The place was like a cesspit, it stank to high heaven and the houses here which bordered the River Taff were no better than slums. How people could live like this, he didn't know, but he guessed if that was all they knew or they were forced to live here due to the severe overcrowding in the town, then what chance did they have? In this place, the Irish rubbed shoulders with the Welsh, the English, even the Eastern Europeans, and there was plenty of conflict, he'd heard about that, but for the most part, the communities didn't mix with one another.

He noticed an elderly man stood on the doorstep of his higgledy piggledy-looking house. Scrunched-up pieces of newspaper were stuffed in the windows where the glass had broken. The man's eyes had a defeated look about them, almost as though he'd given up on life.

'Hello, sir,' Elwyn said brightly.

A guarded look swept over the man's features, as if he didn't trust outsiders. 'Whatcha want?' he asked, then he took a puff on his pipe. Elwyn guessed maybe his wife, if he had one, didn't like him smoking it indoors.

'I'm looking for The Forge and Hammer inn . . . ' he said.

'Never 'eard of it.'

Then remembering what Morgan had said about what the locals called it, he added, 'The place people refer to as 'The House of Blazes',' he said triumphantly, then smiled.

The man surprised him by smiling back at him. 'Aye, I know where you mean now. It's just past those few houses there, see, on the right.' He pointed with his pipe to an area where the overlooking houses were almost on top of one another, a right shambles it was.

This place felt so claustrophobic to Elwyn. He tipped his hat at the man. 'Thank you.'

As he walked away he felt as if the man's eyes were boring a hole in his back and he turned around.

' 'Ere, you're not one of those reporter sorts from *The Merthyr Star* or *The Cardiff and Merthyr Guardian*, are you?' the man asked.

'No fear, my good fellow,' Elwyn replied. 'I'm a man of the cloth and I'm just looking for a friend, that's all.' He didn't add female friend because from his understanding it would give the man entirely the wrong impression. Fancy that, people might think, he was a minister seeking the services of a nymph of the pave. He chuckled to himself as he walked away, but then as he saw a vision of Seren before him, his laughter turned to a feeling of dread.

When he entered the pub, he noticed several grimy-looking men and boys seated on wooden benches around large wooden tables. In the middle of each one a candle burned. To his astonishment, even the young boys were supping ale from pewter tankards. Ironworkers or colliers, he guessed; even at their young ages they were doing a man's job so reckoned they deserved a man's privileges, and he wondered if even they sometimes tipped up their hard-earned wages to bed one of the women upstairs. By the worldly look on those filthy faces, he guessed some probably had.

He approached the wooden bar and the red-headed man standing behind it, with chubby cheeks and bushy sideburns.

'Can I help you, sir?' he asked, leaning over the bar with the traditional landlord's bonhomie.

Although Elwyn didn't often drink alcohol, he replied, 'I'll have a pint of your finest ale, my good man, if you please.' He could have come right out with it about asking where Seren was, but thought better of it. There was no way he wanted to risk the man clamming up, so he figured it best to stay and take a pint.

The man handed over the foaming tankard to Elwyn, and he took a few sips. 'Getting dark early now, isn't it?' Elwyn said brightly, trying to engage him in conversation.

'Aye, autumn is upon us and with a vengeance too. I suppose you've heard that King Cholera is back in the town?'

'Yes, we have a few cases where I'm living.'

'Oh, where's that then?' The man quirked a bushy red brow.

'Abercanaid. Not down the village where I am, mind, but in the upper part. Lewis Square.'

The man nodded. 'I know of it. Got to say, mind, I tend to think of Abercanaid as being a bit of a nobs' area compared to some places around here.'

Elwyn nodded. 'I'm not from around here originally, but Pontypridd, and I'm inclined to agree with you. There are some nice parts of the area with plenty of open space, but from my understanding from our local doctor, the small house concerned was packed full of lodgers. Anyhow, there's little hope many will survive, they've been painting lime around the house and surrounding houses.'

'Course, I remember the last outbreak,' said the landlord. 'That was truly terrible, that was, and all the wrong advice was given at the time.'

Elwyn nodded. 'I heard that too.'

They spoke amicably for some time as he watched him serve other customers and sometimes the young barmaid popped by to take drinks to tables on a tray. Finally, Elwyn decided to chance his arm. 'I'm looking for someone, actually . . . '

'Oh, yes?'

'A woman . . . '

The landlord smiled and tapped his nose with his index finger. 'Well, there's a few sorts upstairs, I'll go get one for you if you like. Any preference? Blonde? Brunette? Red head?'

Elwyn chuckled. 'No, not like that. This woman is a friend and I believe she was brought here . . . Seren James.'

Immediately, the landlord's demeanour stiffened and a guarded expression appeared on his face. 'No, sorry, don't know anyone by that name.'

'Look, let me explain, I'm a minister of a chapel in Abercanaid and I know both Morgan and Seren James.'

The man's body language relaxed a little. 'Oh, yes?'

'I've spoken to Morgan and he's told me all what's happened and that his wife's been staying here. He'd admitted to beating her badly, I just want to check she's safe and well.'

The man's eyes began darting around the place as if fearful he might be overheard. 'Look,' he whispered, 'I can't tell you anything. You need to speak to Mr Watkin.'

'And when might he return?'

'I don't know.' Then he turned to serve another customer and then kept well away from Elwyn.

Was Seren somewhere upstairs here? he wondered. He was just about to leave when he felt a tug on the sleeve of his jacket. 'Sir, I heard what you said to my dad there . . .'

He turned to see the young barmaid at his side. Puzzled, Elwyn frowned. 'Your father?'

'He's the landlord.' She lowered her voice. 'Meet me in the alleyway in a couple of minutes, I have something to tell you.'

He nodded and smiled. Then gave her a sixpence as if he was tipping her for her services at the inn.

He said farewell to the landlord and left the inn, somehow imagining that the man heaved out a sigh of relief as soon as he saw the door close behind him.

It was a short while before the girl followed

after him, still with tray in hand. 'I can't be long,' she explained. 'I've pretended I had to go over to the wash house for something.'

'All right,' he whispered, as he didn't want to get her into trouble with her father. 'What do you know?'

'Seren, Mrs James, left here with Mr Watkin about an hour ago.'

'Any idea where they were going?'

'Aberdare. They went by horse and cart.'

'Is she all right?'

'Yes, I've spoken to her several times, she's well rested and has eaten. I don't know why she has all those bruises on her face though, but I can tell you she was like that when she arrived and I don't think Mr Watkin did that to her, he seems to be helping her, like.'

Elwyn nodded, relieved that was the case. 'Thank you for letting me know, young lady. I might call again to see if I can find out more. But thinking about it, as your father seems a bit suspicious of my motives, if you hear anything and have the time, please could you call to see me at The Manse at Chapel Street, Abercanaid? I'll pay you handsomely for any information given.' He smiled at the girl, who nodded at him.

'I'll see what I can do . . . ' Her eyes darted this way and that in case she was being watched.

Not wanting to get her into any trouble, he said, 'Go on, you'd better go back inside. What's your name, by the way?'

'Molly, sir.'

'Thank you. I appreciate your help today!' He tipped his hat at her and walked away. Now he was going to have to find his way out of this blessed hell hole. Dodging the stream of waste trickling near his feet, he quickly sidestepped it. With cholera sweeping through the town, he needed to avoid anything that could be a potential source.

His next step was to visit Anwen, but he wouldn't go tonight, that would only alarm the woman. He'd go first thing in the morning. She was always up at the crack of dawn and he could go to pray for Seren at his special spot on the mountain.

Why, oh why, had he been placed in Merthyr Tydfil and fallen for a married woman? So far he had done no wrong, he knew that, but his heart was with her and it wouldn't rest until she was safely back home where she belonged.

⋆ ⋆ ⋆

Anwen was having a bad dream. She saw a black cloud hovering ominously over Merthyr Tydfil, people were dying, families were crying at gravesides for their loved ones. The outbreak of cholera wasn't stopping at the village, it was travelling down the village and taking all in its path. Along with the tidal wave she saw Seren, who was slipping under the water which had turned into the River Taff itself. Anwen stretched out her hand to save her, but she disappeared beneath the surface. Then she woke up in her own bed, a bath of perspiration. What could it all mean? Was it another prophecy? There had been no word as yet and last night Seren's mother and sister had called to the farm to enquire about her and Anwen had told them all she knew. They were distraught, of course they were. Who wouldn't be? But she'd promised as soon as she'd heard news from the minister she'd pass it on to them.

She pulled herself out of bed and looked at the clock on the bedroom cabinet. It was only just shy of three o'clock. She had intended getting up at five as usual, but now she realised she was in such a state of anguish due to that blessed dream that she'd never get back to sleep no matter how much she tried. So, she put on her dressing gown and slippers and went to get herself a glass of goat's milk. She was just about to pour it from the jug when she thought she heard footsteps outside. 'Who the heck could this be this time of the morning?' she muttered to herself, then realising it must be Elwyn with news for her, she went to unlock the door.

'Am I glad you're here, Mr Evans,' she said. But her eyes weren't as good as they used to be and for a moment, she failed to realise the person standing in front of her was not the minister.

'You'd better come in out of the cold,' she said.

Then as the visitor stepped over the threshold, Anwen recoiled in horror as realisation dawned.

'Yes, it's me, Mrs Llewellyn. Morgan James . . . '

'I'm not afraid of you!' she shouted at him when she got over the initial shock, her heart pounding madly, and she lifted the poker from the fireside. The fumes of alcohol coming from him almost knocked her over. He'd been drinking, that was a cert, and she guessed it was probably at the Llwyn-yr-Eos pub. Maybe he'd been drinking for hours and only just left there. Maybe the alcohol had given him time to think.

He threw back his head and laughed at her. 'Don't think you and your poker are any match for me!' he growled.

'Maybe not, but then again, you only hit women, don't you?'

His laughter faded away; she knew then she had found his Achilles heel. He didn't like her saying that to him.

'If I was a man and years younger, I'd go ten rounds with you to have the satisfaction of you getting your comeuppance! It's a shame that no man in this village would dare take you on. But it's my guess that there are others in the town who would and I'd gladly pay them to do it and all! So, what are you going to do to an old woman? Knock me flying with your fists? How would that look to the villagers, eh? They'd know it was you because Seren has been living here. What have you done with her?' Anwen spoke with such fierce conviction that Morgan calmed down.

'It's not what you think. I haven't killed her. I did lay into her, mind, until I found out about the baby. I've sent her to China where someone is caring for her.'

Anwen scoffed, then dropped the poker from her hand with a clatter to the floor. 'Let's hope she doesn't lose your poor baby. I pity that child. Now get out of here before I turn the air blue because I don't much like the sight I see in front of me!'

To her surprise, he turned on his heel and walked out through the door. She quickly bolted it behind him and drew the kitchen curtains; her heart was in her mouth and she fought to bring her breathing under control. That had been a close one. Never mind a glass of goat's milk, she needed a tot of brandy, and now she definitely would not go back to sleep for some time yet.

* * *

There was a furious knocking on the door, and for a moment Anwen feared that Morgan had returned, but when she lifted the curtain to look outside into the yard, she could see Elwyn there. She glanced at the clock. It was almost six o' clock. She must have drifted back to sleep in the rocking chair after that incident, though it felt all of five minutes.

She unbolted the door and allowed the minister into the kitchen. 'Well?' she asked, impatient for news.

'Good morning, Anwen. I heard Seren was in China, but when I went there last night, a maid at the inn I visited informed me she's been taken to Aberdare.'

'Aberdare? By whom?' The elderly woman blinked several times.

'Twm Sion Watkin. He owns an inn and the wash house next door. He's a pimp by all accounts, runs several women at the inn.'

'*Oh, fy ddaioni!*' Anwen's hands flew to her mouth, she was so shocked she began to jabber away in the Welsh language.

'I'm sorry, Mrs Llewellyn. I am mainly English-speaking, I can understand some of what you are saying but not all.'

She blew out a long breath. 'Oh, I am sorry, Elwyn. I get like that sometimes. This is the second shock for me. Do you think Mr Watkin has an ulterior motive, maybe?'

Elwyn shook his head. 'Not by the sound of it. It appears to me from what the barmaid told me that he was taking her away to safety from Morgan, where he'll not find her.'

'That's a relief then.'

'You said second shock, what was the first?'

'He, Morgan, turned up here a couple of hours ago.'

Elwyn lifted his brows in surprise. 'Good gracious. What happened?'

'I had just awoken from my sleep when I heard footsteps outside. I assumed it was you. I saw someone standing outside my door, but my eyes these days are not so good. I foolishly allowed him inside. He'd been drinking again. I thought he was going to attack me, so I picked up the poker and he just laughed at me, so I got nasty with him. And do you know the strangest thing, when I stood up to him, he went all meek and mild on me like a little boy, then left me alone. I don't think he'll return.'

'I hope not. Funnily enough, he was the same with me yesterday when I spoke to him.'

Anwen stood shakily, her knuckles bearing down on the table beside her. 'Oh, what are we going to do, Elwyn?' she said, then bit back the bitter tears that were threatening to spill down her cheeks. 'What has Morgan done to his poor wife?'

12

Seren and Sioni were greeted at the door by Sioni's friends, Jim and Marged. 'There's good to see you, Sioni,' Marged said with a warm, reassuring smile, which was what Seren needed right now. It had been hard to feel safe for a long time, even at Anwen's. With the farmhouse being in such close proximity to her old home, she'd found herself waking up several times during the night on occasion, fearful her husband had broken in with the intention of dragging her back home.

'Now let's get you inside,' Jim said, opening the door fully for them to step over the threshold.

Marged looked hopeful for Sioni to introduce her to Seren, but he just stood there nodding, so Seren nudged him. 'Oh sorry, Marged. This is Seren James, she's been staying at the inn and I wondered if she could stay here with you for a while if you've a vacant room available?'

Marged shook her head. 'I'm sorry, I rented out my last room this very afternoon to a young solicitor's clerk.'

Seren felt a lump rise in her throat as Jim stared at her.

'You see, Seren is in confinement,' Sioni explained to the pair.

Jim narrowed his eyes. 'You haven't got that woman into trouble, have you, Sioni?' he asked, as if Seren wasn't present. She could tell he wasn't as warm and welcoming as his wife. But maybe it was because, after all, she was a stranger to the couple, they hadn't got to know her as yet.

'Oh no. It's nothing like that.' He turned to Seren. 'Do you mind if I explain, like?'

What did she have to lose? She'd done nothing wrong herself. She took a deep breath. 'It's all right. I'll tell you myself. I've been married for almost a year and I'm having a baby. It is my husband's child and I haven't known Sioni for long; he was kind enough to put me up at the inn and bring me here after I was beaten up last night by my husband.'

Sioni held up a fist. 'I used to think that man was a friend of mine!'

Jim glared at Sioni, and Seren wondered if he mistrusted their story.

'Aw, I can see those bruises now under the light, you poor thing,' Marged said sympathetically as she held up a candle to examine Seren's face. 'You could do with a cold compress on those.'

'Would you happen to know of anywhere else around here what takes in lodgers?' Sioni asked.

'There's Mrs Mason lives down the road, she's kindly enough, but I wouldn't disturb her this time of a night as she's quite elderly.'

Jim whispered something in his wife's ear. Marged smiled. 'Jim just reminded me we could clear out the box room. It's full of all sorts at the moment, but if you wouldn't mind sleeping in the parlour overnight, dear, I'm sure we could get it sorted by tomorrow night for you?'

Seren nodded eagerly. 'Yes, please,' she said as quickly as possible before they changed their minds. She couldn't believe the kindness from the pair of them to someone they didn't know.

'Now, where are my manners?' Marged said. 'We'll go through to the parlour right now and have some tea.'

* * *

By the following evening, the box room had been sorted out for Seren and she'd settled in well to the house. Marged was very amenable to the fact that as well as Sioni paying something for Seren's keep she'd offered to help out in the home. Meals needed to be made for paying guests, beds changed, laundry washed, dried, ironed and put away, and Seren was more than happy to roll up her sleeves to give the woman a hand.

But she realised the first thing she needed to do when she had time was to write a letter to Anwen and Elwyn, explaining what had happened to her, with a contact address. She decided to address it to The Manse as there was more chance of it reaching its proper destination than at the farm.

So, the very next day she found herself sat at the kitchen table penning a letter whilst Marged sat by the fire with a well-earned cup of tea in her hand. 'Sorry, that's the only piece of paper and envelope I have left,' she explained. 'You won't be able to write a long letter, mind.'

'That's quite all right, Mrs Hopkins. I only need to tell my friends that I'm safe and well and leave a forwarding address. They can tell my family as well.'

Marged nodded. 'No need to be formal with me, *cariad*, just call me Marged.'

Seren smiled, realising she was going to feel at home here. Jim seemed a bit more forthcoming as well now, especially when he'd seen her at work helping out Marged to dish up bowls of porridge and plates of toast early in the morning to the men. It was a large house and a couple of coal miners lodged there, so they were up at the crack of dawn, but Seren was used to rising early after living on the farm with Anwen.

'If you leave your letter on the mantelpiece, Jim can post it later when he pops out.' Marged smiled.

Seren nodded as she began to pen the words.

Dear Elwyn and Anwen,

This is to let you know I am safe and well. You wouldn't realise it but that night when I was alone at the chapel hall, Morgan showed up and dragged me back to the house. He used his fists on me again, so much so that I passed out and I awoke in a strange place the following morning. It was at the wash house at China. He and his girlfriend, Mari, had taken me there. Fortunately for me, I was then shown to the inn owned by a Mr Watkin who has taken me to stay with friends in Aberdare. At the moment, I think it's best that I am away from Morgan as I fear for my unborn child. There is the Merthyr Mountain separating me from you at the moment, but if you are able you are more than welcome to visit. Please could you inform my family of where I am but please be careful not to worry them too much. For obvious reasons, please do not pass this address on to anyone else besides them.

Thankfully yours,
Seren.

She let out a little sigh as she folded the letter and placed it in the envelope. At least now the people she loved would know she was safe and well.

Sioni had returned to Merthyr the same night he'd dropped her off with a promise he'd return in a few days to check up on her welfare. Other than with him and sending off the letter, she now had no contact with her hometown whatsoever.

* * *

'Can you bring the tray containing the basins of faggots and peas through, *cariad*?' Marged called through the open kitchen door.

'I'll be right with you!' Seren replied, and she smiled as she made her way over to the men's table. There were four of them seated there. Ivor and Stanley Bridges, who were brothers and both colliers at the local pit, John Lewis who worked in a solicitor's office in the town, and Gordon Griffiths who was a local policeman. Gordon's wife had suddenly upped sticks and left him for another man, Marged had told

Seren, and warned her he was on the lookout for a new wife. As a result, she was very careful how she spoke to him. But so far, none of the men had given her any grief and she was thankful for that.

'You're a mighty fine cook, Seren!' Gordon said, rubbing his stomach as she laid down the bowl of steaming faggots and peas in front of him. Ivor and Stanley exchanged glances with one another.

'Aye, she might be a mighty fine cook, Gordon, but I don't think she's looking for a husband in her condition!' Ivor said, winking at her. 'When's it due, love?'

Marged breezed into the room carrying a plate of bread and butter for the men. She plonked it down in the middle of the table and with hands on hips said, 'I don't think it's anybody's business but Seren's, and she is a married woman, you know! Her husband is away overseas at the moment.'

Ivor's face reddened with embarrassment and Gordon lowered his head. Marged had a way of keeping the men in check but Seren reckoned she could have handled them anyhow, she'd seen far worse and dealt with more raucous behaviour than this back at the Llwyn-yr-Eos pub in Abercanaid. Truth be told, she knew the difference between a bit of light-hearted banter and when things were getting out of hand. After all, she was used to it, sensing her husband's moods and when he became a threat to her, and so far, she'd sensed none of that at Jim and Marged's home.

When the men had left the room — Ivor and Stanley going for their usual pint at The Horse and Hounds down the road, John studying in his room and Gordon off for a night shift — the women cleared up and then settled themselves down in front of the fire in the parlour.

Marged picked up the blanket she was in the middle of knitting as Seren closed her eyes to the comforting sounds of the click-clacking of the needles and the crackle of the flames in the hearth. Marged left her in peace for a moment, then said, 'What are you going to do though when the baby's born?'

Seren's eyes flicked open. 'To be truthful, I haven't thought that far ahead, but one thing's for certain, I need to keep well away from my husband.'

'Aye, you're doing right by there . . .' Marged set down her knitting on the small table beside her. 'Men like that never change; you take me and my first husband . . . '

'You were married to someone else before Jim?' Seren blinked in surprise.

She smiled. 'Yes, many moons ago. Arthur, his name was. At first I thought he was a good man, but then he got into the drink and took his moods out on me. Luckily for me, Jim came along and gave him a good pasting, else I don't think I'd be here to tell the tale now.'

'I had no idea,' Seren said gently.

'Why would you? And to tell you the truth, me and Jim, we're not really wed. We've been living in sin for the past twenty years.' She chuckled as her middle-aged eyes shone and sparkled like a young girl's at the mention of his name. 'Between me and you, no one around these parts knows. I used to live in the Rhondda Valley, see. Jim didn't want to sully my reputation and we couldn't marry.'

'How was that?'

'Well, Jim is Arthur's younger brother, so that made things difficult within the family for a start, but as well as that, divorces cost money, and in any case, Arthur would have refused one.'

Seren nodded. 'What happened to Arthur?'

'I heard he's shacked up with someone else and that poor blighter is also getting a pasting.'

'That's so sad, but I can well understand why women put up and shut up; it's not easy to leave when your only source of income is from your husband.'

'What does yours do?'

'He's a cobbler, got his own shop. Is very well respected in the village, or I should say, was.'

'Was?' Marged stared at her with her vivid blue eyes.

'People have noticed the way he's been treating me of late.'

'Aye, but I bet they're not staying away from his shop when they need their old boots tapped?'

'You're right there, it doesn't seem to have affected his business as far as I'm aware and it's the only shop of its kind in the village, otherwise they'd have to go to Merthyr town.'

The door opened suddenly and Jim stood there. 'Sioni's just arrived,' he said.

The women exchanged glances with one another and Seren wondered if he'd brought news from Merthyr.

As he swept into the room behind Jim, his cheeks red from the biting wind outside and his eyes watering, he said, 'The cholera in Merthyr, it's spreading fast . . . '

Seren opened her mouth and closed it again. 'My family . . . ' was the last thing she remembered saying before she passed out.

* * *

'Hold the smelling salts under her nose, Jim,' Marged was saying. 'Seren, I've brought you a glass of water.'

Seren opened both eyes. The room seemed to be moving and her sight was blurry. 'Did someone mention cholera?' she asked, blinking.

'Aye, it was Sioni. You're worried about your family then, *bach*?' Marged handed her the glass.

Seren managed to sit up straight and took a few sips of water. 'The reason I'm so worried is because it's already reached Abercanaid. It's in a house a couple of doors away from my aunt's home, and I'm worried about the rest of the family too who live further down in the village.'

'Well, one thing's a cert,' Marged said with big worried eyes, 'you can't go back there now, not like this as you have another life to think of.'

Seren nodded, realising the truth behind the woman's words. 'You're right,' she said.

'I'll go and make us some cocoa,' Marged said wisely. 'Jim, fetch a bucket of coal for me . . . '

After they'd both left the room, Sioni settled

himself down in the armchair, warming his hands in front of the fire. He caught Seren's eyes and appeared to study her face. 'They've been treating you well by the look of it?'

She nodded. 'Oh yes, they've been ever so kind to me. Thank you for bringing me here.' She bit her lip. 'Any news about Morgan?'

He shook his head. 'No, I reckon he's gone to ground.'

Seren chewed on her lower lip. 'And Mari?' she asked finally.

'She's gone and all. Disappeared from the wash house all of a sudden.'

Seren nodded. She supposed the woman wasn't in her right mind anyhow after losing her baby.

They sat in silence for a few moments until Marged turned up with a tray of cups, but there were only two upon it. 'The men will go to the pub for a pint instead. It's that they want, not cocoa!' she explained.

Seren sighed. It was a man's world all right. She watched Jim leave a bucket of coal near the fire and don his tweed jacket. Then Sioni rose from his chair and, leaning over Seren, he tilted her chin to take a look into her eyes. 'Those bruises are beginning to fade.' He paused for a moment. 'We won't be long. I'd suggest bringing back a jug of porter for you and Marged but . . . '

Marged smiled. 'I don't think that would be a good idea in Seren's condition. I think we can bypass the evils of drink for one night. We'll be fine with our cups of cocoa and our womanly chat.'

When both men had left the house, Seren laid her head on the back of the armchair and rubbed her eyes. This pregnancy was making her tired; she found herself nodding off quite often if she had the time to sit in an armchair or lie on the bed.

'You don't want to worry, *bach*,' Marged said, 'the cholera is far worse in Merthyr than over this valley. Though the first case here this time was a little girl from Cwmbach who was seized by the illness and was pronounced dead within hours. It was that quick.'

'Oh, that's dreadful,' Seren said, staring into the flames of the fire.

'Aye, I know. But at least it hasn't taken hold as much as it has in the Merthyr Valley.'

'That's true, in Merthyr there are so many outsiders now rubbing shoulders with the rest of us. Severe overcrowding in slum dwellings, is there any wonder it's so bad?'

'That China district where Sioni lives is filthy.'

Seren nodded. 'Yes, there's an open channel of sewerage running down to the River Taff. It stinks to high heaven there! No matter how clean folk are, if they're surrounded by filth, there's not a lot they can do.'

'Well, one thing's for sure, *cariad*, you'll be a lot safer here regarding the cholera and well away from your husband.'

Seren felt tears spring to her eyes when she thought of the people she'd left behind in Merthyr who she did want to see. She wondered what they were doing right now.

* * *

'But you must go and see Seren,' Anwen was telling the minister. 'You have that letter from her.'

Elwyn looked into the woman's eyes. 'But I feel she's telling me she wants to stay away, and it's probably safer we don't get too involved as it could lead Morgan to her whereabouts.'

'What are you saying?' The old woman stuck out her chin in determination. How could he ever make her realise just how much he felt for Seren and how he was trying to protect himself from falling for her? Of course he cared, he really did, but it wasn't as simple as all that. He let out a long sigh and held up his hands as if in some kind of defence. 'I'm sorry, Anwen, I think we should let things lie for time being.'

'How can you say such a thing? I'll go over there myself, I'll take the horse and cart first thing in the morning.'

'No, you can't do that, you're not well enough, anything could happen to you on the journey over,' he said, surprising himself with how sharp his tongue was. 'She's safe where she is and she doesn't need us meddling in her affairs.'

'Then you're saying you're washing your hands of the whole thing?' Her face creased into a worried frown.

'Far from it. I'll write back to her and explain what we think is best for time being is for her to stay put, but that we will be here for her on her return when she's had the baby and the cholera has died out.'

Anwen tutted and shook her head. 'I just don't want that poor young woman to think she's been abandoned. We don't know who these people are who have taken her in, do we?'

'No, but she speaks highly of them and that is enough for me.'

Anwen nodded, but she had a defeated look on her face, one Elwyn had never seen before and he felt sorry for her.

'Look, if it will make you feel any better, we'll compose that letter together after we've been to see her family. They need to know as they're probably worried sick about her.'

Anwen rose from her chair, her movements stiff and slow. 'You're right, Mr Evans. I'm just being a silly selfish old woman. I'd got used to having her staying here at the farm, it felt less lonely and she was such a help to me.'

'The daughter you never had?'

Elwyn could tell he'd hit a nerve as Anwen wiped away a tear with the back of her hand. 'I'll fetch my shawl,' she said, turning towards the peg on the back of the door.

As he left the farmhouse and walked towards the waiting horse and cart, Elwyn glanced at the village down below. Funny to think that a few months ago he had never set foot in the town of Merthyr Tydfil, though of course he'd heard of it. The town had a notoriety about it far and wide. Who could have guessed that within such a short space of time, he would have fallen for a married woman? That was the main reason he was keeping away: he realised it was morally wrong. She could never be his whilst she was married to that brute, even if she no longer lived with the man. And that Sioni character, how on earth had she got involved with him? He'd made some enquiries around the area, discovering that the man lived off ill-gotten gains and many feared him there. In some respects, he was a little like Morgan, using his fists without thinking. Someone had informed him the man had once been a bare-knuckle fighter in the town and unbeaten at that. On the one hand, he could protect Seren, but what if he hurt her himself? It didn't bear thinking about. He bit his lip and tried to maintain a bright and breezy attitude to keep Anwen's spirits up, there was no use them both worrying. After all, where did worry get anyone?

⋆ ⋆ ⋆

When Sioni and Jim returned from the pub a couple of hours later they were in high spirits, but by then Seren and Marged were dead on their feet. They had to get up early in the morning to see to the men's breakfasts, so they made their excuses and left the men chatting downstairs. If Seren had felt more energetic she would love to have stayed and chatted to Sioni, but hoped she'd see him before he departed.

The women climbed the stairs to bed then stood outside Seren's room talking in hushed tones so as not to disturb the guests. 'Surely Sioni won't drive the horse back home tonight?' Seren whispered.

Marged shook her head. 'When he's had a pint

or two like tonight, he usually kips down on the old sofa in the kitchen. He doesn't seem to mind. Better than him driving over the mountain in the dark, and there's a cold bitter wind in the air tonight.'

Seren nodded, thankful that Sioni would get some rest after all he'd done for her.

Marged held the lighted candle she'd been carrying close to Seren's face. 'You're looking a bit peaky tonight, Seren,' she said curiously. 'Have you been feeling ill?'

'No, just a bit tired, that's all.'

'Well, you have a lie-in in the morning and rest up, if you like?'

Vehemently, Seren shook her head, realising she wanted to catch Sioni before he left for Merthyr. 'I'll be fine after a night's sleep, honestly, I will.'

Marged smiled. 'Very well, you know best. Sleep well, dear.'

Seren watched the flickering shadows of the candle fade as Marged made her way to her own room. She pushed open her bedroom door, not even bothering to light the candle by the side of her bed. She just undressed in the dark and climbed into bed and was fast asleep before she knew it.

* * *

Upon awaking the following morning, Seren heard the front door open and close. At first, she thought that maybe it was Sioni slipping out early to return to Merthyr, but then she realised it was probably Ivor and Stan returning from their night shift at the pit. They'd need feeding for sure after a gruelling night's work. Marged would already be up and about and she felt guilty staying in her bed while the woman was commencing her working day downstairs. Quickly, she washed and dressed and made her way downstairs. It was still pitch-black outside and she could see the shapes of the neighbouring streets as she held up a candle to the landing window.

As she approached the kitchen, she could hear Marged as she clattered around searching for a saucepan to put the porridge on to heat. She glanced at the horsehair sofa bed where Sioni had been sleeping, but there were just a couple of discarded blankets atop of it. Where was he? She spied two Tommy boxes and jacks that belonged to Ivor and Stan on the kitchen table.

And where were they?

'Morning, Marged,' she said, tying the strings of her apron behind her back to begin work.

Marged turned towards her and blinked. 'My, my, Seren, you should still be in bed, dear. I was going to wake Jim to help me with the breakfasts this morning so you could have a good rest.'

'Let him have a lie-in instead,' Seren said, smiling kindly. 'He works hard enough at the pit himself. I was awake anyhow. Has Sioni returned to Merthyr, then?'

'Ah, no, not yet. He's going to have a bit of breakfast first to set him up for the day.' She emptied a small hessian sack of oatmeal into the awaiting pan and then, after pouring a jug of water on top of it, put it on the stove to warm up. 'He's out in the yard helping Ivor and Stan fill a couple of bowls with hot water for them to have a good scrub before they have breakfast and get to their beds. Fair play, he insisted on doing it so I could get on with the breakfasts. He's a good 'un.'

'That's kind of him.' Seren raised her brows in surprise and wondered if Marged had any clue what Sioni did for a living. Would she have him under her roof if she realised that he lived off immoral earnings from the prostitutes in China? In effect the man was a whore master who, under the cover of being a publican and the owner of the wash house next door to the inn, was doing very well for himself in a very seedy manner.

Yet, all of her own dealings with him had been good up until now: he could have abused his station when he'd discovered her in a position of vulnerability at the wash house that morning. He could have tried to put her to work for him, but instead, he'd taken her to a place of safety, and for that she was extremely grateful. Maybe it was only because she was pregnant, who knew. He might even have other plans for her yet, but for time being all she had was trust.

13

The talk in Abercanaid was that Morgan had left his little cobbler shop locked up and there was no sign of him at the house either. Many people were up in arms about how he'd treated Seren anyhow and were glad to see the back of him. Elwyn had his concerns, though — it wasn't like him not to open up his shop even if he'd had a skinful of alcohol the night before, and it didn't help that Maggie Shanklin was setting tongues a-wagging around the place. 'I bet he's taken Seren back,' he heard the woman saying when he was buying a loaf of bread at the bakehouse. 'And I reckon it won't be long before we'll be hearing the patter of tiny feet, you mark my words. 'Tain't right though, in my book, a woman leaving her husband like that. She should have stuck by him and no wonder he was off with a floozie if she wasn't giving him the attention he needed!'

A couple of the customers in the bakehouse, who he recognised as friends of the woman, nodded in agreement and murmured. Elwyn had to bite his tongue. The woman was barking up the wrong tree but she was correct about the pregnancy. Spotting Elwyn stood there, Maggie turned to face him, her sharp beady eyes looking him up and down. 'So, do you know where they are, Mr Evans?' she asked.

Elwyn pasted a smile on his face. 'No, I'm

sorry, Mrs Shanklin, I'm afraid I don't.'

Maggie narrowed her eyes as if she didn't quite believe him. 'I expect that Anwen would know, I might pay her a visit later.'

Oh no, that was the last thing the woman needed, she was at such a low ebb now that Seren was living in Aberdare. 'Anwen doesn't know anything at all, Mrs Shanklin,' Elwyn said calmly. 'The woman isn't very well at the moment, so please don't go troubling her, will you?'

Maggie smiled, then addressing her friends said, 'Perhaps we'll pay her a get-well visit, then. We'll bake her some cakes and offer to help at the farm to ease her burden; she shouldn't be left alone at her age.'

'She's not alone!' Elwyn said sharply. 'Seren's mother and sister are back and forth there to keep a check on her, as am I to chop sticks for her and do other jobs around the place, and she has young Sam Williams as a farmhand.' It was a lie about Seren's family back and forth, but the rest was true enough. God forgive him for having to tell such an untruth but he was sure on this occasion that if it saved Anwen from any unnecessary grief, then it was a lie worth telling.

Maggie said no more after that as she waited in line with the other women. She turned her back on the minister, obviously having made up her mind that she was going to visit Anwen and nothing he could say or do would prevent that. Elwyn decided to leave the shop before further questions might be asked of him. 'Please excuse me, ladies, I've just thought of something at the chapel that needs doing,' he said, tipping his hat to them. A few nodded but Maggie ignored him.

As he opened the shop door and closed it behind himself, he let out a long sigh. People like Maggie Shanklin really worked him up and he could do without it this morning. The real reason he was in the bakehouse shop was to purchase a loaf of bread as his parents were arriving from Pontypridd and the housekeeper was going to prepare a nice tea for them all. It had been a while since he'd last seen them and he was looking forward to it. Mrs Johnson had baked a fruit cake for the occasion and given The Manse a good spruce up — it was immaculate, she was a right treasure. His parents would arrive later by train and he'd arranged for one of his parishioners to pick them up in his carriage from the station.

As he made his way back to the chapel, his thoughts were on Seren. It just wasn't fair that people were tittle-tattling about what was going on. He needed to speak to her mother and sister about keeping an eye on Anwen when he wasn't there. The chapel kept him busy enough, and if Maggie and her cronies were to turn up unannounced, it might all be too much for the woman.

Abercanaid was a lovely village where the people had been through so much, but it did have its downside: as everyone lived in close proximity to one another, it was hard to keep secrets here, he was well aware of that. If someone as much as coughed, their neighbour knew of it.

* * *

Several people had died in that house in Lewis Square, but thankfully, Elwyn had managed to find out that Seren's Aunt Maud was all right, which was a relief for her family. The severe overcrowding in that small neighbouring house had caused all those deaths and people in the area were understandably worried sick. Would one of them be next? Doctor Owen was to hold a special meeting in the chapel hall to pass on advice he'd been given by the medical officer of Merthyr Tydfil. The hall was packed out that afternoon and Elwyn watched as people continued to flood in. Maggie Shanklin was seated at the front with a couple of her friends. There was a lot of chitchat going on. What he had noticed of late though was that chapel attendance had risen since the return of the disease and he guessed it had something to do with the fact people feared sudden death and were concerned about their eternal souls. Still, he shouldn't complain. It was nice to see such healthy numbers at chapel, even if it wasn't because of his preaching.

Doctor Owen stood at the front of the room and when the noise of chatter abated, Elwyn addressed the crowd. 'Welcome, one and all . . . ' Heads nodded as the villagers waited patiently to hear what was being said. 'We're here this afternoon to talk about the recent return of cholera to the area. Doctor Owen has kindly taken some time out of his busy schedule to speak to you about the disease and how you can best protect yourself against it. Afterwards, you can ask him any questions you like to allay your fears.'

There was a collective murmur as people looked at one another. Elwyn smiled. 'Then we'll begin. Over to you, Doctor Owen.'

The doctor stood before the people as Elwyn took a seat beside Maggie in the front row.

'Good afternoon, everyone,' he greeted them. 'As you all know by now, there has been a recent outbreak of cholera in the area, beginning at the north end of the town, and it now appears to be sweeping down the valley . . . '

There was a collective gasp as if the people were hearing the doctor's news for the first time, but Elwyn realised having someone of Doctor Owen's status mention it made it all the more real for them.

'Sadly, it arrived at a house in Upper Abercanaid at Lewis Square and several people living in that house have succumbed to the disease.'

'No wonder,' Maggie whispered to her friend behind her open palm, 'that woman who lived there was taking loads of lodgers into that small house, they were living on top of one another.'

Elwyn looked at her and away again. If there was one person he could bank on to provide a running commentary, it was Maggie.

'Now, in recent years,' the doctor continued, 'we were advised to wash in cold water to kill the germs during a cholera outbreak, but now we realise that was bad advice. You need to use hot water. Boil a kettle or saucepan on the fire or stove, same thing for cooking and washing utensils and clothing. Do not use cold water unless it has been previously boiled. Boiling water kills germs! Ensure you wash your hands after going to the toilet or handling anything unclean, and maintain a high standard of hygiene at all times. You can also use a white lime wash on the walls of your house to help keep the disease at bay. Avoid crowded, dirty areas whenever possible. And at the moment, keep well away from Upper Abercanaid!'

The crowd nodded their heads in unison.

'What about some of the people around here who won't do any of that though, Doctor Owen?' a lady at the back shouted as others joined in in agreement with her.

Suddenly, Maggie was on her feet. 'Yes, there's one well-known house in my street where the mother doesn't keep it clean at all. The kids' heads are crawling with lice and she's got bed bugs in the house, I hear, too. And the stench coming from the place is stomach-churning. What about the likes of her?'

Doctor Owen nodded amicably. 'I quite understand your concerns, ladies, and whilst we can't force people to do any of what I've just said, you can keep your own homes clean and keep well away from those sorts of people. I think I know the family you speak of, and I shall send her a letter with advice, as I'll do for others in the area. Now then, are there any more questions?' Both Maggie and the lady at the back of the room shook their heads and reseated themselves.

A man to Elwyn's right stood with his flat cap

in his hand. 'Any more news of the folk at Lewis Square?' he asked solemnly. 'You see, my sister lives there and I've been afraid to call for fear of catching the disease and passing it back on to my family.' He sat down.

'That's quite understandable, sir. You can be assured you have done the right thing. Of the nine out of the twelve who were attacked by that disease, seven have died, I'm sorry to tell you.'

There was a collective gasp.

'And although, up until now, we thought it was contained only in the streets immediately surrounding Lewis Square, it's thought that someone in David's Square, a little lower down, has also succumbed to the disease.'

'Oh, no, it's the work of Satan himself!' a woman stood and shouted as murmuring continued.

'Let me assure you, madam, and everyone else, this is not the work of the Devil. Cholera is a disease that's been threatening our shores again for some time now. It was on the Continent and it's thought it might have arrived here on ships from the port at Liverpool.'

'But it seems to me,' said the woman who was now quaking with anger, 'that it will take anyone down with it!'

'Not necessarily, Mrs . . . ?'

'Monroe, Mrs Monroe.'

Doctor Owen shook his head. 'That's not necessarily the truth. Take an example of a puddler at the Cyfarthfa Works. He got a bad case of stomach cramps one morning and granted, he died by the night. Death can occur quite quickly in some cases. But then let me explain that the man in question was well over sixty years of age and the neighbourhood he lived in was extremely filth-ridden. He was an out-and-out drunkard and had been drinking alcohol to excess for days on end before succumbing to the disease. If he had recovered it would have been a near miracle.

'The first victim at Abercanaid was the wife of a drunkard. Cholera claimed her life because of the overcrowding at her home and the filth she lived in. At the back of the bedroom was a heap of ashes which was foul with excrement. Then at Quarry Row in Georgetown, there were reeking cesspools that poisoned the health of the cholera victims before the disease even arrived.

'Then take one of the most terrible instances of all, at a house at Sunny Bank. There were many people crowded together in one small dwelling and the walls were fermenting with all kinds of germs, enough to destroy many people. In fact, we haven't found a single case where the disease has come from well-ordered, clean homes as yet this year. There has always been a deciding factor that causes someone to submit to the disease and usually that's wallowing in some sort of filth or being in compromised health to begin with. Cholera is the fruit of abundance of many things, including poverty, filth, degradation and so forth. Where cleanliness exists, you will not find cholera. So, what I'm saying to you all is you need not be alarmed if you follow the guidelines that Doctor Dyke, the medical officer, has put forward. It is not that dreadful scourge which it was many years ago — back then it took the lives of thousands, but now it is more likely to be in the low hundreds in this town.'

Elwyn swore he could hear a collective sigh of relief from everyone in the audience, including Maggie beside him. And he had to admit, he felt a sense of relief himself.

His parents had mentioned in their last letter that they were concerned about coming to Merthyr because of the disease, but he had already assured them that Mrs Johnson kept The Manse clean and tidy to a very high standard and it had a proper flushing toilet, too, in the garden. Thankfully, the cholera outbreak in the village seemed to be concentrated on the upper area of the village, not near the chapel. Now he could reassure them further with what the doctor had told them all.

Mother had mentioned in her letter that they had a surprise for him when they visited and he wondered what that might be. He had no clue.

* * *

As Ivor and Stanley took their seats at Jim and Marged's kitchen table, Gordon Griffiths appeared, his face tinged blue from the cold outside.

'Hard night again, Gordon?' Stan asked as he watched the constable remove his damp cape and drape it over the chair behind himself.

'Aye, a bad robbery a few streets over. You know that big house where the Machens live?'

After setting down some bowls and spoons on the table, Seren paused to listen a moment.

Both men nodded. 'Worth a few bob over that way where the *crachach* reside, mind!' Ivor said, then whistled through his teeth.

'Whoever the thief was, he got in through a small downstairs window and made off with a haul of silver pieces,' Gordon explained.

'Aw no, never,' Marged said, as she walked over to the table and slopped porridge into the men's bowls by the aid of a wooden spoon.

Sioni entered through the back door and took a seat at the table.

'Who's this, then?' Gordon asked in a friendly manner.

'He's a friend of ours from Merthyr,' Marged introduced. 'Twm . . . '

She was about to give his full name away when Sioni said suddenly, 'Most people call me Sioni . . . ' He smiled and Gordon nodded.

'Nice to meet you,' Gordon muttered. Of course, the other two men had already encountered him.

'What time did that burglary happen, then?' Marged asked.

'About half past three this morning,' Gordon explained. 'The owners heard some noise downstairs and the dog began to bark. By the time the head of the house had run downstairs, there was no one to be seen, then he noticed the half-open window and most of the silver from the display cabinet, candlesticks and plates and what nots, had all disappeared!'

A sudden chill ran down Seren's spine. Sioni had been sleeping on that old sofa in the kitchen last night. He could easily have nipped out the back door and made over to that house a few streets away. Surely it couldn't have been him? She looked at him intently, narrowing her gaze for a moment. What did she know of him anyhow? It was a coincidence, mind, that he'd been staying here overnight. He could easily get the spoils back to Merthyr and no one would be any the wiser.

Whilst the men were tucking into their breakfasts, she went outside to check on the horse who was stabled in the yard. He seemed fine, and there was nothing of significance on the cart either — just a couple of empty wooden boxes and sacks. She felt bad for being so suspicious.

When she returned to the kitchen, the three working men had disappeared to their beds and Sioni and Jim, who had just arisen from his bed, were seated by the fireside drinking cups of tea. 'I'm frying them bacon and eggs, would you like some too, Seren?' Marged asked.

Seren shook her head — she couldn't stand the thought of eating anything greasy this time of the morning, it would turn her stomach. 'It's all right, Marged, I'll toast some bread in front of the fire. Would you like some, too?'

Marged nodded. 'Yes, please. I've had nothing either as yet.'

As she knelt with the bread on a long fork, toasting it in front of the fire as the men chatted, she felt Sioni's eyes on her all the while as if they were boring a hole into her back. Jim was chatting about how tough it could be as foreman at the pit as he was sandwiched between the workforce and the managers. She heard the odd 'Yes' and 'No' in reply from Sioni, but she knew he wasn't really paying attention to the man as he was too busy staring at her.

'And the thing is, see, Sioni, they're quick enough to make the men work longer hours and if they could get away with it, they'd reduce their bloody wages an' all!' Jim said vehemently.

'For goodness' sake, Jim!' Marged scolded, as she placed the men's plates of fried food on the table. 'There are ladies present, wash that mouth out with soap and water, will you?'

'Sorry, Marged, sorry, Seren,' Jim said, rising from his armchair as a mark of respect and sitting back down again when he'd apologised for the use of expletives in front of them.

Seren didn't really mind, she knew how fraught things were becoming at the coal pit lately as she'd heard Stan and Ivor mention it. It was a difficult thing for Jim as he was their foreman and they lived under his roof.

There was no chatter during breakfast as Marged kept her beady eye on Jim, and it was almost as though the wind had been taken out of his sails; he looked defeated, almost.

Sioni rose from his seat. 'Well, thank you, Marged, that was right tasty,' he said, patting his stomach.

She nodded. 'So, you're off back to Merthyr, are you?'

'Aye, in about an hour or so, but first I was going to ask Seren to come for a walk with me. That's if she's not needed here?'

Seren felt a blush rise to her cheeks; she hadn't been expecting that.

Marged smiled. 'Yes, of course. I've only got a

few dishes left to wash up. She needs to take it easy anyhow and a breath of fresh air will do you good, Seren.'

Seren smiled. 'I'll just fetch my shawl, then,' she said. There was a faint flutter in her chest. Why did she feel so excited being around this man? He was a rogue, after all.

They left via the front door, to see Jim had fallen asleep back in his armchair by the fire and Marged was almost dozing in her chair opposite. 'They're like a pair of bookends there,' Sioni whispered, causing Seren to chuckle. Although Jim sometimes got the sharp end of Marged's tongue, she realised just how much affection the pair had for one another.

Once outside, it was nice to see the sun shining for a change. 'Where are we off to then?' Seren wanted to know.

'I thought we'd walk as far as the public gardens and have a little sit on a bench,' he said, taking her by the arm. 'I have a proposition to put to you.'

That sounded ominous, she thought, as she walked along with him almost as though they were a couple. People nodded and smiled at them and some men even tipped their hats in her direction.

Once they reached the gardens, Sioni led her to a bench overlooking some colourful flower beds surrounding an ornamental fountain. 'Please sit down,' he urged.

She did as requested, and he followed suit. 'Look, I didn't want to say anything in there in front of Jim and Marged, but you're going to need money in the future for yourself and the baby.'

She nodded. 'Yes, and I am quite prepared to work for it.'

'I understand that, but I'd like to give you something to tide you over.' He reached into his jacket pocket and brought out a black velvet drawstring pouch and handed it to her.

She blinked. 'What's this?'

'There are ten sovereigns in that purse. Keep them for a rainy day and there'll be more if you need it.'

'But I can't accept this from you, it's not fair.'

'You can and you will.'

'The only way I can accept any money from you is if I work for you,' she said quite curtly.

He raised his dark brows in surprise. 'What do you mean? At the wash house?'

'No, I've been thinking about it: you said you need someone to sort out the girls and run things at the inn.'

'Well, yes. But I didn't really think someone like you would want to do something like that.'

She let out a little sigh. 'It's a means to an end. I could get those girls sorted out for you. They could do with some decent clothes and a good wash. I could also vet the clientele who are paying for their services as well. But you'd have to stop allowing the girls to thieve off their clients. I overheard some of the girls at the wash house talking about that. It's not on, taking money off the men for their services and then robbing them blind afterwards!'

His eyes widened. Then he rubbed his stubbled chin as he mulled things over. 'Maybe you're right,' he said finally.

'Another thing . . . If I work for you, there are to be no young girls taken on. That's not right, they're barely out of childhood.'

He nodded. 'Well, at the moment the youngest is eighteen, but I have to admit I've taken them younger than that when they've been driven on to the street.'

'They might get driven on to the street from poverty, but it's wrong for them to get exploited by men for immoral purposes.'

He nodded.

'Well, do we have ourselves a deal?'

He shook her hand. Then she handed him back the pouch of money. 'I'll earn this instead,' she said firmly. 'Now I'm going to ask you once and I expect a straight answer: was it you who stole that silverware from that house last night?'

His face reddened. It depended now on whether he told her the truth if she'd definitely work for him in the future. If he lied, she wouldn't go ahead with it. She could tell by his face he was guilty as his eyes darted everywhere.

Finally, he nodded slowly, and then let out a long breath. 'Yes. Yes, I did. How did you know?'

'Well, I didn't find your stash, if that's what you're thinking. It was just a hunch. Where did you hide it?'

'In the stable beneath the horse's bale of hay.'

'I checked the stable but didn't look under the hay.'

He smiled. 'I don't suppose you think much of me now . . . ' He shook his head.

'What do you mean, I don't think much of you *now*? I didn't before, but you have shown me great kindness nevertheless and I am pleased you told me the truth, as you needn't have done so.'

His eyes widened and then he stroked his brow and looked off far in the distance as if gathering his thoughts. There was a long pause before he brought his gaze to meet with hers. 'Look, I'll take the haul back to Merthyr, sell it to a fella I know who'll pay handsomely for it and then I'll split the money with you.'

Her chin jutted out in defiance. 'You'll do no such thing! I want that silver returned to those poor people.'

'Poor people? They've got far more than you or I will ever have, my darling!'

'Maybe so, but Marged was speaking about them earlier and they've worked hard for that money. The Machens started off with a barrow in the market place, then increased their fortunes by opening a small grocery shop, which led to a string of them, and that was all down to hard toil. They weren't born with a silver spoon in their mouths!'

'I didn't realise that,' he said sombrely.

'So, please return that silver, it doesn't belong to you!' She pursed her lips.

He held up his open palms as if in self-defence. 'Whoa! But how do I do that without getting caught?'

'You had no worries about the risk of getting caught taking it in the first place. I'll tell you what you are to do. You'll stay put here today on some pretence to Jim and Marged, then when it gets dark you are to drop the silverware off on the doorstep of that house.'

He opened his mouth as if he couldn't believe his ears, then closed it again. 'But I can't do that . . . '

'You can and you will, if you want me to work for you.'

'All right, all right,' he said, a small smile appearing on his lips. 'Look, there are refreshment rooms open across the way, let's go inside out of the cold and have a cup of coffee.'

'I thought a whisky or a pint of ale would be more your sort of style.' She laughed, pleased that she had got through to him. Indeed, she wondered why she was able to get through to him when there were others that feared him, and it was then she realised it was all that practice she'd had at standing up to Morgan — that surely counted for something.

* * *

Elwyn stared out of the window of The Manse. They would be here soon. Fair play to Mrs Johnson, she had the place gleaming like a new pin; there wasn't a surface that had missed the flick of her duster, and now the room smelled of lemon and lavender, a very fresh and clean perfume filling the air. On the table was a fresh bunch of flowers in a crystal cut-glass vase, a mix of chrysanthemums and dahlias of varying shades of white and pink. The armchairs were covered in well-ironed and embroidered antimacassars on their backs and arm rests. The lace net curtains had been washed and returned to the windows and the windows themselves cleaned with white vinegar and elbow grease. He reassured himself that Mother wouldn't be able to find a speck of dust in his home.

He became aware of approaching footsteps and found his housekeeper stood behind him. 'Don't worry, Mr Evans, it's all in hand. I've got in a nice bit of ham for their tea that they can have with bread and butter, and there's the fruit cake too. Did you remember the loaf?'

The palm of his hand flew to his head. 'I'm sorry, Mrs Johnson, I totally forgot. I'll go and fetch it from the bakehouse now.' Of course, he hadn't forgotten the loaf of bread, he just hadn't wanted to stay in the shop a moment longer with those gossips around.

'Don't worry, Mr Evans, I'll pop down there now, it shan't take me a moment. I think I'll pick up some Welsh cakes as well. They always go down well, especially if someone prefers something a bit lighter than fruit cake.'

He nodded. 'Thank you, Mrs Johnson, you're an angel.'

'If you don't mind me saying so, you don't seem yourself lately, not since . . . ' She bit her lip and he understood why; she was going to say since Seren had left the valley, but she was too polite to say so.

'Yes, I do miss Mrs James, you are correct. She was a good friend to me. While you're out, perhaps you could pick up some cheese as well? Father's partial to some bread and cheese.'

She smiled. 'Very well. I'll just fetch my cape.'

'You're worth your weight in gold, Mrs Johnson,' he said, smiling at the woman as her cheeks blushed pink. As he watched her leave the room in a rush, he noticed Mrs Shanklin stood outside in the street and he hoped she wasn't going to choose this particular time to call on him. No doubt she was up to even more mischief now that Tom had gone to London. She stood staring at the window for a moment, causing him to step back for fear of being seen, then she turned her back and crossed the road as if she'd changed her mind about calling at The Manse.

By the time Mrs Johnson had returned and got in through the back door with her wares to the kitchen, a carriage had pulled up outside the house. 'They're here, Mr Evans,' she called as he made his way to the front door, with the woman in attendance behind him quickly removing her cape and hanging it on the hallstand in preparation of receiving the visitors.

John Jenkins, who owned the carriage, was helping Elwyn's mother down from it and she had a big smile on her face. She'd obviously dressed well for the occasion in her best emerald-green day dress and around her shoulders she wore a small fur-lined matching cape and fur-trimmed hat on her head.

'How good to see you, Elwyn!' she exclaimed as he went to take her arm to guide her inside. 'I have missed you so.' Then she quickly pecked his cheek. Why was it around his mother he always acted or felt like a young lad?

'It's good to see you too, Mother.' He smiled and he genuinely meant it. Although sometimes she put on airs and graces, she was a good sort who genuinely cared for his welfare.

'Hang on a moment before we go into the house, there's a surprise waiting for you in the carriage.' She giggled.

He turned, expecting to see Father stood there behind his mother, but he was helping someone out of the carriage.

Then he saw her, someone he hadn't seen in years, or so he thought; there was something so familiar about her. She stepped down from the carriage dressed in a blue velvet fur-lined cloak. Her blonde hair was loose in ringlets on her shoulders and her clear blue eyes sparkled and shone like a pair of polished diamonds.

'You don't recognise me, do you, Elwyn?' she said softly. He thought he did, but he just wasn't sure. 'It's me, Lucinda . . . '

He blinked several times. 'Little Lucy who went to school with me?'

'Yes, the one and the same!' She giggled. 'We left to live in Carmarthenshire, do you remember?'

He did, it all came flooding back to him. There was a special party the day the family left Pontypridd behind, and he remembered his nine-year-old self shedding a little tear of regret. 'I do remember it well, Lucinda,' he said, smiling at her warmly as he took both her hands in his own. She had developed into an enchanting-looking young woman. So, this was his mother's special surprise! He'd wondered what she had up her sleeve.

14

Anwen was dozing off in front of the fire with Macs, a young sheepdog, at her feet. She'd bought him from a local farmer as she no longer liked living alone. Suddenly, the dog's ears pricked up and he sprang to life, barking.

'Sssh, Macs, what's the matter with you?' Anwen scolded, thinking he was being far too jumpy of late, but the dog was frantic, his hackles on show as he emitted a low growl. She picked up the poker beside the fireplace, fearful that Morgan James might be up to his antics again, but then when she strained her eyes to look outside of the window, she could see a few women walking with extreme purpose towards the farmhouse. Were her eyes deceiving her? She never normally had that many visitors.

There was a sharp rap on the door and the sound of excitable voices babbling outside, so she went to answer with Macs at her heels. As she drew open the door, she saw Maggie Shanklin's hooked nose, beady eyes and unwavering stare in front of her. 'Hello, Anwen,' she said in greeting. Anwen noticed that most of the women had wicker baskets in their arms.

What's going on here, have they come to buy some eggs or something?

'Good day to you,' she said cautiously, holding the door just a little ajar in case she needed to slam it shut in the woman's face. 'What is it you want from me?'

'Oh, we don't want nothing at all,' Maggie explained. 'We've brought you some provisions we've made for you. We figured as how you might be lonely up here on the mountainside living alone.'

'Lonely?' Anwen scoffed. 'Since when have any of you lot worried about my loneliness?' She opened the door wide, so they could all hear what she had to say to them. 'Was it when you all tried to get me banned from the chapel? Or was it when you slandered my name all over the place? And you, Mrs Donovan . . . ' She pointed to a woman to the right side of Maggie. 'Didn't you walk past me in the street the other day without even acknowledging me?'

The woman shook her head. 'No, that can't have been me, I would never do a thing like that, or maybe I didn't notice you.'

Anwen shook her head. 'And you, Doris . . . ' She addressed a woman stood behind Maggie. 'You were a good friend to me until you got in with this Maggie one stood before me!' She swallowed a lump in her throat when she thought back to how friendly the woman had been at the time but had then turned her back on her.

Doris shook her head. 'We still can be good friends,' she said, then smiled. 'It was all a misunderstanding.'

Should she give them the benefit of the doubt? She wasn't sure. It was perishing cold though and they had come a long way. 'Well, you'd better all come inside then,' she said with a note of resignation, watching them troop into her kitchen, then she closed the door behind them. Maggie exchanged glances with the women and then almost nervously they waited to see what Anwen would say next. 'Sit yourselves down then!' she said, pointing to the old sofa and a couple of chairs next to a low wooden table. The women proceeded to sit, whilst Anwen seated herself in her rocking chair with Macs beside her as her protector. He was looking curiously at the women, angling his head to one side, but he had calmed down at least.

'So,' said Anwen, after she'd rocked back and forth several times, enjoying studying the women's faces as they waited in anticipation. 'I suppose what you've all really come for is the gossip of what's happened to Seren James?'

Maggie's mouth fell open and snapped shut again.

'We're concerned, that's all,' said Doris.

'Pah!' Anwen said. 'Pity more of you weren't concerned when that poor girl was taking a leathering from that brute of a husband of hers!' Then she pointed a gnarled finger at Maggie. 'And you, in particular, Mrs Shanklin, you've been going around saying how she can't keep her husband satisfied and that's why he's gone off with a rum sort from the wash house at China!'

Maggie's face reddened. 'I've said no such thing!' She looked towards her friends for support. 'Have I, ladies?'

The women shook their heads, but no one actually spoke. They began to mutter and squirm around in their seats, unable to cope with the truth.

'Well, what have you brought me, being good neighbours and all, like?' Anwen demanded to know.

'I've brought you an apple pie,' Mrs Donovan said timidly. She stood to remove a covering cloth from her basket and took it to Anwen for her to inspect.

'Looks good. Thank you very much. Please place it on the table by there.'

The woman nodded and did as told, reseating herself.

One by one the women presented their wares, which were mainly home-baked goods and jams. Finally, Maggie stood and walked over to Anwen.

This is killing her! Anwen chuckled inside.

Maggie opened a tea towel to show off some currant buns.

'Very nice, Mrs Shanklin.' She lifted one to inspect it closely and sniffed loudly. 'They're quite hard though. Are they rock cakes by any chance?'

One of the women giggled and Maggie turned to see where the laughter was coming from, but wasn't quick enough as Doris stifled her mirth with the palm of her hand.

Maggie narrowed her eyes. 'I can assure you these were freshly baked this morning,' she said.

Anwen smiled. 'I was only teasing you, Maggie. Now please leave them on the table and I'll make us all a cup of tea.' This definitely wasn't going as Maggie planned, Anwen could tell by the look on the woman's face. And Anwen intended guarding Seren's secret with her life, so for time being she was going to tell a few fibs to throw the old crone off track. While they were sipping their tea, and Doris had handed around the Welsh cakes she'd made, the talk turned to Seren yet again.

'So where is she staying then?' Maggie asked with a gleam in her eyes. 'I've heard she's back with her husband but they've both moved out of Abercanaid.'

'That's right,' Anwen said. 'They're back together and now living in Cefn, so I'm told.'

Maggie gave a self-satisfied grin, turning to her friends as if to say, 'See, I told you so.'

'But is that wise for her to do that?' Mrs Donovan asked with a worried look on her face. 'If she's getting knocked about by her husband?'

Anwen paused, unsure how to answer. She set down her cup and saucer on the occasional table by the fireside. 'Aye, well, it's her choice of course. No one can tell her what to do.'

Maggie rose to her feet suddenly and came towards Anwen as if about to say something, causing Macs to jump up and emit a low growl at the woman, keeping her at bay, his hackles rising as he bared his teeth.

'What were you about to say, Mrs Shanklin?' Anwen asked innocently.

'J . . . just that I'd like to wish them all the best for the future. I wonder who'll take over his shop; it's been closed for days now, he's losing business.'

'Who knows?' said Anwen truthfully. 'He might return to it at some point.'

Maggie retook her seat and stared at Macs. 'Well, 'twill be a foolish person who tries to harm you with that dog on sentry duty.' She sighed loudly.

Anwen nodded. 'Yes, he's a good 'un. Can sniff out trouble a mile away.'

'But is it correct that Seren's having a baby though?' Doris asked, putting Anwen in a difficult position.

She mulled it over for a few seconds. 'Yes, maybe that's why they got back together, for the sake of the baby.'

Maggie exchanged glances with Doris. 'Course, I could tell ages ago. I even told her myself she was pregnant . . . ' she said with a know-it-all tone of superiority. 'Well, I for one am glad they've left the village. It wasn't healthy, her getting so friendly with Mr Evans; people were beginning to talk.'

Anwen looked at Maggie with curiosity over the top of her spectacles. 'Oh, were they now? Let me tell you this, it was Mr Gruffudd himself who asked Seren to befriend the minister as he feared he'd be lonely when he turned up here, not being a Merthyr man himself. She was no more than a friend to him, just as I have been. So, do *these people* who were beginning to talk have anything to say about my friendship with the man?'

'But that's hardly the same, is it?' Maggie said. 'Forgive me for saying this, but you're not an attractive young woman who might turn a man's head.'

Anwen chuckled. 'Maybe not, but I had my moments back in the day. Let me just tell you all this now before you leave . . . ' She'd had enough of the sanctimony of the situation. 'It's *those people* who have filthy minds who are seeing things that are not there, things that are perfectly innocent, like how that young woman helped the new minister at the chapel. The people who are gossiping want to see things that are not there so *they* can spread their evil message. It says in the bible that gossips are to let no corrupt communication proceed out of their mouths — you'll find that's from Ephesians, chapter 4, verse 29. And also 'He that hideth hatred with lying lips, and he that uttereth a slander . . . is a fool!' ' She glared at Maggie. 'And that last one is from Proverbs, chapter 10, verse 18.'

'Well, really!' Maggie said, now seeming affronted as her mouth snapped shut as if she was at a loss for words.

'I have several more I can tell you,' Anwen said, smiling at the woman.

Maggie turned to the group of women. 'I think I've heard quite enough, ladies. I am not going to be accused of spreading slander around this village when all I have is a young woman's welfare at heart, and I am most definitely not going to stay here to be insulted!'

'Where else do you go?' Anwen chuckled.

The women placed their teacups down with a collective rattle and stood, not quite knowing how to handle the situation. One or two muttered their thanks for the tea, but they all realised they had to show their solidarity with Maggie, that much was evident.

'Mind how you go, ladies, do take your time. Macs has got a habit of nipping at fast ankles especially of *those people* who spread slander and gossip around the place!' Anwen called out to them once they were all safely on the other side of the door, then she bolted it, lit the oil lamp and closed the curtains. Then she bent down to pat the dog, who was wagging his tail, on the head. 'That showed them, Macs! Come on, boy, I've got a nice tasty bone in the cupboard for you.' She giggled to herself as she went off to fetch it for him.

* * *

At The Manse, the conversation was both interesting and lively as they all sat around the table. Wilma Evans was facing her husband, Joseph, and Elwyn faced Lucinda, so they naturally fell into conversation with one another.

'So, did you like living in the countryside?' he asked her.

Her eyes twinkled and he noticed she kept looking at him from time to time, almost in a bashful manner. 'Oh yes, but it's nothing like here. Father had a smallholding there and enjoyed working out in the fields, but his heart missed Pontypridd. Mother would have been happy to stay there. She was doing well as a seamstress and had planned opening her own shop, but Father said Merthyr was where the money was to be made and it wouldn't be too far away from our old home neither.'

He quirked a brow. 'Merthyr? I assumed you'd moved back to Ponty.'

She shook her head. 'No, we're living in the

Thomastown area now. My parents have kept in communication with yours for years, so that's how we're still in touch and they helped us to find our new home.'

'Yes,' agreed Wilma. 'Grace and I wrote to one another with our news every month over the years and I couldn't wait for them to come here to live.'

Joseph cleared his throat. 'I have to say, this is a nice piece of ham on my plate. Your housekeeper doesn't skimp, does she?'

Elwyn smiled. 'No, indeed, Father. Though she might have pushed the boat out a little as I told her you were arriving.'

As if on cue, Mrs Johnson arrived with a tray carrying several covered china dishes. 'I've got some potatoes here and some kidney beans, as well, to go with the ham,' she explained.

This was even more than Elwyn had imagined. What had happened to the simple menu of ham, cheese and bread? But he guessed she was out to impress and show off that she was looking after him very well indeed.

After feasting on the meal and then being served small slices of fruit cake with cups of tea, Joseph steepled his fingers across the table. 'So, tell us all what's been going on here then, Elwyn . . . '

Elwyn felt his colour rise. He could hardly tell his parents about his feelings for Seren James or what had gone on regarding her husband, so instead he said, 'I've settled in very nicely here at the chapel; the congregation has been most friendly.' Then after a few minutes of church and village business, they went back to discussing what was going on back at Pontypridd, his parents seeming satisfied that he was happy where he was for time being. When Lucinda left the table to use the facilities, his mother suddenly said, 'So, what do you think then, Elwyn?'

'About what?'

'About what, he says, Father!' she chuckled.

'About Lucinda of course,' his father said.

He was confused. 'Well, she's absolutely delightful.' What were they expecting him to say?

His mother studied his face. 'We were thinking more of her as marriage material. Now that you've entered the chapel as a minister, it's time you were thinking of settling down.'

Oh no, that hadn't been on his mind at all. Lucinda was very lovely indeed, but he still thought of her as being his little friend from Pontypridd.

'Yes,' his father added, 'it would be great to unite both families, particularly as we all get along famously.'

His parents looked at him in expectation as he began to feel slightly hot beneath the collar of his shirt. He let out a breath of relief when his housekeeper disturbed them to ask if they required any more tea.

'T . . . that would be lovely, thank you, Mrs Johnson,' Elwyn said. By now he was silently praying that Lucinda would return to the room, as he kept his eyes affixed on the open door, but so far there was no sign. As the housekeeper departed, his parents gazed at him yet again as if expecting a reply.

'Well,' said Mother in a brusque manner, 'do you think you might like to begin courting

Lucinda? If so, Father can have a word with her parents about it.'

What could he say that wouldn't cause offence? He could hardly let them know he had fallen for a married woman, it would cause such a scandal. So, he found himself nodding in agreement and being patted on the back by his father just as Lucinda breezed into the room.

'What's going on? Have I missed something?' she asked.

Joseph chuckled. 'We might have some good news for you before too long, once I've spoken to your father, young lady!'

Lucinda's eyes lit up. 'Oh, really!' It was obvious to Elwyn that she had some idea what was going on here and now he felt like a fly caught in a spider's web. She was such a beautiful young lady, though, who had a lot going for her, and who knew if he'd set eyes on Seren ever again?

'Yes, really,' Mother said, as Mrs Johnson entered the room with another fresh pot of tea.

'Well, I must say everyone looks so happy here!' she enthused.

'Oh, we are,' Father said with a note of excitement to his voice, and then to Elwyn's surprise he looked at him and winked.

It was then he realised he'd been well and truly set up.

* * *

Seren was sorry to see Sioni set off for Merthyr. He had done as she'd requested and left the sack of silverware on the doorstep of the house and for that, she felt so much better.

'I'll be back in a few days,' he said. 'You have everything you need here for time being. I think it would be better if I ensure Morgan is well and truly away from Merthyr before I bring you back with me, understood?'

She nodded solemnly. Jim and Marged had already said their goodbyes inside the house and had thoughtfully left the pair in peace outside to say farewell.

'You'll never know how much I really think of you, Seren,' Sioni said, lifting her chin and gazing into her tearful eyes.

She swallowed. 'I think I do . . . ' she replied in a husky voice. 'No man has ever done as much for me as you have, Sioni. I need to ask you why, though? As I've never done anything for you.'

'Because you are an absolute lady, Seren. I know you're a strong woman beneath it all, but you looked so vulnerable when I took you in at the inn, as if you'd been through so much and needed taking care of. And when I discovered it was a friend of mine who had done that to you, it hurt me. Don't get me wrong, I've seen several working women beaten by men who were so angry at being robbed of their valuables whilst they slept, but you'd done nothing to deserve being hurt like that and when you were with child and all . . . '

It was then she noticed he had tears in his own eyes. This man, who terrified other men and women in China and beyond, had a sensitive side. 'There's more to it than that though, isn't there?'

He nodded. 'My mother used to take some hits from the fists of my father. He was a right brute. He used to knock us kids around an' all. So as soon as I was old enough, I learned how to fight back, and by the age of thirteen, I was almost as big as he was. One night, when he set on my mother, I showed him what I was capable of and gave him a right hammering. I don't know if it was the shock of me turning on him like that or the blows themselves, but he was never the same again. He became timid around me after that and never touched my mother or us children ever again. It was at that point I realised the power I had in these fists. I used to train regular up the mountain; people would put bets on to see who would win.'

'You mean bare-knuckle boxing?'

He nodded. 'Aye. I never lose a fight as in everyone's face, I see my old man. You see, I wish now I'd killed him. He had a long and cruel death from a disease and no matter how much I hated that man, it was 'orrible to see him suffer like that . . . ' He drew a breath. 'But I have to say my mam was glad to see him go and I couldn't say I blamed her neither.'

It was all beginning to make sense now why Twm Sion Watkin was the way he was in life. If only people understood him like she did.

He leaned over and quickly pecked her lips, then she was in his arms and she felt safer than she had in a long while. She yearned for him to claim her lips, but he suddenly pulled away. 'As much as I want to, I'll wait. You're still vulnerable and hurting over what Morgan has done to you.

I'll be returning and I'll be taking you back to Merthyr with me some day, but for time being, you need to stop with Marged and Jim until after the baby's born.'

She felt a rush of disappointment wash over her. What was he saying? Was it some kind of rejection? She wasn't quite sure.

'Goodbye, Sioni, and thanks for your help . . .' She swallowed a lump in her throat and hoped her trembling voice wouldn't betray her as she wondered if she'd ever see him again. Maybe he'd forget all about her offer to work for him, or maybe he was giving her the brush off.

He smiled, then got on his cart to ride back to Merthyr. She turned away to wipe a trickle of a tear that had found its way down her cheek, and when she turned back again he was a small spot in the distance and her heart ached for him so much.

15

'Are you all right, dear?' Marged asked as Seren walked in through the back door with her head lowered, hoping the woman wouldn't notice her low mood.

She looked up to meet Marged's kindly eyes. 'I don't know what's the matter with me, Marged, I can't stop crying. I hardly know Sioni really and yet I'm weeping like a baby at his departure.'

'Aw, it will be the pregnancy making you like that. Come and sit down for a while. You've been doing too much as well. I'll fetch you a glass of water.'

Within minutes, Seren found herself seated at the table with a cold glass of water in front of her. 'Is it normal to be as weepy as this when you're pregnant?' She sniffed.

Marged nodded and smiled. 'Yes, it is. I was like that on all three of mine, and the babies didn't suffer for it either. They're three strapping lads now. Absolutely anything could set me off: Jim raising his voice, something sad I'd heard, even something that was supposed to make me happy. I was in floods of tears a lot of the time.'

Seren raised her brows and gazed at the woman. 'I didn't realise you had any children.'

'Oh yes, the three are by Jim, thankfully, not my first husband. I didn't want to have any more ties to him.'

'Do they live locally then?'

'Two are in Merthyr working at the ironworks and the youngest works on the Glamorganshire Canal on the barges, so we don't see him that often.' She smiled as she spoke about the lads.

'What are their names?'

'Owain, Glyn and Meurig,' she said proudly. 'Fine upstanding lads they are and all, but to be honest with you, I'd rather the two got out of the ironworks; there are so many accidents there from the molten iron — men have lost eyes because of it, or got burnt and even lost their lives. Glyn told me a young lad was badly burnt only last week. He'll be scarred for life now. Mind you, he's lucky not to have lost his life.'

Seren nodded. 'That poor boy and his poor mother . . . ' Her eyes filled with tears again.

Marged tutted at herself. 'Now I've gone and upset you again, haven't I?'

'No, it's not you, it's me being so sensitive right now.'

Marged took a seat at the opposite side of the table and stretched out to take Seren's hand. 'I think myself it might be more than being pregnant for you, it could be a delayed sort of shock to your system after what your husband did to you recently.'

She nodded slowly as realisation set in. 'Maybe. I am quite used to being knocked around every now and then, but this time it was different, he knocked me out cold for a moment. He only stopped after I told him I was carrying his child, but in all honesty, maybe me telling him that saved my life in the end. By all accounts, he was mortified that he'd hit me when I was pregnant.'

'Was he now?' Marged raised her voice then pursed her lips and raising a fist said, 'If I caught hold of him I'd give him what for. Pregnant or not pregnant, he shouldn't lay a finger on you anyhow. But then again, if I thumped the brute, it would make me no better than he is.' She let out a long sigh.

Seren smiled through her haze of tears. 'Thank you.' There was truth behind the woman's words.

'That's why you must never take him back, not even for the sake of the baby. Once he or she is born, he will start it all up again.'

Seren shook her head, vehemently. 'No, I never will now as I realise I could have lost my child because of him.'

'Have you thought of any names yet?'

She shook her head. In all honesty it had been the last thing on her mind. 'I know it sounds awful, Marged, but I haven't even been thinking that way.'

Marged smiled. 'It's no wonder, too. But at least you have a man from Merthyr who wants to take care of you . . . '

'You mean Sioni?'

'Aye, I do. I can see he thinks the world of you, I've never seen him so protective of a woman before.'

'He's never been married then?'

'No, not to my knowledge.'

Before Seren could say anything else — as she'd longed to ask more about him — Jim entered the kitchen, his face as grim as stone. 'It's all going on at the pit apparently. Thomas

Jenkins was out in the street and reckons the men are revolting over there; they're refusing to work for the bosses.'

Marged's lips set in a firm line as she shook her head. 'They need a peacemaker to speak up for them . . .' She pierced him with a stare.

'Me, you mean?' His eyes widened and he shook his head. 'I can't do that, I could end up losing my job over there, it's hard being caught in the middle of it all. I'm not one of them and I'm not one of the big bosses either.'

'Maybe so, Jim, but someone has to fight for the likes of Ivor and Stan.' She pointed to the ceiling where the men were upstairs sleeping off their night shift.

Jim blew out a long breath. 'I don't know, I have a bad feeling about all of this,' he said, leaving by the back door to go to the yard.

'Where's he off to?' Seren asked. She was feeling worried now.

'Gone to chop some sticks for firewood, I expect. I asked him to do it earlier. I do hope he takes care though, he can get so worked up about things at that coal pit. He's been getting some grief from one of the undermanagers who's on his back all the time. He keeps asking Jim to push the men to fill more trams of coal, but Jim reckons they're treating the men as if they are like a bunch of pack horses and if this carries on, there could be accidents due to tiredness. Speaking of which, I better warn Jim to be careful chopping those sticks, the mood he's in . . . ' She rose from the table and patted Seren's shoulder in an amicable fashion.

One thing was for certain, there was trouble afoot at that pit. Seren wondered how it would all pan out — she hated to see Jim and Marged upset by anything as they were so kind to her.

* * *

As Elwyn composed his Sunday sermon, he found his mind drifting off from time to time as he stared out of his chapel office window. What had he got himself into? How could a simple family tea have changed into a prospective engagement to a woman he hardly knew? Years ago, he had known Lucinda well, of course; she'd been one of his best friends who had played on the mountain behind their house at Pontypridd. But the day the family left the valley behind was the day he realised that life couldn't be just how you wanted it to be, and that all things changed. He'd still had his other friends, the boys and girls from neighbouring streets, but none had been as special to him as his little Lucy. But meeting her once again was like meeting a stranger. They'd had a shared past, granted, one which he was truly thankful for, but time and himself had well and truly moved on. If he had his way, he'd have married someone like Seren. She'd have been the woman for him — kind-hearted, strong, wilful at times, and possessing a beautiful soul. It was a pity she'd ever set eyes on Morgan James.

There had been no word of the man's whereabouts from the villagers and he couldn't afford to ask too much in case it set tongues wagging about him being overly interested. He was well aware that, thanks to Mrs Shanklin, people were already talking about his friendship with Seren.

Before he wrote another word of his sermon he decided he'd pay Anwen another visit. He needed to keep an eye on her, so as well as discussing things with her, he could check on her at the same time. She was a wise woman indeed.

He set down his fountain pen and donned his jacket and made for the mountain. A strong wind was in force today, so it might be an idea if he checked things were well secured around the farm, to save the old lady from having to do it herself.

After the long pull up the mountain, he stood and, turning, gazed on the village below where all manner of life was taking place. Children playing in streets, women pegging out washing, colliers and ironworkers sleeping off their night shifts, people chatting at various shops and in the pubs, even at this hour of the day.

He turned back to head towards the farm and, in the distance, he spotted Sam.

'Hello there!' He waved to the lad.

Sam waved back at him. He was in the middle of knocking a wooden post into the ground with a mallet. 'Hello, Mr Evans!' The lad stopped what he was doing as Elwyn drew near.

'What are you doing there?'

'Mrs Llewellyn says she wants me to make a chicken run, so I'm knocking in these posts and I'll be putting up some wire netting to keep the buggers in . . . ' As if realising what he'd just said in front of the minister, Sam's face reddened, making Elwyn chuckle.

'Don't worry, I understand what you mean. How's your mam and baby sister these days?'

The boy's eyes lit up. 'Mam's a lot better, thanks. She says she'll be back at the chapel to help with the bible class now that Mrs James is no longer here. She couldn't make it last week as my sister had colic.'

'That would be great if she can carry on with the class, though numbers have fallen since Mrs James is no longer around.'

The boy looked at him intently. 'Where is she, anyhow?'

He knew he needed to be guarded with his answer for fear people found out her whereabouts. 'Cefn Coed, I'm told.' Then changing the subject, 'Is Mrs Llewellyn in the farmhouse?'

'Yes, but be careful how you go, that sheepdog, Macs, is very protective of her, he might nip at your heels!'

Elwyn smiled. He remembered the first time he'd encountered the dog and noticed that now if he came to the farmhouse, he entered very slowly and kept his voice quiet to begin with until the dog settled down. It wasn't a bad thing, though, having a dog like that. If Morgan James or any other intruders tried it on, they'd get a shock, that was for sure.

As he walked across the yard, he heard the gate swinging back and forth in the breeze. It was even windier up here on the mountain than down in the village. He peered in through the kitchen window to see Anwen dozing by the fire.

It seemed a pity to wake her but he did need to check to see if all was well. The woman didn't seem as active as when he'd first met her — back then she was doing all sorts around the farm and could hardly sit still for a moment, putting him to shame with how physical she was at her age.

Macs immediately spotted him and began barking, which awoke Anwen. By the time both the woman and dog appeared at the door, Elwyn noticed the dog was pleased to see him this time as he wagged his tail, and tentatively Elwyn patted his head.

'That's good.' Anwen smiled. 'He's accepted you. He doesn't do that to many. I had Maggie and her friends call here the other day and what a commotion that caused! Here, come inside, don't stand on ceremony.'

Elwyn did as told, wiping his feet on the raffia doormat inside. He removed his jacket as it was warm as toast inside the house, which he was glad of. 'Maggie and her friends, you say?'

Anwen took his jacket and hung it on a wooden stand. 'Aye. They decided to pay me a visit. Come and sit by the fire and I'll tell you all about it.'

Elwyn followed the woman to the fireplace and sat opposite her as she rocked in her chair. 'So, what did they want?'

Anwen smiled at the memory of it, feeling like she'd got the better of them all. 'Oh, they came on the pretence that they were being nice and neighbourly as I might be lonely up here now Seren's left. They brought me cakes and all sorts . . .'

'And what did they really want, do you think?'

'To get the gen out of me . . . '

'Gen?'

'Gossip about Seren. They wanted to pump me dry for information but I could see through them and didn't give anything away.'

Elwyn let out a long breath. 'Thank goodness for that. I encountered them in the bakehouse the other day too and have to admit I told a few fibs.'

Anwen chuckled. 'At least we're both singing from the same hymn sheet, as it were. In any case, I don't think they'll call again as they looked scared stiff of Macs. Now then, any news about Seren since we wrote her that last letter?'

He shook his head, then warmed his hands in front of the fire.

'What is it you're not telling me?'

There was no way anyone could put one over on Anwen, she was as sharp as a lemon. 'There is something I wanted to ask your advice about.'

'About you and Seren? About whether you ought to visit her at Aberdare?'

He shook his head. 'No, not that.'

'Well, go on, spit it out, lad!'

'The other day my parents came for tea at The Manse . . . '

'That must have been nice for you.'

'It was, but they brought a young lady along with them, named Lucinda. She's someone I used to know many years ago until the family moved to Carmarthenshire. They recently moved back to the Valleys.'

'So?'

He wriggled about uncomfortably in his chair, then ran a finger beneath his collar. 'So, somehow, they've got it into their heads how lovely it would be for me to be reacquainted with her, which it is, of course . . . '

She peered at him over the top of her specs. 'But they are reading too much into things?'

'Precisely!' He sat up, feeling good that someone could see what he could. 'They seem to be under the impression that it would be an opportune moment for me to settle down. That simple afternoon tea went from a small family gathering to me practically being engaged to Lucinda!'

'And now you don't know what to do about it?'

He nodded. 'Precisely. I'd appreciate your thoughts on this, Anwen.'

She cleared her throat and stopped rocking in the chair to look at him in earnest. 'Well, let me just ask you this, Elwyn . . . '

'Go on.'

'If you had never laid eyes on Seren James and this Lucinda came along for tea at The Manse, would you have considered courting the young lady?'

Now that was a thought and he gave it some consideration. 'To be honest with you, I think I might have, but I wouldn't have rushed things.'

'There's your answer then. Seren is a fine woman, and under different circumstances then you might have been together, but she's not yours to have. By law, and in God's eyes, she is married to someone else and unless that changes, you will forever feel guilty for your association with her.'

'You're right and so wise about things. Maybe I should give Lucinda a chance but explain to my parents I don't want to rush into marriage just yet, there has to be a period of courtship.'

She nodded and smiled. 'Just because you have feelings for Seren doesn't mean you need to act on them. I know I thought you ought to visit her at Aberdare, but maybe it would be better if I pay someone to take me there. Meanwhile, you carry on with your life here in this village, Elwyn. You're needed here.'

It doesn't mean I'll forget about Seren though, he thought to himself.

* * *

Feeling less fraught than he had in a long while, Elwyn went to help Sam in the yard to set up the chicken run. Later, Anwen called them in for a plate of eggs and bacon each. 'You've both earned it,' she said, smiling.

'It's me who needs to pay you for your very good advice, Anwen,' Elwyn said.

'Aw, go on with you, you've done a lot for me, it's the least I can do.'

It was good to see Anwen getting on with life at the farm now Seren was no longer around, and he was quite sure the sheepdog and the company of himself and Sam did a lot to ensure that.

16

By the time Ivor and Stan had arisen from their beds and eaten, they decided to go across to the pit with Jim.

'Look,' Stan said to him when they were ready to leave, 'whatever you tell the bosses and the men, we'll agree with. We know you're a fair-minded man.'

'I appreciate your support, both of you,' Jim said, turning to Ivor so as not to leave him out, 'but it's not as simple as that. The bosses demand their pound of flesh — I've heard it from a good source they plan to lay men off to save money!'

'Over my dead body!' shouted Stan.

'Aye, mine an' all!' Ivor raised a fist.

'Hopefully, it won't come to that,' Jim reassured them. 'But we have to be mindful that our jobs might be on the line, and yours more so than mine.'

Ivor nodded. 'It gets me so angry sometimes. We walk for miles underground and sometimes crawling on our bellies, our clothing gets damp, we have to eat our food with hands covered in coal dust, all the while the bosses get to wine and dine in luxury. Here, we should show them our battle scars, our blue blood!'

Seren and Marged were sitting near the fireside. 'I remember the blue scars my father used to get when coal dust got inside any cuts he had,' Seren whispered. 'They always left a blue mark on the skin.'

Marged nodded. 'Yes, my Jim has several over his body. It's not a job for the faint-hearted, working underground.'

'Whatever's going on, I hope they manage to resolve things today,' said Seren.

'Me too.' Marged picked up her knitting which was lying on an occasional table beside her and began click-clacking away with the needles. It was obvious she was trying to keep her mind occupied to avoid any thoughts of trouble on the horizon.

'We'll be off then, ladies,' Jim said, and he lowered his head to peck his wife on the cheek.

'You take care over there, lads.' Marged wagged a finger.

The men nodded, but Seren noticed a fire in their eyes she'd never seen before.

* * *

It was arranged for Elwyn to call on Lucinda the following week, so he made his way walking briskly alongside the Glamorganshire canal, past Rhydycar and over to the town, where he faced the long climb up the hill towards Thomastown. Although it was breakneck steep, he realised going back home downhill would be easy for him. The large terraced house in question was set just up off the road, facing a spot of green land opposite that people used as a public garden. It was a much nicer area than most other streets in the town. People who lived here were obviously a little more affluent.

Taking a deep breath, he rapped on the highly polished brass knocker and the door swung open. He was faced with a kindly-looking middle-aged lady who wore a long black dress and white lace pinafore. On her head, she wore a lace cap.

'Hello,' she greeted him. 'You must be the minister, Mr Evans, from Abercanaid?'

He nodded. 'Yes, that's correct.'

'Do come inside, Mr and Mrs Samuels are expecting you . . . '

She led him down a corridor and into what appeared to be a drawing room where a table was set for tea with a pristine white cloth, matching china crockery and a cake stand of various dainties.

Elwyn acknowledged with a smile the couple stood before him in front of the fireplace. They looked a lot older since he'd last set eyes on them. Alfred was now completely grey-haired and sported a moustache and Grace had wrinkles around her eyes, but neither had lost the warmth that always exuded from them.

'Elwyn, it's so good to see you again.' Grace stepped forward to greet him. 'My, my, you are quite the young man. Lucinda told us all about your meeting the other day.'

Alfred walked towards him and gave him a firm handshake. 'It's good to see you, you were like another son to me,' he said, continuing to pump Elwyn's hand. Then, whispering in his ear, said, 'I understand that you and I have things to discuss later on regarding Lucinda . . . ' He winked, taking Elwyn aback.

'W . . . where is Lucinda, by the way?'

'She won't be a moment,' Grace said, 'she's just getting herself ready.'

'That young lady takes ages to doll herself up, I really don't understand what she's doing all this time!' Alfred chuckled. 'But that's like most women, I suppose. You've got all this to come, Elwyn!'

Oh dear, he hoped his own parents had informed the Samuels that he wanted to take things slowly.

A couple of moments later, Lucinda appeared, framed in the doorway like a pretty picture. Her golden curls fell in waves on her shoulders and in her hair she wore a cerise pink satin bow that matched the colour of her dress. She looked even more beautiful than the last time he'd laid eyes on her.

'At last!' said Alfred. 'Come and join us, m'dear!'

Even though the man had teased about his only daughter being slow to get herself ready, it was obvious to Elwyn that she was the apple of his eye as over tea he hung on to her every word and extolled her virtues.

It was a relief afterwards when he said he'd show Elwyn around their garden. Elwyn swallowed, realising this must be the man-to-man talk he had ready for him. They left the ladies chatting over another cup of tea while they strolled in the garden. After pointing to some flower beds and the hedgerows and saying how fond he was of cultivating the area, Alfred turned to Elwyn with a serious look on his face. 'I've spoken to your parents . . .' he said.

'Oh yes?'

'We had quite a conversation, and of course, it came round to the fact that it would be nice for you and Lucinda to step out with one another.'

Elwyn nodded, then cleared his throat. 'Yes, that would seem to be the consensus of opinion.'

'Consensus of opinion? What kind of terminology is that, young man?'

Elwyn felt his face grow hot. 'I, er, just meant that my parents seemed to have it in their heads that it would be a good thing for Lucinda and myself to get engaged.'

'I see. And what do *you* think, Elwyn? I'd like to know, seriously.'

Deciding that honesty was the best policy, he took a deep breath and said, 'I have given the matter a lot of thought and think it would be nice to become reacquainted with Lucinda, but I have no plans to rush into marriage just yet.'

Alfred pulled a pipe out of his trouser pocket and lit it with a match. 'I see, lad. But I'm taking it your attentions, as a man of the cloth, would be entirely honourable?'

'Absolutely, sir. I'm not saying I'd never want to marry, I just think a good period of courtship is required first.'

Alfred patted him firmly on the back. 'My thoughts exactly, young man. I'm glad we're of the same mind. There is plenty of time of course, but don't wait too long. I shouldn't want Lucinda to end up waiting around like an old maid.' He puffed out a plume of acrid smoke, causing Elwyn to cough.

'No, of course not, sir.'

'Well, now I've said my piece to you about my daughter, I think we should return to the house for a glass of sherry to celebrate your renewed acquaintance with her!'

After they'd all chit-chatted for a while, Lucinda led him into the parlour with her parents' blessing. 'What did Father say to you outside, Elwyn?' she was eager to know.

'I think he just wanted to know what my intentions were towards you, Lucinda.'

She nodded. 'Just think, in no time at all, I could be running that house for you at Abercanaid.'

'Well, I do have a housekeeper who does that for me, very efficiently too,' he said, trying to keep his tone light-hearted, but he could tell by the gleam in her eye, she had other ideas. By the end of the visit, it had been arranged that Elwyn would be taking Lucinda out to a concert at the local St. David's Church in the town. He didn't mind that too much as he appreciated a good choir and apparently a local soprano would be singing there too, but it did bother him that if they were seen together openly, it would be a given they were now a couple. For their first outing together, Lucinda's parents and his own would be present and later they all planned to dine at a local hotel.

When he finally got to say goodbye to Lucinda on the doorstep, he gave her a small peck on the cheek and watched as a faint blush spread over her face and her eyes sparkled. He could well imagine her as a minister's wife, but he already knew the one who had the best qualities to reach out to people, and that was Seren James. He wondered what she was doing right now.

* * *

There was a furious knocking at the door and Marged, wiping the flour from her hands on her apron, went to answer it, tutting at the same time. 'Hold your horses, will you! Where's the fire?'

Seren set down her rolling pin on the pine table and, following after the woman down the passageway, shadowed her at the door.

'Come quick, it's Jim!' Stan said, and took a big gulp of air. 'Ivor's with him. There's been trouble at the pit and someone hit Jim over the head with some kind of rock.'

'What on earth?' Marged was already grabbing her shawl from the hall coat stand. 'I'll have to go, Seren. You stop here.' Marged's eyes were wide with panic and Seren thought she needed support.

'No, I'm coming with you.' Seren grabbed her shawl too and closed the door behind them.

'Is he conscious?' Marged asked, falling into step with Stan as Seren walked behind, trying to keep up. The pregnancy was slowing her down a little more each day as her stomach swelled with the emerging life inside her. Worry about her husband was obviously fuelling Marged's need to get there fast.

'Aye, just about. I told Ivor to keep talking to him. I think he needs a doctor though.'

Marged nodded. 'There's one living a couple of streets over called Doctor Glover. Could you pop over there, Seren?' she asked breathlessly.

Seren nodded. 'Which street and what number?'

'Number 10 Collier's Row. Tell him I'll pay him later.'

'Will do,' Seren said, flying off in the direction that Marged pointed. She could always ask someone for directions if she couldn't find it.

The road to the doctor's house was up a winding pathway on the hill. She could hardly believe it, one moment she was baking pies with Marged, and the next, she was climbing uphill. Someone started to come towards her, steering a horse and cart. She waved frantically at the elderly man. He pulled up his cart sharply, saying, 'Whoa, boy!' to the horse.

'Anything wrong, love?' he asked, pushing back the rim of his bowler hat to get a better view of her.

'I'm looking for Doctor Glover, there's been some sort of accident at the pit.'

The man nodded. 'Hop on, love, I'll take you to his house as it's a fair walk up that hill.'

Grateful for a lift, she nodded enthusiastically. Noticing her condition, he clambered down and helped her aboard the cart.

Within five minutes they were outside the doctor's house. 'He holds his afternoon surgery at his home,' the man explained. 'I'll wait a while in case you both need a lift to the pit.'

'Thank you, Mr er?' She appreciated his thoughtfulness.

'Williams. I'm Tudor Williams.' He jumped

down to help her off the cart and walked her to the house.

Doctor Glover's wife, on seeing Seren's distress after explaining about the trouble at the pit, immediately interrupted her husband's surgery for that afternoon. There were only a couple of patients left to be attended to, so he told them to return home and he'd see them first thing in the morning as he was being called away on a matter of urgency.

The doctor was grateful for a ride with Seren on the cart to get to the pit as it would have taken up valuable time to get the horses ready and hitched to his own carriage.

The moment they arrived at the pit, Seren's attention was drawn to a large crowd of men, who appeared to be colliers, having a raucous altercation with three smartly dressed gentlemen in suits and top hats. But where was Jim?

'Is that your friend over there?' Tudor asked.

Her eyes scanned the scene and fell upon someone lying prostrate on the ground, where Marged and Stan were attending to him.

'Yes, that's Jim . . . ' Her heart missed a beat at the sight of him.

Tudor assisted her down from the cart and the trio made their way to where Jim was lying.

To keep him warm, Marged removed her shawl to drape over her husband.

Seren gasped. 'Is he . . . ?'

Marged turned and, with tears in her eyes, said, 'No, he's still breathing, Seren, but I can't get him to come around.'

It was then that Seren noticed the trickle of

blood running from Jim's temple, and his wife dabbed at it with the edge of her pinafore.

'It was that bloody lot over there!' Stan pointed at the colliers. 'Jim was standing between the managers and the workforce, and one of them threw a brick, or maybe it was some sort of rock, at them. Poor Jim caught the blow. It wasn't meant for him.'

'Foolhardy of whoever it was, to say the least.' Seren's chin jutted out. She could hardly believe that these negotiations the men were having would resort to violence, but then again, she of all people abhorred any violence whatsoever, no matter the cause.

'Anyhow, it caught Jim good and proper on the temple and he fell to his knees and immediately toppled over, it was awful to see . . . ' he said breathlessly. 'Me and Ivor carried him over here out of harm's way in case any more were thrown and then I ran to get Marged. It was all I could think of to do.'

It had obviously been a terrible ordeal for the man.

'I've brought Doctor Glover,' Seren said firmly, stepping out of the way to allow him through. He had his leather Gladstone bag in hand and knelt beside Jim.

'Sorry to meet you under such dire circumstances, Mrs Hopkins,' he said.

She nodded. 'Thanks for coming, Doctor. Did Seren tell you I'll pay you later? I don't have any money on me, see, as I rushed to get over here.'

He smiled. 'We can discuss that another time. My priority is to examine your husband.'

They watched as the doctor tried to rouse Jim, but to no avail. Then he examined the wound and listened to Jim's chest via a stethoscope and felt for a pulse on his wrist.

He turned to Marged. 'Well, he has a strong heartbeat, so that's a good sign. We should know within the next forty-eight hours or so whether he'll make it or not.'

'You mean he might be unconscious for good, Doctor?'

The doctor's eyes clouded over and he shook his head as Marged's hands flew to her face. 'You mean he might not even make it at all?'

The doctor nodded. 'Look, come over here away from your husband for a moment, as you never know, he might be hearing what we have to say, even if he can't rouse himself. It happens sometimes with unconscious patients.'

'Sorry, Doctor.'

Doctor Glover led her to one side, where there was a lot of nodding and shaking of heads as they discussed the situation. Eventually, he returned and said to Stan and Ivor, 'Have you got any stretchers here at the pit to hand?'

'Aye,' said Ivor. 'We've a couple we use for accidents, like.'

'Well, bring one over and, Tudor, if you don't mind, we'll use your cart to get him back to his home. The next two days will be crucial.'

Tudor nodded. Then Doctor Glover tended to Jim's head wound by dabbing it with iodine and applied a cotton dressing covered with a bandage. The men managed to roll Jim on to the stretcher as the doctor gave them orders to be as gentle as possible, explaining that he might well have broken something they weren't yet aware of.

All the while Marged watched and wept into the hem of her pinafore, whilst Seren draped an arm around the weeping woman. She hadn't seen anything like this since the last pit accident at Gethin Coal Pit, and then the men had been laid out on beds of straw. It brought it all back to her. There had to be some sort of solution for the men to reach an amicable agreement about the layoffs and unreasonable demands at the pit.

By the time they'd got Jim back to his home and in his bed, the men were fair exhausted, so Seren set about making cups of tea for them whilst Marged sat by her husband's side holding his hand. Sometimes life just wasn't fair. Later, Seren took a cup up to Marged. 'I've put a spoonful of sugar in it for you, for the shock,' she whispered.

Marged smiled. 'We never did get to finish our baking, did we?' she said, then she closed her eyes and wept as if the pain of the day was all too much for her.

* * *

It was later that evening when Seren heard a calamity upstairs and she dashed up the steps breathlessly to see Marged stood at the open bedroom door.

Oh, dear Lord! Had Jim passed away?

But there was a huge beaming smile on the woman's face and her eyes were shining.

'Someone fetch Doctor Glover!' she shouted excitedly. 'Jim's just come around.'

Seren's heart gladdened as she hugged the woman then, looking past her into the bedroom, she saw Jim sitting up in bed, staring around him as if wondering what all the fuss was about.

'I'll ask if Stan or Ivor can go for him,' Seren said as she rushed back down the stairs to find both men seated by the fireside. They hadn't even bothered going to the pub that evening as they wanted to keep a check on their foreman.

'Stan! Ivor!' Seren shouted. 'It's Jim, he's come round!'

'Thanks be to God!' said Ivor, momentarily closing his eyes.

'Can one of you fetch the doctor, please?' she said. 'He told us to contact him as soon as Jim shows any signs of consciousness.'

'Aye, of course, Seren!' Stan had already donned his jacket and flat cap and was headed for the door.

* * *

Jim recovered quite quickly and it wasn't long before he was on his feet once again. Marged had warned him he wasn't to return to the pit until he was properly well again. In his absence, the men had formed a committee to discuss the actions of the managers at the pit and money had been collected from the men to help Jim whilst he was in recovery.

'Such kindness shown . . . ' Marged carried a large wicker basket of fruit in her arms and placed it down on the kitchen table. 'This just arrived on behalf of the colliers at the pit!'

Gordon Griffiths looked over the top of his newspaper from the armchair. 'Well, they can wrap it up all they like, but one of those flaming sods hit your Jim with that rock and ought to be behind bars!'

'I know that,' Marged said softly, 'but emotions were running high at the time . . . '

'But the coward meant to hit someone. I tell you now, if someone puts the man's name forward, I'll have no qualms about locking him up!' Gordon said fiercely, throwing his newspaper down on the table beside him. He stood and left the room in silence and all they could hear was the clomping of his boots as he walked upstairs to his bedroom, probably to calm himself down.

Seren exchanged glances with Marged. No doubt Gordon was upset on behalf of Jim as he and his wife had been good to him. Later, when the women were washing and drying the dishes at the scullery sink, she asked, 'Do you think it's true what Gordon said, that someone might put that man's name forward?'

'I seriously doubt it.' Marged began to dry the dishes with a clean tea cloth, rubbing away as if her life depended on it.

'Why do you say that?'

'Colliers are like family to one another, see. They might occasionally run one another down but if someone, such as an outsider or boss, is against that person, they'll do all they can to defend them. The only people who might provide the man's name, and that is if they saw what happened in the first place, are the managers themselves.'

'I suppose, though,' said Seren, scrubbing away at a metal saucepan, 'that you couldn't blame them, as if that rock hadn't hit Jim when he stepped between the men and the management, one of them would have copped it instead.'

Marged stopped drying for a moment and set down her tea towel. Pursing her lips, she said, 'You're probably right, Seren. So, let's hope they didn't see what occurred as that collier could get in trouble with the police and the managers. He could well end up losing his livelihood!'

How was it, Seren wondered, that not so long ago she was living a different life in a neighbouring valley where she had grown close to a handsome minister? And now she was living in another mining community where she cared for Jim, Marged and their lodgers like they were family? She'd tried to push thoughts of Elwyn from her mind, but it had been impossible. Even her little dalliance with Sioni had done nothing to make her forget Elwyn. It was then she realised he was the love of her life, the one she could never have whilst she was still married to Morgan, and that made her so desperately sad.

17

A frantic rapping on The Manse door early in the morning caught Elwyn unawares. What was going on here? His heart pounded as he pulled on his dressing gown, got into his carpet slippers and made for the door to hear the distressed cries of a woman. 'Mr Evans, please, can you help?'

He unbolted the door and there, stood before him in a dishevelled state, was Seren's sister. Her eyes were moist with tears and her dark hair clung heavily to her face as if she'd been caught in the rain.

'Come inside, Gwendolyn,' he said gently. 'Please remove your shawl, I'll fetch you a warm blanket from upstairs.' Within moments he had returned with a towel and a blanket for her, which she gratefully took from him. She proceeded to rub her hair dry and wrapped the blanket around herself.

'I'll make us a cup of tea,' he said firmly, but as he was saying the words, Mrs Johnson arrived from her bed. It was almost time to begin her day anyhow.

'I heard the knocking, anything I can do to help?' she asked, worry lines etched on her face.

'Could you make us both a cup of tea and bring it into the drawing room, please?' Elwyn asked. 'Then bank up the fire?'

The woman nodded then set about her

business whilst Elwyn led Gwendolyn into the drawing room, gesturing for her to take a seat.

She sat huddled with the thick woollen blanket wrapped around her, teeth chattering. Elwyn couldn't make out whether it was the cold or shock that was causing it.

'Now then, Gwendolyn,' he said, looking into her eyes. 'What's the matter?'

'It's my mam.' She swallowed. 'I think she's caught the cholera.'

Elwyn stiffened. 'And what makes you suspect that?'

'You see, she visited her sister, my Auntie Maud, at Lewis Square the other day. I know we were warned to keep away from that place.'

'So, have you called Doctor Owen out?'

She shook her head. 'I thought he may get angry after the advice he gave us to keep away from that place.'

Elwyn smiled. 'I very much doubt it. I'll get dressed after the tea and see if I can fetch him. What are your mother's symptoms?'

'She's been feverish overnight and vomited several times. I've left her in bed . . . ' She chewed her bottom lip, nervously.

'And had you been taking the doctor's advice about boiling water and keeping things clean?'

'Oh, yes. I wish Mam had stayed put and hadn't gone to see Aunt Maud. Seren will need to be told, of course. You have her address, don't you?'

He nodded, unsure what to do if their mother did have cholera. He wouldn't like to think of a pregnant woman risking two lives to visit. 'I'll see if I can get word to her but I wouldn't want Seren to risk coming here if it is cholera. How do you feel yourself? Any symptoms?'

She shook her head. 'Physically, I feel fine.'

'That's good, then. Right, once we've had the tea, I'm walking you back home so you can attend to your mother, while I'll fetch the doctor. We can think of contacting Seren later when we confirm what it is ailing your mother.'

Gwendolyn nodded as Evan realised just how like Seren she looked physically, but Seren had copper tones in her hair that seemed to match her fiery spirit.

He walked the young woman back to her house and went straight to Doctor Owen's home. The curtains were open, so he knocked the door.

The doctor's housekeeper opened it and stood there blinking — in amazement at someone turning up at such an early hour, he assumed.

'Mr Evans! What brings you to our door?'

'Is Doctor Owen available, please? I need his help, urgently.'

She nodded and led him inside the house. 'He's just getting himself ready for his daily surgery. Please take a seat.' She showed him into the doctor's office where he took a chair. How many people had sat in this seat, he wondered, with the weight of the world on their shoulders, no doubt, as they awaited the doctor's diagnosis?

It was a good few minutes before Doctor Owen appeared. 'Sorry to keep you waiting, Elwyn,' he said. 'I understand you require my services?'

Elwyn stood. 'It's young Gwendolyn Edwards; she knocked on my door as she fears her mother might have contracted cholera.'

'But why didn't she come straight here?'

Elwyn cleared his throat, then hesitated a moment. 'Apparently, her mother's been to visit her sister at Lewis Square and the girl was embarrassed to tell you after the advice you gave everyone about keeping away from that area in particular.'

The doctor's eyes widened. 'Ah, yes, but she should still have come here, I wouldn't have bitten her head off. I'll just go and get my bag. You'd better return to The Manse, in case it is cholera. I'll keep you informed.'

'Thank you.' Elwyn walked back home, all the while thinking of Seren. If this did turn out to be another case of cholera, what then? It didn't bear thinking about.

* * *

Sioni hadn't called to see Jim and Marged for a couple of weeks. 'Does he know about Jim's accident?' Seren asked Marged one afternoon as they were peeling potatoes at the sink for the evening meal.

Marged laid down her knife and potato on the wooden counter. 'I did manage to send a message to a friend who was off to Merthyr, but so far there's been no reply. I thought he might have turned up here by now as he's very fond of Jim.'

Seren nodded. 'Has he been known to keep away for long?'

'No, not really.' Marged let out a long sigh of

disappointment. 'We tend to see him about once a month. I need to go over to Merthyr Market soon, perhaps you'd like to accompany me and we'll see if we can find him?'

Seren was unsure of that but curiosity was getting the better of her. 'What do you want from the market, anyhow?'

'A roll of material to make some new curtains. I want to brighten this place up. I can get it locally of course, but Merthyr has such a vibrant market place and there's much more choice. I haven't been there for almost a year. There's a wagon that goes there and back that runs twice a day.'

'Yes, I'd love to come with you!' Seren found herself saying with great enthusiasm. It would be good to get out and about for a while and maybe she could pay a visit to Abercanaid if they took the early wagon.

Marged smiled. 'That's settled then. Maybe you could purchase some linen to make bedding for the little one and some nightgowns and daywear for him or her whilst we're there.'

Seren smiled. At least it would give her something else to think about other than having her mind on either Elwyn or Sioni.

* * *

Doctor Owen turned up at The Manse about an hour later. By the smile on his face, Elwyn realised it was good news and he invited him into the drawing room.

'Please take a seat, Doctor,' he said, gesturing.

The doctor removed his hat and coat and the housekeeper took them, then he placed his bag by his side as he sat. 'Not cholera, fortunately, I think it's more likely to be a case of a simple upset stomach. Gwendolyn might have overreacted as her mother told me she'd made herself a meal with some meat that might have been left sitting around in the pantry a little too long. I think she'll be all right. I've told her to just drink cool boiled water for now until her stomach settles, so that the poison or whatever it is will be flushed from her system, and of course, not to return to Lewis Square for a while. But between you and me, I think we've seen the worst of the deaths there. The last one was well over a fortnight ago. Dr Dyke says he thinks there hasn't been an outbreak now for about ten days anywhere in Merthyr Tydfil, and it was nowhere near as bad as the last severe outbreak in this town.'

Elwyn huffed out a sigh of relief, though in a way he felt slightly disappointed that now he need not rush to send word to Seren, but her mother's health was of most importance.

'I think it's safe to conclude,' said Doctor Owen, 'cholera has now left Merthyr. Lessons must have been learned since the last time regarding the spread of the disease, and we'll be more prepared for it in future.'

Elwyn was glad to hear it.

* * *

A few days later, before daybreak, Seren and Marged took the wagon to Merthyr Tydfil.

Marged reckoned it would be best to take the early one as the later vehicle would be packed. Even so, they had to share it with several business-men, a man with a cage of chickens, and several others who would be plying their wares at market. Seren guessed this time of day was more for people in some sort of business than ordinary shoppers. Marged said the early bird got the worm and she was in business herself, the business of running a lodging house, and she wanted to spruce it up with new curtains, come hell or high water.

It was a bit of a bumpy ride over the mountain as the wagon rolled over uneven stretches of road, and the odd misplaced stone or rock here and there shook the living daylights out of them. As they reached the top of the mountain that overlooked the Merthyr Valley she gasped as she took in the belching chimneys of the Cyfarthfa Ironworks and the splendour of the Crawshay family castle just behind it.

Marged draped an arm around her in excitement. 'How do you feel about this today, *cariad*?' she asked. 'Is it difficult for you returning after all that's happened?'

'No, not really, Marged. I'm glad of the chance to do some shopping today and visit my family at Abercanaid.' Of course, it wasn't just her mother and sister she wanted to see, it was Elwyn too. Her mind had cleared lately, and although initially, as Sioni had been her rescuer she'd seen him as a knight in shining armour, being parted from Elwyn made her realise it was him she really felt something for. There was a strong emotional attachment. But why hadn't he bothered to visit her at Aberdare? He knew the address. That hurt a little, but she had placated herself with the fact he sometimes had a busy job seeing to the needs of his congregation. And then there was her dear friend Anwen, of course. How she longed to see how she was, she had been that worried about her.

'I'm glad you feel all right returning here,' Marged said, interrupting her thoughts. 'It is your home, after all, and I have no doubts that someday you shall return to it again.'

Seren smiled. Merthyr had a magnetic draw for her and, after they'd visited the market place, she planned to leave Marged to her own devices whilst she visited her nearest and dearest in the village.

* * *

Elwyn and Lucinda were walking arm in arm along Merthyr High Street. With Christmas on the horizon, the young woman was becoming most excitable and he could tell by the way she was pausing to peer in every jeweller's window in town, she had one thing only on her mind and that was getting an engagement ring on her finger.

'You see, I can't quite make up my mind whether to go for a solitaire-style ring, you know what I mean, with a single stone . . . ' She let out a breath before beginning again. 'Or something a little more adventurous such as a ruby surrounded by diamonds,' she said as she snuggled up to him and pointed in the shop window, but he was no longer listening.

For across the street, standing outside St. David's Church, was someone he recognised all too well — Seren. She did look right bonny, as though she'd put on a little weight, but it suited her. As she turned side on, he could see a small bump — so the pregnancy was going well then. She was wearing a flowered dress, cream shawl and blue-ribboned bonnet. In his excitement he released his grip on Lucinda's hand and said, 'There's someone I must see, please excuse me.' Not waiting to hear her reply, he walked across the main High Street, dodging a horse and carriage.

Seren appeared to be in a world of her own, gazing at the church entrance as if wondering if she should go inside. She seemed to be studying the sign outside inviting people to step inside for free refreshment and the chance to visit the beautiful church with its stained glass windows.

'A penny for them, miss?' he said.

She turned, her blue eyes sparkling, and there was a faint blush to her cheeks. She did look ever so well.

As recognition dawned, he was amazed to see how pleased she was to see him stood before her.

'Elwyn, but how did you know I would be in Merthyr today?'

'I didn't. I just came out shopping . . . '

For the first time he felt awkward. How could he explain that during her absence he had become betrothed to someone?

Deciding honesty was the best policy, and

after all, she was a married woman, he said, 'There's someone I'd like you to meet.' He glanced at Lucinda who was still staring in the shop window, mesmerised by all it had to offer. No doubt she thought Seren was just another member of his congregation he had bumped into in the town, and today there had already been a few.

Seren's face suddenly paled as her eyes clouded over. Then he watched as she swallowed hard. 'Is that young lady a friend of yours?' she asked in a shaky voice.

He nodded slowly. 'Actually, she's someone I've known since we were children in Pontypridd, but her family moved away to the countryside and now they've returned and settled in Merthyr at Thomastown, so we've become reacquainted.'

'I see.' She bit on her bottom lip and said stiffly, 'And what precisely does she mean to you, Elwyn?'

Her body language was now guarded, he could tell as her chin jutted out and her face took on a look of determination. Seren and Lucinda suddenly exchanged glances across the road at one another, as if each was checking the other out. What a mess he'd got himself into. He took a deep breath and then exhaled. 'Lucinda is about to become my fiancée,' he said, then he wiped his moustache with the back of his hand as if he'd just drunk a glass of milk and was wiping away the evidence. His manner just seemed so awkward.

'Fiancée?' Seren blinked several times then she gave a nervous laugh. 'But you're having me on, aren't you?' she said, half expecting to see a mischievous twinkle in his eyes, but there was none.

'I know this will have come as a shock to you, Seren, but it all happened so suddenly . . . '

'You make it sound as if you played no part in it whatsoever!' She took a step back from him just as Marged appeared at her side.

'So, this is where you got to!' she said brightly, quite unaware that she was interrupting something so serious.

'Yes, and I was just leaving.' Seren turned towards the woman, and taking her by the arm led her away.

'Wait, Seren!' Elwyn called after her. 'I wanted to tell you something about your mother!'

On hearing mention of her mother's name, she turned to face him as he closed the space between them. 'It's just your sister had thought she had contracted cholera.'

'Cholera!' She stared at him and began to feel a little light-headed.

'It wasn't what Gwen thought though, I went for Doctor Owen and he said it was a stomach upset. She's perfectly fine, I saw her myself the other day.'

'Well, I don't know who you are, young man,' Marged said, 'but you could have chosen your turn of phrase more carefully and not frightened Seren unnecessarily like that in her condition!'

Looking into Elwyn's eyes, Seren could see just how sorry he was and she wondered if he regretted mentioning his engagement like that to her without warning. Now, at least, she knew he could never be hers. And although it hurt so badly inside, finally, she could carry on with the rest of her life.

★ ★ ★

After they'd purchased the roll of material from Merthyr Market, asking the stall holder to hang on to it for them until they picked it up later, Seren decided to take a hansom cab to Abercanaid. Ordinarily she'd have walked the couple of miles, but she was becoming more tired and out of breath these days as the pregnancy became more evident. Marged insisted on accompanying her and Seren was thankful for her company as she knew Mam and Gwen would give the woman a good welcome. But now she wished she hadn't left Elwyn in such a huff as she'd forgotten to enquire how Anwen was. How she missed the elderly lady who had been like another mother to her. If she had time she'd try to call to the farm, but it would be difficult for her climbing all that way uphill.

By the time they arrived in the village, they'd already been in Merthyr for several hours.

Seren knocked on the well-polished oak door. Mam took great pride in her home as the brass door knocker gleamed in the early afternoon sun. As a rule, Seren would normally waltz into the house without knocking, but she figured it might be a tad rude to do so when she had a stranger with her.

As the door swung open, her mother's face said it all as her mouth opened to speak, but no words were forthcoming. Then tears sprang to her eyes. 'Oh, Seren, how have you been, *cariad*?' Then she was sobbing in her mother's arms. It was several moments before she spoke.

'Oh Mam, sorry I went away without warning like that but I had no other choice . . . ' Memories of the brutal beating she'd sustained from Morgan came flooding back to her.

Her mother nodded slowly in understanding. 'I heard all about it from Mr Evans and it fair near broke my heart.' Tears filled her mother's eyes. 'He told me about the letter he'd received, so at least I knew how you were.' She looked at the woman stood behind her daughter. 'Aren't you going to introduce us, then?' she asked.

'Mam, this is Marged from Aberdare, the lady who has been putting me up this past couple of months.'

'Hello,' Marged said softly. 'Your daughter is a credit to you, Mrs Edwards, she has been a great help to me around the home.'

'Thank you for taking care of her. Please come in, both of you, we shouldn't stop on the door-step too long or Mrs Shanklin will be busybodying around the place!'

Seren chuckled. Some things about Aber-canaid never changed. They enjoyed a lovely afternoon chatting and catching up on all the news as slices of *teisen lap* were offered around. Mam was such a fine baker that Seren was truly proud of her offerings, and she really brewed a nice cup of tea as well. She didn't scrimp on the flavour either like some did, drying out tea leaves and reusing them to make more. Mam only reused them on her precious roses in the garden. Then the talk got around to Anwen Llewellyn.

'Don't you worry about Anwen, Gwen and I have both been to see her several times. She's even got herself a collie sheepdog now who keeps a close guard on her. Macs won't let anyone near her . . . I wish Gwen had been here today to see you but she's started work.' Mam smiled proudly.

'Work?' Seren quirked a brow.

'Yes, she's working as a maid at a big house in Thomastown now.'

The word Thomastown made her think of Elwyn's new fiancée and she bristled at the mere mention of the area. Surely Gwen couldn't be working for that particular family? It would be too much of a coincidence, unless Elwyn had arranged it? After all, he had mentioned Gwen went to him recently for help when he thought their mother had cholera.

Seren cleared her throat. 'Who is she working for, Mam?'

Please don't let it be Lucinda's family, it will be more than I can bear.

'A very nice young married couple. The husband owns a jewellery store on Merthyr High Street. They're Jewish.' Her mother smiled. 'And they're very generous to Gwen too. They treat her very well indeed. And guess what? Mrs Solomon is expecting a baby and she's asked Gwen if she would become a nursemaid to the child!'

Her mother looked so happy and proud about it all, and Seren was too, now that she realised her sister wasn't working for Lucinda's family.

'That's wonderful news, Mam.'

The talk turned to Jim's injury outside the pit.

'He was very fortunate,' Marged explained, 'but I find it hard to forgive those men responsible who just throw their rocks and stones without thinking about the consequences of their actions.'

Seren nodded. 'There was a lot of unrest here in the village when Dad died at the Gethin Pit, wasn't there, Mam?'

Her mother's eyes filled with tears, and Seren feared for a moment she'd said the wrong thing as it was a recent bad memory when thirty-four men and boys had been killed and the village was shrouded with grief. But that grief had eventually given way to anger at the circumstances that caused the explosion beneath ground. It had been a case of human neglect, the coroner had said, so, understandably, once people got over the initial shock, tempers were frayed.

'Yes, it was a terrible time and families are still suffering here.' Mam shook her head. 'There have been hardships because of it as so many lost their head of the house.'

For a moment, it was as if both women were united on common ground. Even though Jim hadn't died, it could easily have happened after that blow to his head.

Eventually, when the time came to say goodbye, Seren felt torn. It was painful to leave her mam behind. Taking both her mother's hands in her own, she said, 'Please take care of yourself, Mam. As you can see I'm doing well with Marged and when it's safe to return to Abercanaid, I'll be back.'

Her mother's eyes flashed. 'I'd like to horse-whip that Morgan James, that I would!' She raised a fist. Then, as if realising maybe she wasn't showing the best side of herself to Marged, she dropped her arm to her side. 'I can't wait until the day you return forever and I can see my bonny new grandchild,' she said, as she hugged her daughter to her chest. 'And don't have any worries about Mrs Llewellyn, I'll keep an eye on her.'

'Thanks, Mam.'

Mam turned towards Marged and smiled. 'It's lovely to meet the woman who is taking such good care of my daughter.'

'It was lovely to meet you, too.' Marged touched her hand.

Both women walked along the canal bank at a brisk pace towards Merthyr town as they couldn't afford to be too late back or they'd miss their transport.

'We'll have an hour before the wagon leaves for Aberdare,' Marged said. 'Anything else you wish to do?'

'I'd like to see if we can find Sioni,' Seren said. What was the use now in holding a candle for Elwyn? He was spoken for and that lump in her throat was a sign that later, when she was alone in her bedroom, she would shed some painful tears over him for she realised that with a potential wife on the scene, they could no longer even be friends, knowing she had such deep feelings for him.

'Very well,' Marged said. 'It is strange he hasn't been in touch since I sent him news about

Jim's accident. It's so unlike him.'

After how he'd helped her when she needed it most, she had to agree it seemed out of character that he hadn't paid a visit in weeks.

18

The House of Blazes was heaving when they arrived, which surprised Seren as during the time she'd stayed there, she hadn't seen it half as busy.

As if reading her mind, Marged said, 'It's probably crowded here as there are so many visitors to the town today with it being a popular market day.'

Seren nodded. Then she scanned the throng of people to see if she could spot Sioni amongst them, but her heart slumped when she realised there was no sign of him. He could be upstairs in bed, she supposed, sleeping off a heavy session, or . . . She realised with some regret that, as he was a whore-master, he probably took liberties with the girls in his keep.

Then through the crowd, she spied young Molly, who was taking a tray of empty tankards towards the bar. As she walked away from the bar, she wiped the sweat off her brow with the back of her hand. The poor love looked so tired, she was probably exhausted from all the fresh custom.

Seren grabbed her by the arm and smiled. 'Molly!'

The young girl smiled as her eyes flickered with recognition.

'Hello, miss!' Her eyes lit up.

'Have you seen Mr Watkin today?'

The girl shook her head vigorously, then her eyes began darting around the room. It seemed obvious to Seren that she knew something but wasn't prepared to say what that something was in case she got into trouble for it.

'Look, I understand you might not want to be overheard,' Seren whispered. 'Meet me outside in the alleyway in a few minutes.'

The girl chewed on her bottom lip, then nodded.

Once outside, and hidden around the side of the pub, Seren and Marged waited until finally the girl made an appearance, breathless as if she was in a rush.

'I can't stop long or it'll go noticed,' she explained. 'I'll tell you what I know . . . '

'Go on, please,' Seren urged.

'It was around a couple of weeks ago, a man I recognised came to the pub; he was about the same stamp as Mr Watkin, looked as if he could 'andle himself. Anyhow, he began drinking with him and before the night was over a few punches were thrown between them. It was as if they started off as friends but ended up foes that night.'

'And what happened then?' Marged asked, as if she wanted to know as soon as possible.

'Well, they went outside, and Sioni, I mean Mr Watkin, never returned. A couple of coppers called here as well asking after him. There's been all sorts of rumours flying since then and no one has set eyes on him neither.'

'What sort of rumours?' Seren asked.

'People seem to think something bad has

happened to him. I overheard some men talking and they said they think he was 'done in' by someone called Morgan! That's your husband, isn't it?'

Seren's heart skipped a beat. 'And you think that's the same man who was in his company the evening he went missing?'

Molly nodded. 'Aye, I do.'

It was all beginning to make sense now. From Molly's description of the man it could well have been Morgan who had got into that fight with Sioni. There was only one thing for it: she was going to have to find Mari who, in turn, might lead her to her husband and she could ask him outright. But by now she realised there was only a half an hour or so remaining until the last wagon returned to Aberdare.

'Make your way towards the wagon, Marged,' Seren said with some authority, 'there is some-one I need to find.'

'But you might miss our ride home, *cariad* . . .'

Seeing the worried look on Marged's face made her feel awful, but she knew she couldn't rest until she discovered what had happened to Sioni. He had helped save her, she owed him this much at least.

'Don't worry, if I don't make it I shall pay to stay somewhere overnight and catch one back to Aberdare tomorrow.'

'But I don't like the idea of you being left alone in this place in your condition,' Marged protested.

'Maybe not, but I feel something is wrong.' Then she turned to face Molly. 'You go back inside, love,' she said kindly. 'I should not want you getting into any bother because of me.'

Molly nodded and smiled.

Reluctantly, Marged turned to make her way to the wagon, only to retrace her steps and, facing Seren, she said, 'I've decided, if you miss the wagon then we shall both miss it. I'll spend the night with you.'

'But won't Jim be worried about you if you don't return tonight?'

'With any luck he'll know nothing about it as he's on a night shift. As for the lodgers, they can fend for themselves for once. I've told them before now, if I'm not around they're welcome to take anything from the kitchen.'

So that was settled then. Seren had to admit she was glad of Marged's support as she didn't know what sort of reception she'd get this time at the wash house as some of the girls had been a little hostile towards her that time she'd first encountered them.

As they walked down the muddy pathway with filthy waste around their ankles, the women lifted their skirts and Seren tried not to breathe in the foul stench.

'Ye gods, this place is horrendous!' Marged protested. 'No wonder they call it 'hell on earth'!'

Seren couldn't disagree with that, and she was well aware that they could be in danger of contracting something from the foul muck swilling past their feet on its way down to the River Taff, but concern for Sioni spurred her on.

When they arrived at the wash house, a memory came back to her of someone carrying her to the door, something she hadn't remembered before. But who was it? It could not have been Mari, she was too slight to carry her full weight. The arms, she remembered now, thick-set and muscular, and the smell of alcohol . . . It was him! Morgan. Her stomach somersaulted at the memory.

Taking a deep breath outside the wash house door, she rapped the tarnished knocker. Within half a minute a small wooden hatch was drawn back and she spied the face of a haggard-looking middle-aged woman. 'Whatcha want?' she asked, as if annoyed at being disturbed.

'Is Mrs Gowerton around?' Seren asked.

'Yes.' The woman just stood behind the door, two beady eyes staring at her.

'Well, can I see her?'

The woman coughed. 'I'll check she's not indisposed. Wait there.' Then she sharply slid the hatch shut as Seren and Marged exchanged glances.

'What charm school did she go to, I wonder?' Marged asked, causing Seren to chuckle.

Within minutes the door was opened fully and Mrs Gowerton stood there. A big smile on her face appeared as she recognised Seren. 'What brings you to our door again, m'dear?' she asked, her kindly blue eyes twinkling. 'And you look so much better than the last time I saw you, too.'

'I'm looking for Mari,' Seren explained.

Mrs Gowerton shook her head. 'I'm sorry to tell you this but Mari has passed away.' Her eyes looked sad at the mention of the woman's name.

Seren felt as though her head was swimming. Surely, she must be mistaken? Had Mrs Gowerton really said Mari was dead? She felt Marged take her arm as if she realised what a shock she'd had. 'B . . . but what happened?'

'Come inside, dear, I'll tell you all about it.'

Thinking quickly, Seren thought about the wagon. 'We'd better not, thank you, we don't have much time left to catch our transport for Aberdare.'

'I see. Well, all I know is her body was found washed up on the banks of the Taff. Most people seem to have come to the conclusion that she did away with herself. But I'm not so sure of that . . . '

'Why do you say that?' Marged asked.

'She was getting better. She'd been low after losing her baby, but she was picking up. She'd even started to sing in front of all the girls again. Oh, she had a beautiful voice. I think she started to pick up after leaving your husband,' she said, looking at Seren.

Oh, dear Lord, does Morgan have something to do with her death? Her blood ran cold at the thought of it. *There but for the grace of God go I.*

Remembering something, Seren opened her reticule and handed Mrs Gowerton a shilling. 'Please ensure Connie gets this,' she explained. 'She kindly loaned it to me last time I was here.'

Mrs Gowerton nodded with understanding as Seren left with tears in her eyes.

* * *

As the women headed back from the market place after picking up the roll of material Marged had purchased, Seren felt almost in a stupor.

'You look pale, *cariad*,' Marged said, 'come on, let's get to that wagon . . . '

She hardly remembered the journey back home as her thoughts were so awful. Had Morgan killed Mari and also done something to Sioni? She could hardly discuss this right now with Marged as there were others on the wagon. The man with the chickens had obviously had a profitable day as he was returning with an empty cage, and the businessmen looked worn out. She wondered if they made the trip on a daily basis? If so, how did they manage when the weather was bad? They'd be soaked to the skin.

When they returned to the lodging house, there was a lantern lit in the windowsill of the downstairs parlour. 'Jim's up early out of bed,' Marged said.

But when they got in and offloaded their packages, they could see it wasn't Jim who was up and about but Gordon Griffiths. His face was ashen.

'What's wrong?' Marged asked. 'Is there something wrong with my Jim?'

Gordon shook his head. 'No, nothing like that. He's still sleeping off his night shift upstairs. It's you I need to speak to. Please sit down, Marged.'

Without even removing her shawl, Marged sat in the armchair nearest the fire and Gordon took the armchair opposite her. He sat with both palms of his hands together.

'That gentleman you had staying here recently from Merthyr Tydfil . . . ' he said.

'Sioni?'

'Aye, that's the one.'

Marged sat forward in her chair. 'Why? Has something happened to him?'

Gordon cleared his throat. 'Er, not exactly. It's the police at Merthyr, they've contacted us at the station in Aberdare. It appears he's on the run!'

Seren felt her heart pound with fear, her mouth now dry. 'On the run?' She blinked. 'What has he done?'

'He went missing at around the same time as a prostitute was found drowned in the River Taff. But it has recently transpired that the woman didn't die from drowning as first thought. There were several blows to the head, so the Merthyr police believe she was killed and then thrown into the river.'

'But what makes you think that Sioni was responsible?' Marged shook her head in disbelief.

'Because she worked for him at the wash house.'

Seren was about to butt in and mention her husband's dealings with Mari when Marged shot her a glance as if to warn her to say nothing for now.

'So,' said Gordon, 'I just want you to let me know if he turns up at your door, Marged. Does he know that I'm a police officer?'

'I don't think I told him that, Mr Griffiths, and you weren't in uniform when he last stayed here and he only came into the kitchen on the tail end of your conversation about the stolen silverware, so wouldn't have been aware you are a police constable.'

Gordon smiled. 'That's good. So, he could well show up at some point.' Marged nodded. 'And if he does, I'll be waiting.' He stood and, picking up his police cape from the back of the chair, made for the door. Turning to both women, he said, 'Just be sure to tell me if you see him, right? Withholding information from a police officer is a criminal offence.'

Both women nodded. Seren felt relieved when she heard the front door close behind him but then she began to tremble at the thought of it all. 'Oh, Marged, what are we to do? I think it's more likely Morgan has killed Mari than Sioni.'

Marged's eyes widened. 'In all the years I've known Sioni, I've never known him to be a murderer, but he is capable of great violence towards those who have crossed him in some way.'

Seren nodded. 'I think the key to all of this is for me to search for Morgan to find out what exactly has happened.'

'Oh no, Seren, you can't do that, not in your condition. He might hurt you again.' Marged's eyes were wide with horror.

'No fear, no, he won't. Whilst he knows I have this child inside me, he won't harm a hair on my head.'

'Well, if that's how you feel, you must still have someone with you for protection. Take my Jim with you, or Ivor or Stan.'

Seren shook her head. 'It had better not be a man as he's insanely jealous.'

Marged stuck out her chin in a determined fashion. 'If that's the case, then I shall come with you and we'll get to the bottom of all of this.'

Seren chewed on her bottom lip. Something about it just didn't add up. It sounded out of character from what she was hearing for Sioni to go to ground, he wasn't that sort of person as a rule. People in the area feared him. But then again, if he had done something that would cause the police to go after him, he'd disappear, particularly if he were facing the gallows.

It had been a long day for both women. 'I'll make us a cup of tea before Jim wakes up,' Marged said. 'We could both do with one.'

Seren couldn't argue with that.

⋆ ⋆ ⋆

Elwyn had attended a meeting in the town about the evils of drink in Merthyr Tydfil and all the other things that went along with it, such as gambling and prostitution, which had got him thinking about targeting certain areas to bring people to the churches and chapels in the town. A group of ministers and other clergymen decided it would be a good idea to go preaching in the more deprived areas like China to save fallen women and men. Today was his turn to go there with a group of parishioners, and even Lucinda had decided to tag along. She was going to get a right shock when she entered the Devil's Lair, Elwyn thought, almost chuckling to himself, especially as Maggie Shanklin had insisted on being one of the deputation. Mary Williams would also be there to speak with the women. She was thriving at the chapel since Seren had encouraged her to come along. How good Seren would have been speaking to the people and winning them over. Lucinda didn't have that sort of touch. Although she was nice enough, she couldn't seem to connect in the same way Seren could.

'And I'm telling you now,' Elwyn preached from outside The House of Blazes to a small crowd which included some of the workers from the wash house, 'flee fornication before it's too late! Every sin that a man doeth is without the body; but he that committeth fornication sinneth against his own body!'

Maggie Shanklin stood beside him and when he paused, she raised her index finger and shouted, 'And the wages of sin is death! Death, I tell you, so repent right now! Throw away your evil alcohol and stay away from the bed chamber of those you are not married to!'

Elwyn glanced at Maggie and shook his head in frustration. 'Please, Mrs Shanklin, don't go frightening people. Remain quiet for time being.'

Maggie nodded. 'Sorry, Mr Evans, I got carried away there for a moment.'

Mary beside her was doing her best not to laugh as Elwyn realised that Maggie was quick to judge others but not that quick in removing the splinter from her own eye.

A few in the crowd began to mutter as a couple began to walk away. 'It's not too late, though, for redemption!' Elwyn shouted at the two women in their gaudy dresses, which made him think they might be prostitutes. 'Remember Mary Magdalene and what our good Lord said to her?'

Both women turned. 'No!' one of them replied.

'Then I shall refresh you. Mary was known as an immoral woman but she washed the feet of Jesus with her tears and used expensive oils, and when Simon, one of his disciples, contested this, Jesus told Mary that her sins were forgiven and her faith had saved her. She was to go in peace . . . So you see, no sin is too big or too small, he saves and forgives all.'

The women paused for a moment, then, whispering to one another, they stayed to hear what else Elwyn had to say to them. Then afterwards, he prayed with the people and told them they were welcome to visit any of the churches and chapels in the town. He also mentioned several coffee taverns and tea shops that were welcoming people to drink there instead of partaking of the sin of alcohol in the area.

For once Maggie remained quiet. Even she seemed to be in awe of Elwyn's preaching. Lucinda though, he observed, kept well away from the women and he noticed she occasionally sniffed, as if to make out they were filthy, when in fact it was the area itself that had an unbelievable stench. Could he really make this woman his wife if she weren't prepared to properly support him and be at his side?

* * *

Seren racked her brain as to where she could search for her husband — she had to find out what had gone on. It appeared he'd left Abercanaid, but first she needed to be sure. A couple of days later, she and Marged left

Aberdare and went to her old house. She still had a key and decided to enter via the back entrance as she felt they'd be less visible that way.

She gently tapped on the back door and when there was no answer, she inserted the key in the lock and turned.

'Oh, do take care,' Marged advised.

A memory was flooding back at her of the evening she had last set foot in the scullery. Morgan had forcefully removed her from the chapel hall and marched her back to the marital home. As she entered the small room, she remembered him pushing her around and demanding answers about what was going on between her and the minister.

He'd been taunting her. The words he said came echoing towards her.

'That man has turned your head!'

'Now go and pay attention to me like you do to him, woman!'

'Whore! Hussy!'

His jealousy had been evident. Then there was the slap across the cheek, slight and stinging at first, but then the slaps became harder and faster and hurt far more as her head snapped back.

'Are you all right, Seren?' Marged's words pierced her memory, like bursting a bubble of despair.

She nodded. There was a big lump in her throat. She swallowed hard. 'Yes, I was just remembering something . . .'

'Then I shall keep quiet in case you remember something of importance,' she reassured her.

Seren was thankful for that. She closed her eyes. Morgan was telling her something about the butcher that Sioni had mentioned. Somehow the beating she'd received had temporarily wiped that memory, but it confirmed what Sioni had said. If she'd been in any doubt that he'd been telling the truth before, now she had no qualms about it. The words came ringing through her ears. 'I'm offloading you to Frank Smedley!' Then he threw back his head and laughed. 'You're soiled goods now! Be thankful he's prepared to take you on!'

She was protesting, saying she didn't want to go, but he was forceful and he knocked her to the floor. That was it, she'd hit her head on the corner of the table and was out of it for a while. But as she came around she knew she had to tell him she was carrying his baby or else they'd both end up in danger.

The house sounded deadly quiet and smelled musty from her absence. There was no sign of anyone keeping it clean and tidy. All the effort she'd put in to keep it spruced up and a home to be proud of, was to no avail. This was now a house and not a home. 'I have to leave,' she said quite suddenly, knowing if she stayed, she'd throw up the contents of her stomach in disgust.

Once outside in the back lane, Marged spoke. 'I don't know what happened to you in there, Seren, but is there anything I can do to help?'

Seren let out a long breath of relief. 'It was horrible. I could see all these pictures before my eyes and feel things that went on that last time I was here. Things I haven't remembered before.

He . . . he . . .' To her horror she began to weep as Marged put her arm around her and hugged her close.

'There, there. It must have been an awful ordeal for you.' Then she allowed her to cry on her shoulder.

Finally, when she'd stopped crying and Marged had passed her a clean handkerchief to dab at her eyes, she said, 'The good thing is, though, the name of the butcher from Cefn Coed that Morgan planned to sell me to came to mind.'

Marged's jaw fell open and then snapped shut. 'He planned to sell you? His own wife?'

'Yes, it is true,' she sniffed. 'Sioni had mentioned it to me and at first I didn't believe it, but when that memory came back at me, the name Frank Smedley came to me. Apparently, according to Sioni, as well as selling me he was going to exchange shops with the man. His cobbler shop for the butcher one. I've no idea though if Morgan had planned turning that into a cobbler shop or keeping it as a butchery business, but it did sound as if he wanted to get away from the village and set himself up somewhere else.'

'Then what we must do is find Frank Smedley to see if he can shine any light on matters,' Marged said softly.

Seren nodded. It was the best lead they had for now and the only option available to them.

* * *

Lucinda was studying the furniture in the long front display window of Argyle and Sons on the High Street. Elwyn sighed. He couldn't for the life of him imagine why she needed to look at furniture right now, it wasn't even as if he'd asked her to marry him as yet. So far, he'd avoided purchasing any of the engagement rings she'd shown him. Why wasn't she getting the message? It wasn't as if she needed to rush into marriage either, time was still on her side, she was only twenty-one years old. At least her father understood, though Elwyn had got the distinct impression that he didn't want his dear daughter messed around. It wasn't that he intended to cause any problems, he just didn't see the point in rushing anything, but Lucinda seemed to have other ideas.

'See here, Elwyn, that's such a beautiful walnut cabinet!' She pointed excitedly at a piece of furniture in the corner of the window. 'And it's a good price too. Couldn't we buy it now ready for later?' She looked at him and blinked several times in expectation.

'Look, Lucinda,' he sighed, 'we aren't really going to need any new furniture at The Manse, there's quite enough there already. And it's good quality too as it's been well looked after by the previous minister!'

She pushed out her bottom lip and pouted, which she was prone to do when she couldn't get her own way. 'Most of it is so ugly and old-fashioned though . . . If you won't buy that one for me then I shall have to ask Daddy!'

Elwyn bristled. *And that will have your father thinking I'm some sort of cheapskate who can't support his dearest daughter*. He shook his head before saying, 'Very well. But that's all I'm paying for today, and we shall ask them to keep it by. I'll place a deposit on it.'

Suddenly, her eyes sparkled and her mouth curved into a huge smile. 'Thank you, so much!' She hugged him to her. She was beginning to remind him of a petulant child, one whose behaviour he didn't much care for. Seren would never have acted this way, in fact he sincerely doubted she would have asked for anything new in the first place as she understood the need to save pennies.

'And don't forget we have that concert to attend tomorrow evening at the church,' she reminded him. He was no longer listening as the vision of the woman he really loved danced before his eyes and he wondered what she was doing right now.

* * *

After taking a horse-drawn omnibus to Cefn Coed, both women alighted at the High Street. Glancing around, the pair kept watchful eyes for a butchery business, but they couldn't see anything that looked remotely like one.

'Are you sure it's Cefn Coed we want?' Marged asked.

Seren nodded. 'Positive. Come on, we'll ask someone.'

A lady in a fur-trimmed hat and bonnet strolled towards them, holding on to the arm of a gentleman in a top hat and a frock coat. They both looked quite well-to-do.

'Excuse me, please,' Seren said, causing the man to tip his head towards her. 'I wonder if you could tell me if there's a butchery business around these parts run by a man called Frank Smedley?'

The man smiled. 'Ah, yes, if you carry on up the street and turn next left, you'll see a side street, it's there.'

'Thank you, sir.' She smiled.

The man nodded and, replacing his hat, went on his way chatting merrily to the woman.

'Well, you were given the correct information then, Seren.' Marged smiled.

When they arrived at the turning, Seren immediately spotted the shop set inside the cobbled street. It had a big white sign with black letters written in Olde English style: F. C. Smedley Purveyor of Best Quality Meats.

As they stepped inside the small shop a little bell jangled overhead and Seren noticed the iron-infused aroma of blood, which almost caused her to gag. She took a deep breath and tried to concentrate on why they were here in the first place. The man behind the counter was in the middle of serving a customer. He was quite rotund and he wore a navy and white striped apron over his white coat and a straw boater hat on his head. His hair was neat and short, he sported mutton chop whiskers and a moustache, and Seren noticed he had nice, kindly-looking eyes.

'Thank you, madam,' he said to the elderly customer as he slipped a newspaper-wrapped package into her basket and took some coins from her outstretched hand. Seren held the glass-fronted door open for the lady and when she'd departed, the butcher looked at them with a big expectant smile on his face. 'And what can I do for you ladies today?'

Seren drew up to the counter. 'Hello, Mr Smedley. I understand that you have had dealings with a Mr Morgan James from Abercanaid?'

He nodded. 'But what of it?'

'I am Mrs James,' she explained, causing the man's eyes to light up. It was then she realised that perhaps he still thought he was buying Morgan's wife! 'Please, you misunderstand. I have heard that he wanted to sell me to you and exchange shops? And to be frank with you, selling me sounds like something from the middle ages!'

The butcher shook his head and held up his hands. 'Look, I haven't done anything wrong, it was his idea . . .'

'No, I'm not saying you have, Mr Smedley. All I want to know is the whereabouts of my husband.'

'B . . . but I've no idea where he is, Mrs James. He was supposed to have called here last week to seal the deal. We'd only conducted a gentleman's handshake previously, but my solicitor had drawn up papers that needed his signature so we can exchange business premises.'

'How do you mean 'seal the deal'?' Seren glared at him. 'Sell me, I suppose!'

'N . . . no actual money was going to change hands, it was to be a simple exchange of properties, that's all. I'm telling the truth, I have employed a solicitor for this.'

'And I bet your solicitor, whoever he is, didn't realise that Seren here was part of that deal?' Marged tapped her foot on the floor.

Frank's face reddened and he ran a finger under his shirt collar as if it was now choking him. 'No, of course not. Look, I'm sorry if I got the wrong end of the stick, but I thought you were a willing party in all of this?'

Seren thrust her chin in the air. 'Evidently not, sir!'

Then her eyes filled with tears. To think her husband could treat her this way, as if she was a mere chattel, was the ultimate humiliation.

Seeing how upset she was, Frank pulled up a chair for her. 'Look, Mrs James, please sit here. It's not good for a woman in your condition to get so upset.' She nodded gratefully and sat. Then he locked the door and turned the sign to 'closed'.

'I am sorry. Truly I am. It was just too tempting an offer for me to refuse. I'm looking for a wife and thought my business would do well in Abercanaid,' he explained.

'But I couldn't be your wife in any case as I am already married,' she protested.

'Well, companion, then.' He smiled.

She shook her head. 'So, you'd have been happy to live in sin with another man's wife?'

Seeing how affronted she was, he shook his head. 'I am sorry, honestly I am. I hadn't thought it all through properly. I have since been offered other women but none of them came up to scratch.'

'By whom?'

'Pardon?'

'By whom were you offered these other women, might I ask?'

'A Mr Watkin who lives in China. For some reason he seemed to get involved and was trying to persuade your husband not to sell you to me.'

At the mention of Sioni's name, Seren's heartbeat quickened. So, he hadn't been lying when he said he'd try to get the man set up with someone else from the wash house or the inn. But obviously none were good enough for Mr Smedley. Probably because he'd seen their loose morals and sampled some of the women already. He obviously wanted someone who looked the part of a respectable wife.

'How did you come to meet Morgan in the first place?' Seren asked, glassy-eyed.

'I don't like admitting this, but I don't see no point in lying to a lady like yourself. It was at that House of Blazes place at China, the place Mr Watkin owns.'

'And you were both there for the same reason, I suppose?' Marged said harshly. 'To sup the ale and sample the goods!'

Frank nodded slowly as his cheeks reddened. 'Yes, we were. We'd often run into one another, either in the bar room or on the upstairs landing . . .' His voice trailed away as if he'd said too much.

'It's all right, Mr Smedley,' Seren said softly, smiling. 'I've known for some time what Morgan was getting up to. Where was he when you last encountered him?'

'It was at The House of Blazes and he was

with that Mari one.'

'I take it you don't know, then?' Seren looked at him to gauge his response.

'Know what?'

'Mari is dead.'

He gulped, then closed his eyes for a moment and opened them again. 'Dead? But how can that be?'

'Her body was found washed up on the banks of the Taff, but apparently she'd struck her head on some sort of rock, which must have happened when she went into the water. The police are looking for Mr Watkin.'

Frank frowned. 'But what would he have to do with it?'

'I've no idea, that's why I'm looking for Morgan as both men have disappeared.'

Frank's eyes flashed and then narrowed. 'You don't think they're both in on it, do you?'

She shook her head. 'I've no idea what's gone on to be honest with you, but if Morgan shows up, please let me know as I want a word with him.'

He nodded, open-mouthed.

'I'll write down Marged's address where I'm currently staying, you can contact me there. But whatever you do, please don't pass the address on to Morgan, will you? He was very cruel to me in the marriage and I fear he could harm me again.'

'No, ma'am. I certainly will not, you and your unborn child could be in danger yourselves.' He laid a comforting hand on her shoulder.

When the women left the shop, Marged took

her by the arm. 'Do you think you did the right thing there, giving Mr Smedley our address?'

'I don't know, Marged, but for now it's the only hope we have.'

* * *

A couple of nights later, Seren was washing up the dishes after the evening meal in the scullery. Marged was upstairs tidying the bedrooms of those men on night shift. The only male in the house was John Lewis, who was studying in his bedroom for his upcoming exams. As it was all quiet, Seren began humming softly to herself, but she was startled by a tapping on the window.

'Seren!' a voice she recognised said. 'Open the back door, please!'

Her heart hammered as she went to unbolt it to see Sioni stood there. The whites of his eyes shone through his grimy face, alert as they darted this way and that as if he feared someone was after him.

'B . . . but what are you doing here? Do you know the police are looking for you?'

He nodded. 'Aye, I do.'

It was then she noticed he was looking as though he'd lost weight and there were bags beneath his eyes. He hadn't shaved for days either. 'Gordon Griffiths is on night shift tonight. I don't know if you realise it but he's a policeman, and he's the one who informed us the Merthyr police are after you. It's not safe for you to stay here as he'll be back early in the morning, but I can give you something to eat if you like?'

He nodded gratefully. 'Look, if I can sleep in the shed overnight, I'll be gone first thing in the morning before that copper returns.'

She nodded. 'I'll have to tell Marged though, she's been worried sick about you.'

'All right, but no one else for now.'

'I'll just nip upstairs and explain to her so she can keep John Lewis out of the way. He's studying in his room but should leave for the pub shortly, all right?'

'Thank you,' he said.

'Keep out of sight in the shed until I tell you it's safe to come out.' She dragged over a blanket that had been covering an old armchair by the fire and handed it to him. 'Here, take this, it's perishing.'

He nodded gratefully as he took it from her and for a moment their eyes locked, and then he left through the back door.

Marged was shocked when Seren whispered to her what had just occurred. Marged said she'd remain upstairs where she could keep an eye on John's movements, until it was safe for Sioni to enter the house.

Eventually, the lodger shut his bedroom door and there was the sound of footsteps and the front door opening and closing behind him. Marged rushed down the stairs to join Seren, where she found Sioni seated at the scullery table with the blanket draped around his shoulders and a plate of bread and cheese in front of him with a steaming mug of tea.

'Aw Sioni, *bach*. What's going on?' Marged asked.

He chewed then swallowed. 'It was the night I was drinking with Morgan. I've never seen him so drunk. Usually he handles his drink well, but he was particularly aggressive that night. I asked him to come outside and have a fight with me. I didn't like the way he'd been shoving Mari around as I knew she'd recently lost their baby. I told him if he was really a man, he'd hit me instead.' He put his head in his hands and for a moment, Seren feared he was about to weep.

'Then what happened?' Marged urged, as Seren stood by patiently waiting, arms folded.

'He threw a few punches at me outside in the alleyway, but I ducked and missed them, but then he started to taunt me, so I knocked him out. I thought I'd killed him so I wasn't about to hang around.'

'Did anyone witness it?' Seren asked.

'No, luckily. But I was so angry for what he'd done to you when you were pregnant, I did want to kill him, mind, Seren. I really did, but somehow I'd stopped myself from laying into him any further. Anyhow, I went for a walk to cool down but when I returned, I couldn't find his body. I'd dragged it around the side of the inn.'

'So, you think he got up and walked away?' Seren blinked.

'I don't know, but then later I couldn't find Mari either . . . so I kept a low profile, stayed at a friend's house. But next day I heard the news that Mari was found drowned. I thought people would blame me and they have. I didn't do anything to her, I swear.' He held up his palms in defence. 'But I might have killed Morgan . . . '

Seren gently touched his shoulder. 'It doesn't make any sense though, Sioni. I don't think you'd killed him, but probably knocked him out for a few minutes and then he got up and walked away. And I do believe you.'

He nodded and smiled.

'Well, you can sleep in the shed tonight,' Marged told him. 'I'll get you a couple more blankets, it'll be cold, mind. Whatever you do, don't come inside the house unless we tell you the coast is clear. What do you intend to do now?'

'Move on, I suppose. I don't want to go to the gallows for something I haven't done.'

'Then you have got to find Morgan!' Seren said sharply.

Sioni nodded. 'If he's alive, that is.'

'No body has been found, has it?' Marged folded her arms and looked at him. He needed sense talking to him as he seemed to be blaming himself for something that might not have happened.

'I don't know . . . ' He rubbed his chin.

Marged shook her head. 'Don't be daft, Sioni. Of course a body hasn't been found, it would have been all over the newspapers.'

'That's where you might be wrong, people have been known to disappear in China, never seen or heard of again, it's that sort of place.'

Seren supposed he did have a point, but she wasn't about to agree with him: they needed to keep his spirits up and she'd help him any way she could. It was the least she could do after all he'd done for her.

Later when she said goodbye to him, she handed him a small bundle wrapped in a large cotton scarf.

'I've put some food together for you,' she said.

He smiled and thanked her, looking all but worn out.

'I have a friend in Merthyr who will take care of you. He's a godly man, a minister. I've written a letter to him, he knows of some of the circumstances regarding my husband. You can trust him; his name is Elwyn Evans and he lives at The Manse beside the chapel in Abercanaid. I've jotted down instructions for you of how to get there. Show him the letter immediately and explain who you are and he will understand.'

Sioni nodded. 'I don't understand why you're being so kind to me, Seren. Why do you trust me so much? I could be telling you any old tale.'

She smiled and, taking his hands inside her own, said, 'I've come to rely a lot on instinct over the years. You did a lot to help me in my time of need, and now you must allow me to help you.'

He nodded. 'I thought the first time I saw you that you reminded me of an angel.' He took her hand and planted a kiss on the back of it.

19

'I think we'll have the Christmas tree in the corner there,' Lucinda was saying. Mrs Johnson rolled her eyes and tutted under her breath as she dragged the large fir tree across the floor.

'Very well,' Elwyn said with a note of resignation. 'Here, let me help you, Mrs Johnson . . . ' The pair exchanged knowing glances. Lucinda was taking over the place and annoying his housekeeper too. Goodness knew what would happen if he did marry her — he had a feeling Mrs Johnson would be out on her ear. The woman had her own way of doing things, as she had for years, but Lucinda had grand ideas that didn't quite fit in with Mrs Johnson. The last thing he wanted was the women at each other's throats, so he was quite pleased when they were all interrupted by a knock at the door.

Respite at last!

As Mrs Johnson went to answer, she was called away by Lucinda to try the tree in yet another corner, so Elwyn went to answer the door himself. He pulled the door open to be met with the eyes of a man who looked like he had seen a lot of life. His face was ingrained with dirt but his eyes sparkled beneath the grime. He was a large-set man who had a physique very like Morgan James.

'Mr Evans?' he asked, clutching his cloth cap in his hands.

'Yes, sir, what can I do for you?'

'I'm Twm Sion Watkin . . . ' the man said.

Elwyn trembled. So, this was the man who had taken care of Seren and was feared by most, particularly in China, the man he had been trying to find — and now, without warning, he was on his doorstep.

'What brings you to my door?' Elwyn asked, worrying if he was now in danger and how he'd found his address.

The man cleared his throat. 'We have a mutual friend, Seren James. She sent me here. Please, I need a place of safety.'

Elwyn breathed out a sigh of relief, then nodded at him. 'Come through to the chapel and we'll speak in my office.' He beckoned. He didn't want to risk Lucinda or Mrs Johnson seeing him at the house. He decided not to inform either of the women where he was going. He hoped they were too wrapped up in decorating The Manse for Christmas to notice his absence, and ushered the man inside the chapel and towards his office.

'Please take a seat.' Elwyn closed the door behind them and took a seat himself. The man glanced around the room as if in awe of the religious works of art on the wall. 'So, Mr Watkin, why do you need a place of safety and is Seren all right?'

He nodded and smiled. 'Aye, she's fine. It's the police; they're after me, see, but for once, I've done no wrong.'

Elwyn frowned. 'I don't understand. What is it they think you've done, Mr Watkin?'

He frowned. 'Please, call me Sioni. It's that

prostitute Morgan was knocking around with. She was found dead on the banks of the Taff, but I swear I didn't kill her.'

'Then why do the police assume so?'

'Because on the night of her murder I was in the company of Morgan. We started out as butties but ended up as enemies, fighting one another . . . ' He carried on explaining all that had happened that fateful night and how the finger of suspicion was now pointed at him as he thought he was the last one to see the man alive.

Elwyn rubbed his chin. 'I am inclined to believe you, but I don't really know you. I've learned that you were kind to Seren and for that I'm grateful. But there's no way I can harbour you at The Manse though.'

'How about the chapel then?' Sioni asked hopefully.

Elwyn shook his head. 'That wouldn't work as parishioners are back and forth here a lot, particularly as it's the Christmas season. I have an idea though,' he said, as Sioni looked at him in expectation.

* * *

'What? Me put up a known criminal from China?' Anwen's jaw almost hit the floor with shock. 'I've heard talk about that man and he has a fearsome reputation.'

'Look, the man helped Seren escape Morgan, he can't be all bad, can he? Better than Morgan James at any rate,' Elwyn said firmly. 'It was Seren who sent him to me in the first place.'

Anwen nodded. 'I'm still wary though, Elwyn,' she said, glancing at Macs who was lying contentedly on a rug by the fireplace.

'And I understand that. But if he comes here, it could be protection for you in case Morgan returns. After what happened the last time he showed up, you could be at risk yourself!'

'*Oh fy ddaioni!*' Anwen was off jabbering in Welsh as she did when she was alarmed or upset by something. Finally she paused and, holding the palm of her hand to her chest, said breathlessly, 'Sorry, Mr Evans, but you've shocked me so much this morning.'

'It wasn't my intention to do so, but it seems the best solution all around. Mr Watkin can remain hidden here as it's far enough away from the village and he'll be around if Morgan should bother you. You have to remember Morgan's on the run himself as it looks as if he was the one who murdered Mari. He could well bother you again if he's seeking a place of refuge.'

Anwen shook her head. 'Macs here will see him off.'

As much as Elwyn didn't doubt that the dog would try to protect his owner, he might be no match for Morgan's hobnail boot, or any food the man might have laced with poison. 'Please, Mrs Llewellyn, think about it for your own sake until the man is brought to justice.'

'Well, how does anyone know the man murdered Mari in the first place? There's no evidence of that, is there?'

'No, but you know full well how cruel he was to Seren and apparently . . . ' he paused for a moment as Anwen watched him in anticipation, 'it was his fault that Mari lost her own child.' He shook his head sadly.

'His fault?' Anwen narrowed her eyes.

'He kicked the woman to the floor.'

'Any man who can kick a pregnant woman is not a man in my book! It's just as well Seren is living in the other valley. Is there any news of her?'

'According to Sioni, she's fine, she's the one who sent him to me looking for help. Look, if you decide to take him in, he can tell you all about it and how she's doing.'

Anwen's eyes lit up and Elwyn realised he had got through to the woman at last. 'All right, fetch him here. I can well understand you can't keep him at The Manse with nosy parkers like Maggie Shanklin around.'

Elwyn smiled. 'I knew you'd do the right thing, Mrs Llewellyn. He's outside. I left him by the barn, not too close to the house, not to alarm Macs.'

'I'll tell you what I'll do.' Anwen's chin jutted out. 'I'll see if Macs takes to him or not, he's a good judge of character.'

Elwyn sighed. He hoped the dog would take to the man for Seren's sake as if he had to turn Sioni away, he'd feel he'd let her down, yet again. 'Is it all right if I bring him in to meet you then?'

Anwen nodded and then looked at Macs. 'Aye, go on, we'll soon see.'

Elwyn left the farmhouse to return to Sioni's side. The man stood slumped against the wooden wall of the barn with his head down. He seemed as if he needed some luck and for the first time, the minister's heart went out to him. He touched him on the shoulder. 'Mrs Llewellyn seemed reluctant to take you in at first, and to be honest, I can't say I blame her. She's had a lot of opposition from folk in the village who over the years have turned against her, so she finds it hard to trust people. You are, after all, a complete stranger to her. But . . .'

Sioni lifted his head, his eyes questioning. 'But what?'

'But I think she is prepared to give you a chance as you have taken care of Seren lately. Seren is so precious to her, the daughter she never had. But there is one condition.'

Sioni angled his head curiously and pushed back the brim of his flat cap so he could see the minister more clearly. 'Oh, aye?'

'Yes, she's only happy to take you in if her sheepdog, Macs, takes to you. She reckons he's a good judge of character.'

Sioni, who had been looking quite serious up until now, chuckled. 'She sounds a right character herself. Why did some of the villagers turn against her then?'

'Oh, she is quite a character, believe me. Some think she's some sort of witch.'

'A witch?' Sioni narrowed his eyes. 'How come?'

'Because she makes lotions and potions for various ailments.'

'So, she's a healer of sorts? Not a blessed witch?'

'Precisely! Now do you still want to meet her and see what her dog makes of you?'

'Aye, lead the way, Mr Evans!' he said, slapping the minister on the back. Elwyn was beginning to like Sioni and could see why Seren maybe liked him too. Although in stature he looked quite similar to Morgan, he had another side to him that probably not many got to see, he decided.

As Elwyn opened the farmhouse door, Macs leapt to his feet and headed towards them. For a moment, Elwyn felt a prickle of fear run down his spine, but instead of attacking, the dog began sniffing around the man's legs. Then Sioni was on his knees, patting the dog on the head and hugging him. 'Macs looks just like a sheepdog I had as a young boy!' he said, looking up at Elwyn with a big grin on his face. 'He used to try to protect us whenever my father got angry.' Elwyn looked on in awe as he watched the man's eyes become glassy with unshed tears. He was right about Sioni; he had a softer side that few would have suspected.

Anwen stood looking at the scene in front of her with great amusement. 'You'll do,' she said. 'There's not many he'll take to straight away like that.'

Sioni stood. 'Thank you, Mrs Llewellyn. I am grateful for you taking me in here. I won't be no bother to you and I'll help you around the farm while I'm here.'

Anwen sniffed. 'Yes, I'll work you hard, mind,' she said, winking at Elwyn. 'Meanwhile, you can both join me for a bowl of cawl and some bread

I baked this morning. Then you can tell us all about how Seren is doing. I'm really missing that girl.'

Sioni nodded enthusiastically.

As they sat eating the meaty soup, Anwen's eyes were on Sioni. '*Duw, duw*, you look like you haven't eaten for weeks!' she said, as he shovelled great big spoonfuls into his mouth.

He laid down his spoon for a moment. 'Please excuse my manners, Mrs Llewellyn, but this is the best grub I've tasted in ages.'

'Well, it's nice to see someone enjoy their food.' Her eyes fell on Elwyn. 'The same can't be said for you though, Elwyn. Is anything wrong?'

He shook his head. There was no fooling Anwen, but how could he discuss things with Sioni around? As if reading his mind, Anwen said, 'Mr Watkin looks dead beat. I've got a spare bedroom set up that Seren used to use, you can sleep there when you've finished your food.'

Sioni nodded and yawned. 'I've been sleeping rough for so long I've forgotten what a real bed feels like.'

Before too long he had risen from the table and Anwen showed him to the bedroom. When she returned, she put the kettle on the fire. 'Now then, Elwyn, tell me what's wrong. We'll have a nice cuppa while we chat.'

It was no use, he couldn't keep things from Anwen, she was a trusted friend. 'Yes, you're right. Something is wrong; I'm missing Seren terribly.'

'But aren't things going well with Lucinda?'

He shook his head. 'No, they're not. I feel my life is no longer my own. She's trying to take over The Manse and getting under Mrs Johnson's feet! The women just don't see eye to eye. But it's far more than that. I don't feel she shares my passion for things!'

'How so?' Anwen quirked a puzzled brow.

'I've been very involved in preaching around the streets of China and other rough areas of the town, talking to the prostitutes and drunkards. A group of us ministers are trying to save these people from themselves, but Lucinda, she just looks down on them. She pretends to care but I know she doesn't really, not like . . . '

'Like Seren, you mean?'

He nodded, then gazed into the flames of the fire.

Anwen sighed deeply. 'Aye, she's a good 'un, is Seren. When Sioni wakes up I'm going to try to find out more about what's going on with her. He's the last of us to set sight on her. It shows how caring she is to send him here. But Elwyn, what if Morgan has killed that Mari? It might mean that he'll come in search of Seren.'

Elwyn looked at the woman's rheumy eyes which now looked glazed over. 'I have thought of that. If he comes anywhere near Abercanaid, I'm calling the police. I was ready to give him a chance when he came to the chapel that time to talk to me, but people like him never seem to change. They make all sorts of promises to get what they want. At least you'll be safe here with Sioni to protect you.'

She nodded. 'And Macs too.' She smiled. Elwyn had no doubt that the dog was a comfort for Anwen, but he could see the old woman was missing Seren dreadfully. 'So, then, what are you going to do about Lucinda? You're not officially engaged as yet?'

'No, we're not, but it would upset both my parents and hers if I called it all off; it would bring humiliation on both families.'

'And Lucinda herself, of course,' Anwen added.

'Yes, her more so than anyone. Oh Anwen, what should I do?'

She stood and patted his shoulder. 'Pray about it, *bach*,' she said. 'I'll go and wet the tea.'

He didn't want to break down in front of the woman, but what was the matter with him?

When Anwen returned with the cup of tea, she handed it to Elwyn while she took the seat the other side of the fire-place. 'It seems to me that you're thinking so much about everyone else, Elwyn, that you rarely have time for yourself these days.'

He nodded, then took a sip of the strong brew. If there was one thing he could say about Anwen, it was that she made a good brew, unlike Lucinda who hadn't a clue in the kitchen. And if she wanted to run The Manse, she'd need someone like Mrs Johnson on board — that woman was worth her weight in gold. A domesticated lady, Lucinda was not.

'Look, Elwyn, I know it was me who sort of encouraged you to enter into a relationship with Lucinda in the first place, but if you are going to end it, you need to do it now before it's too late to get out of. Once you've slipped that engagement ring on her finger, there'll be no stopping her then. Her parents will be throwing good money at a trousseau for her, a wedding gown and breakfast. There'll be people at your wedding you simply do not know. It shall be humiliating for all concerned if you jilt that young woman at the altar!'

Elwyn blinked several times. 'I'd never do that to her. I wouldn't want to hurt her.'

'Maybe you think you wouldn't, but it's easy to get swept along with things. If I were you, I'd speak with her as soon as possible. Thrash it all out with her to find if you're singing from the same hymn sheet, but I doubt you are from what you're telling me today.'

He grimaced. This was going to be far harder than he ever imagined. What on earth was he going to do?

20

Seren felt a flutter in her tummy as she stood in the scullery wiping the dishes. She set down the final dish on the draining board and took a seat by the table as she patted her stomach.

'What's wrong?' Marged's eyes were full of concern.

'I think I just felt a sharp kick then. Not just that butterfly sensation I experienced a few weeks back, but a proper good kick. Ooh, I just felt it again.'

Marged chuckled. 'I know what that feels like. Well, at any rate, felt like. It was quite some time ago, mind. Maybe you should be resting in the afternoons now. We've done most of our work here for time being, so off with you to have a lie on the bed for an hour or so. I'll bring you up a cup of hot milk.'

Seren smiled. 'There's good you are to me.' Then she removed her pinafore and hung it on one of the nails on the back of the scullery door along with the shawls, men's overcoats and jackets. She'd worked it out with Marged, she was about five months gone and it was now mid-December, so the baby would be due sometime next April. She still couldn't take it in that soon there'd be a newborn about the place.

Once she got to her room, she let out a long sigh and sat on the bed to unlace her ankle boots which she placed in the corner and lay back on the bed, well propped up with pillows. It was such a relief to be able to rest as she'd been up since five-thirty to catch the men coming in from their night shifts. She'd prepared their breakfasts whilst Marged had helped them scrub off the coal dust of a hard night's graft in the yard outside. It had been freezing too. They'd looked blue as anything when they'd tramped into the scullery and had stood around the fire-place, stamping their feet and flexing their fingers to keep warm. Then after several hot cups of tea, bowls of porridge, plates of thick toast spread with jam and a couple of kippers, they'd made their way to bed. For it was not really their breakfast in the normal sense, more like their evening meal, so they'd eaten well. Marged was mindful of that, being married to a collier herself.

Sometime later, there was a gentle knock at the door. Marged entered carrying a cup of milk.

'Thank you, Marged,' Seren whispered, conscious of not wanting to wake the sleeping men in the other rooms.

'Is there anything wrong, *cariad*?' Marged whispered back at her, then she handed the cup to Seren and sat on the side of the bed with her hands folded neatly on her lap.

'I'm hoping Sioni has found sanctuary with Elwyn at Abercanaid,' she said thoughtfully.

'Yes, let's hope he has. If your husband turned up it might put paid to all the speculation around the place.'

Seren nodded. The mystery was, where was Morgan and what had he done?

* * *

Morgan awoke with a start and grunted. Where was he? He had a raging headache and his tongue felt sore and swollen, about twice its usual size.

As he took in his surroundings and recognised various items of furniture, he realised he was back in his own familiar bed in Abercanaid. But how had he got here and why was he back here?

He remembered, as fragments of what had happened came flying back at him like shards of glass from a shattered windowpane. He was supposed to have signed that damn contract to exchange business premises with the butcher. But in the event, he hadn't bothered going to the solicitor's office as he'd got himself in a drunken stupor in the company of Sioni at The House of Blazes. He fought to think what had happened next. Yes, he'd got into some sort of disagreement with the man, so bad that they'd ended up having a fight outside the inn in the alleyway. Fists had flown, and although he was strong, he'd been no match for the man as he'd once been a mountain fighter and never lost a fight yet. He was still as strong as an ox.

But what had it been about? One moment they were putting the world to rights, the next thing they were arguing over . . . Seren! Yes, that was it. It had been obvious to him from the way Sioni had spoken about her that he was after her for himself. He'd seen red then and, fuelled by the alcohol, thrown the first punch. And what a fight it had been too. He'd held his own for all of two minutes, then got knocked spark out by the man's furious fist! He'd gone down like a sack of spuds and when he'd recovered consciousness, Sioni was nowhere to be seen. He'd recalled now how he'd dragged himself to his feet and carried on drinking at the inn. When he'd asked the barman where Sioni was, he didn't seem to know.

Mari had shown up later, but she'd played on his wick during that time. Flaunting her breasts in front of him, and then when she realised he wasn't playing the game, preferring to sup his pint of ale in silence, she'd flounced off in a huff to sit on the knee of one of the men from the ironworks. Humiliated, he'd dragged her by the hair, kicking and screaming through the door of the inn, and once outside, he'd given her a good hard slap to bring her to her senses. But she'd taunted him big time. The next thing he remembered was they were near the river and he was dangling her from Jackson's Bridge with his trembling hands around her throat, threatening to drop her over the side. He'd seen real fear on her face then as the whites of her eyes were on show and appeared to bulge out of her head. He swore he didn't mean to, but he released her and she let out a blood-curdling scream as she fell from his grasp, tumbling in the air and hitting the water below with a huge splash as her scream faded to oblivion. There'd just been the sound of the river fast flowing towards the port of Cardiff. Then her lifeless body drifted down south and when she was out of sight, he'd turned and walked away. No one was around, no one to see or hear what had just happened. It was like it had never happened at all. He'd reckoned though if he had been spotted it might be dangerous for him, so he'd made his way to Abercanaid to ensure if the police arrived looking for him, they'd think he'd been there all the time. So, he'd made a point of calling into the Llwyn-yr-Eos pub and having a pint, so that he was seen by some of the villagers. He'd even nodded to Maggie Shanklin in the street, who had scowled at him and retreated inside her house like a scalded cat. But he'd reassured himself, at least he'd been seen by people. Now he had an alibi. He was going to pretend he'd been working in his shop in the back room most of the evening, out of sight, and then gone for a pint to the pub. Anyhow, prostitutes in China were ten a penny. Mari wouldn't be the first to meet her Maker in such a gruesome way, and she certainly would not be the last.

* * *

The Salvation Army were playing Christmas carols in Merthyr town and Seren was Christmas shopping alone. 'Hark the Herald Angels Sing' brought a tear to her eye as she thought of her own dear father who'd loved that particular tune. She planned on taking some presents to her mother and sister and something for Anwen too, though she'd have to leave her gift with her mother as climbing that mountain would be near impossible in her condition.

The shops on the High Street were nicely decorated with wreaths of holly and ivy in their windows and their displays were more prominent than usual. All sorts of poultry hung from the eaves of the poulterer's store: chickens, geese, ducks, and there was a huge turkey on display on a silver platter in the window. Seren wondered who on earth could afford that? Maybe someone from the Thomastown area? And definitely the Crawshay family. They'd wine and dine like kings and queens this Christmas whilst the poor in the hovels of the town would barely scrape by. Some would go hungry no doubt and some, maybe those dosed up to the hilt on alcohol, would not even realise it was Christmas Day at all.

She purchased a pretty straw bonnet edged with a green silk ribbon for her sister from the milliner, who proudly packed it away in a hat box tied with string. For her mother, she bought a pearl brooch, and for Anwen, a new shawl to keep her warm. Her eyes darted around the High Street wondering if she'd encounter Elwyn and his fiancée-to-be once again. She wished him every happiness in the world now she had got over hearing about his new love interest. It had hurt to begin with, but she couldn't expect him to hold a candle for her for the rest of his life. Divorces weren't easy to come by for working-class folk. They were too expensive and there was a lot of stigma attached to them. Marriage was expected to last a lifetime in her world, unfortunately. The only divorces she heard about were those of society folk in places like London. They weren't for the likes of her.

She had toyed with buying him a present too, but she guessed that Lucinda wouldn't be happy about that, so she let that idea float away from her.

She was just rounding the corner at John Street in search of a hansom cab when she glimpsed a familiar-looking face. Those sharp beady eyes and beak-like nose meant it was none other than Mrs Shanklin! She was about to retrace her footsteps but too late, the woman had spotted her. A big smile appeared on the woman's face and her eyes gleamed like two lumps of coal on the fire.

'Seren!' she exclaimed. 'How lovely to see you. 'Tain't too often I'm in Merthyr town and to see you today 'tis surprising. Where are you living now? Cefn?'

Seren cleared her throat and deliberately decided to lie. 'Yes. Cefn Coed, Mrs Shanklin. And how are you?' She hoped to change the subject, but Maggie Shanklin was having none of it. 'I'm fine, dear. 'Tis glad I am to see you an' all as I wanted to tell you I saw that husband of yours in Abercanaid last night.'

Seren's mouth fell open with surprise and she blinked several times. 'Where, Mrs Shanklin?'

'Back at the family home. Looks like he's ditched that floozie sort. There's been no sign of life in the house for days on end, it's been as dark as a coal cellar whenever I've passed by. No candles lit in the evenings, and despite it being perishing weather, no smoke coming from the chimney, either. Then your Morgan comes back all alone one night; I saw him going in after he'd been to the Llwyn pub, staggering he was, blind drunk. If I were you I'd get down there now to keep your eye on him, my girl! You're in with a good chance if that floozie one is out of the picture!' She shot a knowing nod at Seren.

A shiver skittered down Seren's spine. Maggie had worked her up again and she couldn't help her emotion getting the better of her. 'I'd rather have no father for my baby than have that man anywhere near either one of us!' she said, sticking her chin out in determination and trying not to cry in front of the woman. Maggie would love to see that.

'Ah, I see, dear . . . ' A salacious smile curved her lips. 'So, what you're hinting at is that baby you're carrying, 'tis not Morgan's child after all?'

'Certainly not, Mrs Shanklin. Though it's none of your business, this baby is definitely Morgan's child!'

'I see, it's just that some in the village were speculating since you're very friendly with Elwyn Evans, like,' she lowered her voice a notch, 'and he is such a handsome man to be sure, that maybe . . . *you know* . . .'

Seren gritted her teeth. 'Maybe I know what, Mrs Shanklin? Go on, spit it out!'

'Well, maybe 'tis the minister's child you're carrying and not Morgan's? Rumour is that's why Morgan took up with that floozie in the first place.'

A burst of anger shot around Seren's body, making her realise she had to get away from the woman before she did or said something she'd later regret. She spotted a hansom cab pulling up at the kerb, so she pushed past the woman to get to it before a couple walking down the street could do the same.

'Well, really, some people don't like to hear the truth!' was the last thing she heard Mrs Shanklin say as Seren clambered into the cab. She turned her head away so she wouldn't have to face the interfering busybody. She'd had more than enough from her for one day. But it had been useful bumping into her though, as now she knew Morgan was back in Abercanaid and she could have it out with him to get Sioni off the hook.

* * *

Elwyn had to escape The Manse for a moment, he couldn't stick hearing Lucinda wittering on for one more second. At the final hour of deciding to tell her he wanted to break off their relationship, she had looked at him with doe eyes and began jabbering on about how excited she was about Christmas and how she'd help host the Christmas dinner at The Manse. It would be a lovely day as, after the morning Christmas service at the chapel, both families would sit together and enjoy their dinner. On and on she was going, driving him to distraction, so he made an excuse about going to see one of his parishioners, which up until now he hadn't intended to do, but he thought he'd call to see Maggie Shanklin to see how she was coping with Tom being away and to enquire if he would be returning during the festive season. As he rapped on the door, he became aware of a familiar figure striding purposely towards him.

It couldn't be! Yes, it was. Seren!

He released the door knocker and bounded

towards her. On seeing him there she almost dropped her packages, looking as if she didn't know quite what to say or to do.

'Seren? Are you back for good?' He blinked.

'No,' she said breathlessly. 'I'm just visiting Mam today and leaving some gifts. I decided to call to my house as I bumped into Mrs Shanklin in the town and . . .'

He banged the palm of his hand against his forehead. 'Oh, and what has she been saying now? I was just about to call to see her.'

'You won't find her in, she's still in the town. She was digging for dirt as usual and baiting me into losing my temper!' Seren said crossly. She could hardly tell him the woman had suggested it was he who was the father of her baby. 'But the most important thing is that she told me Morgan returned to the house last night.'

'Goodness gracious me. But you mustn't go in there alone.' He narrowed his eyes.

She shook her head. 'I need to find out if he harmed Mari. I have to, I'm the only one who understands what that woman must have gone through. I think if he'll tell anyone, it will be me. What about Sioni, though, did he call to see you?' she asked, suddenly remembering how she'd sent him to ask Elwyn for help.

'He's fine. I couldn't take him in at The Manse, people would realise he was around, so I took him to Anwen's home.'

Her eyes grew large. 'Anwen? I can't imagine she'd take him in.'

'Well, she has, and they're getting along famously. She only took him on the provision that her sheepdog liked him. And he did, immediately.' He smiled, causing Seren to smile too. Was he imagining it, or was she blushing?

'That's good to know.'

'Please, Seren, let me come in the house with you?' he implored.

'No, you must stay outside, please. Take my packages. I'll scream and shout if anything happens, all right?'

He nodded and took the packages from her arms.

'Take care in there,' he warned. 'I'll head around to the back entrance, make sure you leave the scullery door unlocked.'

* * *

As she entered the house using her key, she wondered if there was anyone there at all. All seemed silent except for the ticking of the mantel clock, which she realised indicated that Morgan had definitely been to the home as it was set to the correct time.

In the stillness, she listened carefully. Apart from the soft tick of the clock, she heard nothing. The place looked untidy and uncared for, but it no longer upset her. This wasn't a home to her any more.

Then she heard it, a gentle snoring sound coming from the upstairs bedroom above. Remembering what Elwyn had said to her about ensuring the back door was unlocked, she tiptoed out there and turned the key. She opened the door a fraction to see him stood outside, with her packages neatly stacked against the wall.

'Any sign?' he whispered.

She nodded. 'Yes, he's in bed sleeping by the sound of it. He's probably had a skinful of beer. I'm going to wake him up and confront him about Mari's death.'

'Let me come with you, please?' Seren could see the pleading in his eyes.

'I can't, as soon as he sees you, he'll go mad. He's such a jealous man and he already thinks something has gone on between us. I need to hear the truth first.'

'Very well.' Elwyn nodded his head in silent contemplation. 'Remember though to shout or scream if you're afraid. I won't have him touch a hair on your head.'

She smiled, realising for the first time just how much he cared for her.

She touched his hand to reassure him, then made her way tentatively up the stone staircase to the sounds of her husband's snores, which were now getting louder by the second. The fumes of alcohol hit her hard and she felt like retreating. After all, he need never know she'd been here in the first place. But if she did that, then maybe they'd never discover the truth about the night of Mari's death and Sioni might remain in the frame for it — a marked man. A man who might swing from the gallows at Cardiff or Brecon sometime in the future.

As she approached the bed where her husband lay fully clothed on his stomach, she resisted the urge to lift one of the pillows and smother him with it. It was no use, she had to know the truth.

'Morgan,' she said softly.

He grunted, but otherwise did not stir.

'Morgan!' she said louder this time and she shook his shoulder.

The dribble from his mouth had pooled on his pillow and he slowly opened one eye. 'Mari,' he said quietly. 'Mari, you're back here with me.' A smile danced upon his lips and he turned himself over and pulled himself into a sitting position, then rubbed his sleep-encrusted eyes. He blinked when he saw it was Seren stood before him. 'Seren?' He narrowed his gaze. 'What are you doing here?'

She sat on the bed beside him. 'Morgan, you know that Mari is dead, don't you?'

He shook his head. 'For a moment, I'd forgotten all about it. I thought you were her come back to life as I was dreaming about her.'

'Morgan, tell me what happened.'

He looked at her as if gauging her response. 'And if I do that, will you come back home? I need a woman to warm my bed!'

She realised she was going to have to lie to get the truth out of him. 'Yes, I'll come back, of course I will,' she said with a slight tremor to her voice. He was inches away from her and inside her there was a life that needed protection. Maybe she was stupid to have asked Elwyn to remain outside, but she was right about one thing though, if he saw another man at her side, he'd get so angry.

He smiled. 'Come and lie with me now,' he said, patting the bed.

This wasn't what she was planning at all, she

realised with dread. 'All right, but first, I want to know what happened.'

He wiped his forehead. 'Water!' he demanded. 'My mouth feels dry.'

'Very well, I'll fetch you a cup of water, but then you need to tell me what happened that night.'

He nodded.

Her heart was beating so fast and hard she feared he'd hear it. She was back at his side within minutes and handed the cup to him. But he refused to take it. 'Go on, hold it there like you'd hold it for that bloody minister!' he snarled.

Why had his previous good mood changed?

'I don't know what you mean.' This wasn't going well at all.

'At the chapel, I bet you were always making him cups of tea and baking him cakes to butter him up, like?'

She cleared her throat, realising the need to keep her composure. Swallowing her disappointment down, she said, 'Yes, I helped at the chapel, but it was the villagers I was helping and making tea for, not Mr Evans.' She was trying to keep her voice level. 'And as for baking cakes . . . I only bake them for my own husband.' The last part was a lie because she had once baked Elwyn a cake and taken it to him at the chapel, but telling Morgan that would make him furious.

'He denies any wrongdoing on his part, so I reckon it was you who took a shine to him, throwing yourself at him — he's still a man after all.'

She looked at her husband blankly, hardly

believing her ears. 'Of course I haven't thrown myself at him!'

'Then what about that night I showed up at the chapel hall? I could see two cups there then, and you looked as if you were waiting for him to return!'

'Yes, I was. He'd gone to see Mrs Shanklin who wanted to speak to him in private, and although I'd wanted to walk back to Anwen's on my own, he insisted I wait for him to accompany me as it was getting dark.'

'How very charitable of him!' Morgan spat out the words, then he was on his feet, barefoot on the floorboards. He snatched the cup from her hands and drank it down in one go, wiping his mouth with the back of his hand.

'It's not what you think,' she said nervously, now feeling like screaming for help. 'So, tell me, what happened to Mari?'

He threw back his head and laughed. 'What do you think happened?' There was a long pause as she waited for him to speak, which made her feel uncomfortable. Then her heart began beating like a drum as she realised what the answer would be, but she had to hear it from him. 'The bitch wound me up so much that evening, humiliating and taunting me in the pub, so my intention was to teach her a bloody lesson!'

'A lesson?'

She saw the wild look in his eyes that she recognised all too well.

'Yes, a lesson she'd never forget. I dangled her over Jackson's Bridge. It was to frighten her at first, but once my hands had clamped around her throat, I found myself squeezing harder and harder. Her eyes were bulging out of her head and then I let go. It was one way to silence the slut!'

He was looking quite pleased with himself and that annoyed Seren. 'So, you killed her?'

'Yes, I did!' She noticed a small smile dance upon his lips as he revelled in the memory of it all. 'And then she fell in the water.'

'And you didn't go in after her to rescue her?'

'Nah, it was no use by then, it was evident she was dead as her head must have hit some rocks below . . .'

Seren closed her eyes at the thought of it, then opened them again. She needed to know everything. 'So, Sioni wasn't responsible for her death nor involved in it at all?'

He shook his head. 'No. I can show you what I did if you like?'

'No!' she shouted, shaking her head as she realised he meant what he said. She quickly stepped back from him to the top of the open stairs as he came lunging towards her with arms outstretched, hands splayed as if ready to repeat what he'd done to Mari. But as she side-stepped out of the way, he fell forwards and tumbled down the stone steps, crashing heavily to the bottom.

In horror, she screamed loudly. It was a guttural scream as she couldn't believe what had happened, and it brought Elwyn running inside the house. He glanced at Morgan's lifeless body and then up at her.

'Is he dead?' she asked.

Elwyn's face was ashen as he nodded. 'It looks

like it to me.' He knelt down to check for any signs of life. Looking up at her, he said gravely, 'I can't find a pulse in his neck. I'd better go and fetch Doctor Owen. What happened?'

It was only then she burst into tears as huge wracking sobs shook her body. 'I . . . I'd got him to a . . . admit he murdered Mari, then he said he was going to show me how he strangled her. He lunged at me but I stepped out of the way and he tumbled downstairs. I feel so guilty, Elwyn,' she cried. 'It was an accident!'

He stood and made his way up the stairs, then took her in his arms, allowing her to cry it out. 'You've done nothing wrong, you were only trying to protect yourself and your baby,' he soothed, stroking her hair as he allowed her tears to soak his jacket. Finally, he dipped his hand into his pocket and offered her his handkerchief.

'But it's the number of times I've wished he'd fall down those stairs.' She sniffed, as she wiped away her tears. 'Many a time when he was drunk and I've helped him up them, I've wished I had it in me to let go so that he'd topple down them and I'd never have to suffer at his hands again . . .'

He held her closer to him and kissed the top of her head. 'But it's still not your fault and in any case, even if you thought such things, the thing is you never acted on those thoughts, you're too kind a person to do so. He brought his own death on himself by trying to get at you. If he hadn't tried to strangle you, he'd never have fallen, and I'm convinced if you hadn't moved out the way when you did, it would be you and your own unborn baby lying dead at the foot of these stairs, not him.'

She nodded, realising the truth behind his words as a shiver coursed down her spine. 'I suppose you're right,' she said finally. 'Maybe it was my protective motherly instincts that saved us both in the end.'

He smiled. 'I'm certain it was, Seren. Now I'm going to fetch Doctor Owen.'

'Please don't leave me here with him.' Even though there was no sign of life in Morgan's body, she couldn't bear to stay under the same roof as him.

'How about I take you round to Mrs Shanklin's?'

'Oh no!' She held up the palms of her hands in protest. 'The last thing I need is to go there, she'll have the guts out of me in no time and it'll be all over the village. In any case, she's probably not arrived home yet.'

'All right, I can see the sense of that,' he said. 'I'll walk you to your mother's house and I'll bring the doctor back here on my own and explain what happened.'

Relieved, she nodded. Draping an arm around her shoulders, he led her down the stairs.

* * *

As Elwyn accompanied Seren to her mother's home, someone was watching from The Manse window. There was *that woman* again, the one who'd been on the High Street in the town a few weeks ago. What did she mean to him? The way he was guiding her protectively along Chapel

Street with his hand placed on the small of her back, what was going on here? She wasn't just a parishioner, this was someone Elwyn was in love with. When she thought back to that day in Merthyr town, his eyes had lit up when he went off to speak to her. With a sinking heart, Lucinda realised that Elwyn wasn't in love with her. He never had been. It had all been an illusion on her part and it felt as if she'd just been deluged with an ice-cold bucket of water.

21

'Yes, life is definitely extinct.' Doctor Owen removed the stethoscope from his ears and closed Morgan's eyes gently with his fingertips. Then he stood and, facing Elwyn, asked, 'So, what exactly happened here?'

Elwyn explained the circumstances as the doctor stood on, nodding gravely. 'Well, I know he wasn't easy for Seren to live with and he caused her a great deal of grief and harm. In my opinion, as I can tell he was still under the influence of alcohol going by the smell of him, there is no need for anyone to know the details. We'll just say you called to the house and found him dead at the foot of the stairs, then came to get me. No need to involve Mrs James at all as it won't be good for her or the baby.'

Elwyn let out a long breath. 'Thank you, Doctor. Mrs Shanklin would make a mountain out of a molehill and say Seren had pushed him, probably.'

The doctor nodded with understanding. 'I think it would be a good idea if I called to see her to check her over as it must have been a huge shock for her, especially as he'd threatened her beforehand. I've no doubt if she hadn't stepped out of the way like that, he might have killed both her and their unborn child.'

'You're right, Doctor, my thoughts exactly. He admitted to Seren he killed Mari. The only problem is if we keep the circumstances quiet, Seren can't explain to the police what he told her. Maybe it would be best to come clean and explain she was with him when he died?'

Doctor Owen rubbed his chin in thoughtful contemplation for a moment. 'Maybe it would be best if we allow Seren to decide that, don't you think?'

Elwyn nodded, realising the doctor was right.

* * *

Seren had just settled down with a cup of tea in her hand when there was a knock at the door.

Her mother frowned. 'After all you've just been through, *cariad*, I'm in no mood for any visitors today.'

She went off to answer and Seren could hear the sound of a refined female voice she didn't recognise at the door.

'But I must see her at once!' she heard the woman say.

'My daughter has just had a nasty shock and needs to rest!' her mother was protesting.

Seren placed her cup and saucer on the small table beside her and slowly pushed herself out of the chair to make her way to the door. The young woman framed by the doorway looked familiar to her, but for a moment she couldn't place her until she spoke directly to her.

'I saw you with Elwyn earlier, he was escorting you here! I asked Mrs Johnson where you lived and she told me your mother lived here . . . ' She huffed out a breath, then looked Seren up and down. 'Are you having his baby?'

Seren smiled and shook her head. 'Oh, no, most certainly not. He was walking me here as I was a bit upset, that's all.'

The young woman's long blonde hair swung back and forth as she gesticulated, a fierce gleam in her eyes. 'I want to know what's going on!' she said, throwing her arms up in the air.

'Look, Mam, we can't leave her like this on the door, please invite her inside. You're Lucinda, aren't you?' Seren said softly as recognition finally dawned.

She nodded. 'So, you are aware of me, then, are you?'

'Of course I am. When I bumped into Elwyn in Merthyr a few weeks ago, he mentioned you to me when you were looking in a shop window opposite the church.'

She sniffed, then stepped inside and followed Seren into the living room whilst her mother tactfully withdrew to the kitchen.

'Please sit down,' Seren said.

Lucinda did so. It was as if the wind had just been taken out of her sails. Seren followed suit, sitting opposite the woman. 'So, what is it you want to know?'

'Just what Elwyn really means to you.'

Seren hesitated for a moment. 'He was a good friend to me when I was going through a bad time and I used to help him at the chapel, running the bible classes. Until I had to suddenly leave Merthyr as my husband was violent towards me.'

'I see. But do you have feelings for Elwyn?'

Deciding she couldn't tell a lie, she let out a long breath. 'Yes, I suppose I do, but that doesn't mean I have to act on them. I was quite prepared to see you both get married. I just want Elwyn to be happy.'

'I suppose that is the same thing as love, isn't it?'

'I suppose it is. But I would never stand in the way of anyone's happiness.'

To Seren's horror, Lucinda began to weep. Seren stood and laid a gentle hand on her shoulder. 'It's not as bad as all that, surely? Is it?'

She looked up through tear-glazed eyes. 'I'm afraid it is. I think I've always known really that he doesn't love me. He just tolerates me for the sake of our families. I thought, once we were married, things may change, but today I could tell he'd had enough when he left The Manse all of a sudden like that. Then when I saw him walking with you, I just knew it was you he's in love with. It was the way he was treating you, like you were a precious piece of porcelain. He never treats me that way.'

Seren nodded. She could hear the pain in the young woman's voice and felt desperately sorry for her. 'I don't know what to say, this is between you and Elwyn,' she said softly.

'I know what I have to do,' Lucinda said quietly. 'Please don't tell him I've been to see you. Not until after I've spoken to him.'

'Very well.'

Lucinda rose from the chair and left the room with her head bowed low. Then Seren's mother came into the room. 'What happened?'

'I'm not really sure,' Seren said thoughtfully. But one thing she knew, from the determined look on Lucinda's face, changes were afoot for the young woman.

* * *

By the time Elwyn and Doctor Owen arrived at the house a little later, Seren had managed to compose herself. It was down to Elwyn and Lucinda whether they married or not. For herself, there was other, more pressing business to contend with.

Her mother brushed down her pinafore as she went to answer the front door. 'I hope that Lucinda one hasn't decided to return.' She huffed out a breath. 'Upsetting you like that after what happened to you earlier, you could do without it!'

'I don't think she'll be back, somehow.' Seren sighed.

Hearing the sound of men's voices at the door, Seren straightened. She half feared the police had shown up to arrest her. But she was comforted to hear the sounds of both Elwyn and the doctor's voices.

Doctor Owen removed his top hat as he entered the living room and laid his leather bag down on the floor beside her. 'You've had a right nasty shock today, Seren,' he said, with a look of compassion in his eyes.

She nodded and took a quick glance at Elwyn, wondering what exactly he'd told the man.

'Would you both like a cup of tea?' her mother asked.

Both men smiled. 'I'd love one, please,' the doctor said, as Elwyn nodded and smiled in agreement.

When her mother had left the room, the doctor looked at Seren. 'How are you feeling, my dear?'

'I'm fine, Doctor.'

'You know, you might be suffering from delayed shock, so if it's all right with you, I'd like to examine you and baby after I've had my cup of tea. I've been working flat out today . . . '

She arched her brows. 'Oh?'

'Don't look so alarmed, it's just to check everything is as it should be. Have you felt any kicks since, er, you know, what happened earlier?'

She nodded. 'Yes, I just felt a hard one a few minutes since.'

He smiled. 'Splendid!'

After they'd all had tea and the doctor had examined her and was satisfied all was well, he said gravely, 'Elwyn tells me that Morgan admitted to killing that prostitute at Jackson's Bridge?'

'Yes, that's correct. I got it out of him in the end.'

He let out a long breath. 'The thing is, I was going to write in my report, so as not to involve you, that Mr Evans called to the house and found Morgan dead at the foot of the stairs.'

'Yes?'

'But if I do so, you're not going to be able to go to the police with the evidence you have as you might be implicated, even though your husband's death was accidental . . . '

She nodded, then turning to both, said firmly, 'I appreciate the sentiment from both of you but I feel honesty is the best policy. I shall tell the truth even if it means going to court to do so.' She realised she couldn't live with herself if she lied to the court about the circumstances.

The men exchanged worried glances. Elwyn gave her hand a reassuring squeeze. 'Are you quite sure you'd want to put yourself through that, Seren?'

She nodded. 'Yes. Quite. I don't want to keep anything from the police about this. And I owe it to Sioni to clear his name.'

Doctor Owen stared at her. 'And who is this Sioni you speak of?'

'Twm Sion Watkin, he runs The House of Blazes inn in the China district of the town.'

'And a house of ill repute in the guise of a wash house next door,' Elwyn added.

She felt her cheeks redden. What must Doctor Owen think of her associating with someone who was no more than a pimp? Yet, he wouldn't know him like she did.

The doctor cleared his throat. 'I believe I have heard the name, but how do you come to know this person, Seren? He doesn't sound your sort at all.'

'He was a friend of Morgan's. He helped me to get to a place of safety when Morgan beat me up badly. If it wasn't for him . . . ' Oh no, she felt the tears spring to her eyes and she swallowed.

'Ah, I see, Seren,' the doctor said gently. 'Well, that fellow can't be all that bad if he did that for you.'

Looking at him through a haze of tears, she nodded. 'The problem is, as Sioni went missing at the same time as Morgan, and as Mari was one of his working girls, people assumed she died by his hands.'

'So, he's still in hiding then?' The doctor's eyes widened.

Seren and Elwyn exchanged glances. Then Elwyn spoke. 'Yes, but Seren and I both know where he is and he's safe. I think we're all right to tell Doctor Owen?' he said, looking at her for confirmation.

She nodded. 'He's with Anwen at the moment.'

Doctor Owen raised his silver brows but didn't comment on what he thought of that. 'Then I think we need now to go to the police with the information we have. I'll take you in my carriage, if you like, Seren?'

She nodded. 'Thank you.' She bit her lip. 'But what about my husband's body?'

'Don't you worry about that,' the doctor said. 'I'll make arrangements for a horse-drawn ambulance to collect him.' Then turning to Elwyn, 'Can you be on hand when it arrives?'

'Yes. I'll sort it all out.' He touched Seren gently on the shoulder. 'All will be well, you'll see.'

* * *

Doctor Owen and Seren both made statements later that evening at Merthyr Police Station. The investigating officer shook his head when they finally scribbled their signatures at the bottom of the document. 'I have to admit, I always thought Morgan would meet with a sticky end.'

Surprised, Seren's eyes widened. 'You knew

my husband, Sergeant Greening?'

'Yes, he's been in here several times drunk and disorderly, and a couple of times for beating Mari up. It's no surprise to us that she's died at his hands, and no shock either he fell down the stairs back at home.' He sniffed loudly. 'It was all on the cards. It seemed to me he was living one sort of life in China while trying to maintain an air of respectability back in Abercanaid.'

'What about Twm Sion Watkin?' she asked.

'What of him?' He peered at her over the top of his silver-framed specs.

'Well, now that you realise it was Morgan who killed Mari, is he a free man, as I hear the police are after him?'

'Not exactly free, no. We don't suspect him of the murder as the Aberdare police did. They don't know him like we do and, to be truthful, I think there was a miscommunication with them and us as to why he was out as wanted for murder anyhow, but we needed to speak to him about another matter regarding what goes on at the inn. We understand prostitution is the oldest profession in the book, but some of his girls have been stealing from customers. I want him in here to give him a ticking off about that, that's all. He needs to keep a grip on that place. So, if you know where he is, tell him I want to see him here at the station within twenty-four hours if he doesn't want to be fined or go to prison.'

Seren nodded, and then smiled at the officer. 'Message understood, Sergeant Greening,' she said.

As they left the police station and made their

way to the doctor's carriage, it was beginning to get dark. Funny to think she was in the town earlier, Christmas shopping, and now she was here making a statement about her husband's death.

'Would you like to return home at some point?' Doctor Owen asked.

'I honestly don't know. I think when I see those stairs, they'll always be a reminder of what happened.'

'I suppose they will. You could always sell the property, but one thing's for certain, Seren . . . now you can move back to Abercanaid without fear if you so wish. Just because you've told the police you were there when your husband took a tumble, you don't need to tell anyone else. We can say as I suggested, that Elwyn called to the house, discovered the body and then called me.'

'I think that might be a good idea,' she said. Her eyes filled with tears as she caught the sight of a small wooden nativity scene in the fruit shop window. Mary's boy child was born in a stable, the light of the world. If He could survive such harsh conditions with the unconditional love of His mother, then her child could survive too. Whatever happened in the future they would have each other. And as she looked up at the sky, snowflakes started falling on her head. Maybe it was a celestial sign all would be well from now on.

Epilogue

Christmas morning at the chapel, and it was packed full to the rafters this year, upstairs and down. Seren watched as Elwyn preached from the pulpit on the message of love and forgiveness. Maybe given time she'd find it in her heart to forgive Morgan for all he'd put her through, but right now she wanted to leave the past behind and concentrate on the future. She patted her tummy with affection. Her unborn child meant the world to her. She didn't want to become one of those mothers who brought their child up with bitter words about their father. She'd look for the good that had been in her husband and pass that on to her child instead. No one was all bad, though right now she found it hard to remember any good times with the man.

She smiled when she noticed Maggie Shanklin in the front pew surrounded by her friends. Some things never changed, but she did feel sorry for the woman as her husband wasn't around for the festive season this year, he was still in London. *She's to be pitied*, she thought to herself. *She can't be that happy if she constantly has to find fault with others and stir up trouble*.

Turning, she glanced at Anwen by the side of her. The woman's eyes were shining as she listened to Elwyn's Christmas message and she gave her hand a gentle squeeze of reassurance.

Their reunion when Doctor Owen had taken her to the farm to relate what the police had said about Sioni had been so emotional. They'd both wept as they held on to one another, Anwen saying how much she'd missed her. Even Macs had taken immediately to Seren.

Sioni had given himself up to the police as asked, and later, she was pleased to discover they had allowed him to leave there without charge. He'd come searching for Seren to ask her something in particular. 'The police want me to clean up my act. You know you once said you'd work for me, Seren?' he'd asked in earnest.

'Yes, I remember that well.' She'd chuckled, but then his voice had taken on a serious tone.

'Well, the police have asked me to sort out the girls and stop them thieving from clients and such, so I do need someone to take charge of them. When the baby's born, would you do it?'

She'd smiled. 'I'm sorry, Sioni, I would have done that for you, but what will people say when they hear that a minister's wife is running a brothel? I'll be the talk of the town!'

His mouth had opened wide and then he smiled. 'Minister's wife?' He scratched his head. 'So, Elwyn's asked you to marry him?'

'Yes, but I've told him to wait until next summer. We're engaged for time being, but he's just come out of a relationship and I've just lost my husband. It's too soon for either of us to wed right now.'

He'd nodded, looking a little confused. But then he'd smiled and said, 'Well, I can't think of a better husband for you. Morgan was all wrong.

At least the reverend will take good care of you and you won't have to worry about him getting drunk!'

That was true, she supposed, but it was more than that. She'd had feelings for him from the very beginning, and Anwen had recognised she was in love with him even before she did. She hadn't been able to act on those feelings, but now she was a free woman and didn't that feel good!

'Would you like to come to The Manse for Christmas dinner?' she'd asked Sioni. 'We did invite Marged and Jim but they're too busy at the lodging house. They were so good to me and I'll never forget their kindness towards me, nor yours.'

He'd thrown back his head and laughed. 'You'll have people thinking I'm a reformed character if I dine at The Manse! You all enjoy yourselves and I'm glad that you're so happy, Seren, but I'll be busy working at the inn that day.'

She could see the rueful look in his eye to have lost her to another, but he belonged in a different world, one she had flirted with for a short while. She didn't belong there, and she knew in her heart that he realised that too and that she belonged to another.

In the event, Lucinda had called off the relationship with Elwyn and he hadn't lost any sleep over it. As soon as she'd left, he'd bounded over to see Seren and asked her to be his wife and she'd happily accepted his proposal.

The final Christmas carol was now being played as the congregation stood to leave the chapel. Seren, Anwen and her mother and sister would be remaining behind to dine with Elwyn at The

Manse. Now wouldn't Mrs Johnson be pleased about that, Seren thought with a wry smile.

When everyone had left the chapel and the five of them were all seated around the Christmas dinner table along with the housekeeper, Elwyn watched as Seren rose from her chair and slipped into the kitchen as Mrs Johnson had forgotten to bring out bread sauce. Seizing his chance, he followed after her and, holding up a sprig of mistletoe over her head as she searched the wooden counter, said breathlessly, 'Seren, I've waited a long time for this: would you do me the honour of allowing me to kiss you?' He chuckled as she turned to face him. Her cheeks blazed, then he closed the door behind himself and she was in his arms where he planted a kiss on her lips and she melted into his embrace.

In the dining room just outside was the mumble of voices as everyone waited patiently for Seren and the minister to return so they could begin their Christmas feast.

'I wonder what's taking them so long?' Gwen asked, making to rise from the table.

Anwen clucked her teeth and smiled knowingly. 'Sit back down a moment, gal. I'd leave them be for now, they've waited a long time for this . . .'

Everyone nodded and Mrs Johnson filled their glasses with a tot of sherry. 'The bread sauce can wait a moment,' she said. 'A toast to the future Mr and Mrs Evans!'

Everyone murmured their agreement as they took a sip.

Anwen nodded and, raising her glass, said, 'And Merry Christmas, one and all!'

Other titles published by Ulverscroft:

A DAUGHTER'S PROMISE

Lynette Rees

London, 1888: Eighteen-year-old seamstress Kathryn Flynn lives in Whitechapel, London, struggling to support her widowed mother and younger siblings. But when her work starts drying up and her mother falls ill, she is forced to consider desperate measures. Then she meets Squire, an older city gentleman; and claiming to be Miss Bella Cartwright, she attempts to draw some charity from him as he buys her a drink. Squire has an offer for her: work in the West End, where he would take her under his wing and she could have the life she's always wanted — plenty of money, gifts of fancy dresses, the companionship of people of means — and never have to sew again. But is there something darker lurking beneath his kindness?